Since cricket is one of the novel, the writer, like a typ— — —..— .... bat to talk, would like his words to speak on his behalf. He served for the best part of his life in the Indian Navy as an officer and later switched to the mercantile marine. Although a first class graduate of the Andhra University, he learnt more in the Indian Navy, on his trips around the world and in the school of life. He has published many humorous short stories and a range of articles in various magazines and newspapers in India.

www.gvramarao.com

Acknowledgements

I am most indebted to the support and help from both Mr C. Krishna Kumar and Mr B. Kumar both of whom read the novel in its various states. Without them, I might still be writing it!

I would like to thank Libros International, who believed in my work, and to Sue, my judicious editor.

THE COLONEL'S LAST WICKET

GV Rama Rao

Libros International

For Vani, my wife

AUTHOR'S NOTE

This book is neither a cricket manual nor a critique on the Indian army. It is purely a work of fiction and should be read as such. Some facts have been altered slightly to suit the novel.

SIGHTSCREEN

The sightscreen is the largest item in the game of cricket; it is kept outside the field and plays a small, but significant role in the game. It is nondescript in that it is a blank white screen when the players wear whites and play with a red ball but coloured black when players use coloured clothing and a white ball, as in day and night matches. The crucial role of the sightscreen is not in proportion to its size. Although the minimum size is prescribed in the International Cricket Council (ICC) rules, some cricket grounds employ bigger sightscreens.

The main and only function of the screen is to enable the batsman to spot the ball properly. It provides a uniform background and a contrast so that the batsman can see the path, or the likely path, of the ball and take appropriate action. The screens are also movable and are adjusted to stay behind the bowler so that the batsman can see the movement of the bowler's arm precisely. Whenever a left-handed batsman comes to bat and takes up his stance he invariably asks for the sightscreen to be shifted to suit his line of sight. Any significant movement near the sightscreen upsets the line of vision and concentration of the batsmen. In short, the sightscreen helps the batsman immensely in spotting the ball correctly.

The Superintendent of Police, a young Indian Police (IPS) Officer wearing the pips of a Lieutenant Colonel, knew all this but could not make out any connection with the sightscreen and the leopard which was troubling the populace of the villages under his jurisdiction. Colonel Seth, an ex-army man, had asked for a sightscreen when requested to help the police in hunting the beast. The animal had been making repeated forays into a cluster of villages and had been taking both life and limb of the inhabitants regularly for a few days.

An agitated crowd demanded quick action and the immediate response of the District Forest Officer and the police personnel produced no tangible results. The SP (Superintendent of Police) and the District Forest Officer held a mini conference with the village elders and discussed various measures to trap the animal dead or alive. During the meeting one of the village's headmen suggested seeking the help of Colonel Seth, reputed to be a good *shikari*. The SP had some training in firearms at the Police Academy but was not sure of taking on the wild beast himself.

When contacted, the Colonel readily agreed and reported with an assortment of weapons. He requested that a few animals be kept as prey at a strategic place outside the village and then requested the sightscreen. Fortunately, for the SP, the cricket association at his headquarters provided one readily. The Colonel arranged the sightscreen so it was covering the trees and tethered three goats a few metres apart in front of it. He took up a position in a tree opposite the screen and started his vigil, fully armed with his BSA Magnum 303 rifle and a shotgun.

He did not have to wait for long. The beast fell for the bait; it approached with confident strides and assessed the animals tethered ready for its feast. It jumped on the first animal and gorged itself. The Colonel waited for the appropriate moment and, when he had the animal in his cross sight, fired his powerful rifle, believing he had felled the animal with one shot. The wounded leopard staggered up to see where the shot had come from and launched itself into an attack.

The Colonel however was a marksman of great repute. He gave no second chance to the animal and fired two rounds in rapid succession. The leopard got the second where its heart was and the third right in its head. The immense bullets stopped the heart and split open the skull, shattering it to smithereens. With the last remnants of life extinguished, the animal collapsed and lay sprawled on the ground. The Colonel jumped from his lofty perch and approached the animal with caution and the rifle ready to fire. Fortunately, for him, the animal showed no more signs of life and the Colonel stood on the carcass like a king who had vanquished the invaders.

When the Colonel returned to the village and announced that the job was done and the villagers had nothing more to fear, everyone heaved a sigh of relief. They made a beeline to have a look at the dead animal that had caused them so much consternation for quite some time. The SP and the DFO praised the Colonel and thanked him for what he had accomplished. The Colonel underplayed his success as though it was child's play and left for his quarters. The villagers decided to present the skin as a trophy to the Colonel at a later date.

On the appointed day, the Colonel drove to the centre of the village, where the SP, the DFO and other village headmen received him. They presented him with the trophy and praised his valour. The SP grudgingly acknowledged that the Colonel saved him from considerable embarrassment for it was the task of the DFO and SP to provide protection to the villagers from any marauding wild beasts. The SP could not help asking the Colonel as to why he asked for the sightscreen.

"It helped me in spotting the animal. I was a cricket player before turning *shikari*. I played first-class cricket for quite some time and I found a sightscreen very helpful for taking a proper aim and for executing a shot either with a bat or a rifle."

"Surely you must have used weapons in your army career and you couldn't have had sightscreens then?" said the SP with more sarcasm than admiration.

"Yes, I fought in the 1965 and 1971 wars and received medals too. Shooting in the army though is a different ball game entirely. You don't shoot at wild animals but at intelligent humans who follow some patterns and tactics. You also formulate a plan before attack and eventually you fight for your life."

The SP let it pass and gave a ceremonial send-off to the Colonel, who was greatly relieved for he never liked such shows of unnecessary praise for simple acts. He drove out of the village as the sun was going down and the shadows of the tall trees in the village were lengthening. He switched on some music in his old car and was relaxing while driving steadily. As he approached the outskirts of the village, he saw a vast expanse of empty rice fields. Against that backdrop something caught his eye and he spotted some movement which immediately elevated his spirits. He stopped the car more by instinct and less by intention and looked around.

All that he found was a large field, where a rice crop must have been harvested a few days earlier. A small group of boys were playing a game that resembled cricket. They had no pitch and they were playing in a field with the harvested rice plants protruding like spikes. None of the boys had any shoes or footwear, except for one of them, who was well dressed; the rest had only shorts and nothing else. They had three sticks protruding at one end and a lone stick at the other. The sticks were not of the same height and presented an odd array of stumps. They had a parchment bat, or what was left of it, for it had only half the blade and something that looked like a ball, it had probably been a hockey ball once.

What they lacked in gear they made up for in their ardour and continued to play their game unmindful of the Colonel and his old car, which by then had stopped close to the field. The young lad of a bowler bowled full of enthusiasm. He had no idea of a bowling action and threw the ball over arm instead. For a young boy of his age, he generated enough pace to frighten the batsman. He, the only fellow fully and best dressed of the lot, moved out of the way of the ball to save his legs. However, he was a trifle late in his reflexes and the ball struck him on the knee. He fell in a heap and started to abuse the bowler. Within no time the group of fielders around the batsman rushed to the bowler and started beating him black and blue. No one tried to help the injured batsman as all the boys looked like they were hell-bent on wreaking vengeance on the bowler.

"That's not cricket!" The Colonel shouted and rushed to the aid of the poor lad, who by then was sprawled on the ground having been overpowered by the rest of the boys. The Colonel's shout and his intervention in the game surprised them and they all stopped dead in their tracks. Even the batsman who was hurt stood up and looked aghast. The Colonel went up to the bowler, picked him up from the ground and put him on his feet once again.

"What's the trouble? Why are you hitting the boy? Why did you all gang up against him?" he asked the boys.

"He's bowling fast and he's hurt the headman's boy. How dare he do that!" they all said in unison.

"What do you hold against him? Bowling fast or hitting the boy?"

"Both. Why should he bowl so fast? Why should he bowl so fast especially when the village headman's boy is batting?" one lad asked.

"Is bowling fast not allowed in your game? Is the village headman's son entitled to special treatment?"

"Yes, sir. He shouldn't bowl fast and he should have respect for the son of the village headman," another boy replied.

"While playing a game all players must be considered equal and given equal opportunities. The village headman's son should know how to face all balls or not play cricket at all," the Colonel pointed out.

"But this field is his father's land. He brought the bat and the ball. Without him we can never have a game at all," the same boy countered.

"Okay, I understand you now. Suppose if I provide a bat and

a few balls would you promise to play the game treating all as equals?"

"Yes, sir, we certainly will. In fact, we're fed up of this boy who bosses over us all the time," another of the youngsters responded.

The boys did not expect the Colonel to keep his promise. So they were pleasantly surprised to see the gentleman dressed all in whites coming to the field and presenting the boys with a set of cricket gear. First, he took out a new bat, shining with its parchment cover on the blade. There were multicoloured designs and letters on it, which they could not read and a red rubber grip on the handle. He also gave them a few balls, which were mostly old, a couple of sets of pads and, above all, a set of four stumps, all of the same size. The Colonel gathered the boys around, explained to them how to wear the cricket gear and how to fix the stumps. He measured the distance before setting them up and explained the rudiments of the game. Next, he suggested that they should make the centre of the field even, cut all the sprouting rice stalks and prepare the surrounding area so they would be able to run freely. Finally, he produced a small net and told the boys how to use it. The youngsters caressed the gear with great admiration and enthusiasm as if they were some precious jewels.

The Colonel told them to play the game properly without giving preferential treatment to anyone. "Cricket is always played on a level playing field. Otherwise it is not cricket." He also promised to return after a month to view their progress and to replenish their stock of cricket balls and other items.

He returned as promised and found a sea of change in the whole scene. The first thing he noticed was that the boys had completely transformed the rice field. They had cut all the stalks, levelled the field and made the centre of it very even so it almost looked like a pitch. They had placed the stumps properly and at the correct distance. The boy batting had pads on and seemed ready to brave the fast bowler. The other lad, still dressed only in shorts, commenced his bowling, which now had some semblance of an action and was not just throwing but he still generated enough pace to cause fright to the batsman. The boys played the game with great abandon and without any fighting.

The Colonel stopped his car a distance away, walked slowly and hid himself behind a tree to watch the game without disturbing the lads. The bowler attracted attention most for he bowled with a passion unimaginable for a village boy of his age. The Colonel looked more closely at him and found he was wearing tattered shorts that kept slipping down constantly. He had unkempt hair and his rib cage was showing; he looked almost emaciated. The Colonel wondered how such a weak fellow could bowl fast and become a threat to all the other well-fed boys. As he stepped closer, they stopped their game and ran up to him with their eyes full of admiration.

"We're learning the game, sir. We're enjoying the game and thank you very much for all that you gave us."

"You continue and let me see your progress."

"You've been watching our game. I saw you but didn't tell the others as you were hiding behind the tree," said one of the boys mischievously.

The Colonel gave a hearty laugh and recollected how, in his youth, he had used to play cricket, hoodwinking his dad. Then he took out the cricket gear that he had brought with him and distributed sweets to the children. When he saw them eating the delicious treats with great relish he thought that it had made his day. He noticed particularly the scraggy boy eating them, munching each piece slowly and carefully as though he had finally got his chance after a long wait. The Colonel told them some more rules of the game and taught them how to hold the bat, take the stance and execute a few shots. The boys showed a keen interest and took in every word. He also showed them the correct bowling action and to the great surprise of all of them, he bowled a few balls to the village headman's son. The young lads jumped with joy and yet the Colonel thought he had enjoyed the short game more than the boys. When he left, they gave him a fitting farewell and asked him to return soon and frequently.

The Colonel felt tired and yet very contented. On returning home, he went to his study and relaxed with a couple of drinks before dozing off in his chair.

DREAM GAME

Cricket is a game full of dreams. Every player, irrespective of his talent, dreams of a day when he plays for his school, college, state and finally his country. Every batsman dreams of scoring a century, and every bowler taking a wicket with the very first ball that he bowls and a rich haul of wickets in a match. Even the fielders dream of taking miraculous catches. The charm of the game of cricket lies in these dreams, some fulfilled and some waiting to be fulfilled.

Captain Seth was playing cricket for India and he started his run up with the new ball to start the match. The whole stadium, filled to the brim, egged him on shouting, "Come on, Seth!"

He started his run-up, bowled and surprised the batsman on the off stump with an out-swinger. The batsman played defensively but edged the ball. The man at third slip took a waist high catch without any effort. The batsman, reputedly one of the best in the world, looked at Seth more with admiration than contempt and walked before the umpire raised his finger. His teammates closed around him and hugged him. The captain ruffled his hair and said, "Well done, Seth, a very good beginning to your Test career." The match progressed but the dawn peeped through the drapes and woke Seth. He dreamt a lot. The dream was the same old recurring one, which he must have dreamt umpteen times.

When he woke up, the fantasy ended and reality hit him hard. His dream remained just that: a dream, for he never played for India. He did not even merit selection for the second string team. He was a first-class cricketer but an also-ran too. He played for the Services team but never went beyond that level. Playing for India remained a distant vision and had taunted him in his sleep almost every night for most of his life.

Before getting out of bed, the Colonel looked at the family portrait on the bedside table. His wife standing beside him and his two daughters behind them formed a contented picture of a happy family. His wife after many years of devotion, love and affection had left for her heavenly abode. His two daughters were studying abroad; they would eventually take up jobs and possibly even marry and settle in the USA they loved so much. This left him alone to continue dreaming about his cricket playing days. Feelings of loneliness, gloom and failure overtook him, but he quickly brushed aside such thoughts and started getting ready for his constitutional.

As he walked along the busy park many other morning walkers wished him a very good morning and enquired about his health and his family but he kept thinking of the boy in the village. The young lad, running like a stallion in full gallop and bowling faster than many of his age, stood in sharp focus before him. Surely the boy must be dreaming a similar dream, to play for some big team and if possible for the country and earn name, fame and money, he thought. He felt that the boy was beckoning him, pleading with him to come to his aid and provide the necessary wherewithal to realise his ambition. The Colonel's own dream remained a mere dream but he thought he should be able to make someone else's dream come true and so that was the moment he made up his mind. As he continued his walk back to his bungalow, the resolve intensified and he decided to act immediately.

As he approached the village and contacted the village headman to get the details and whereabouts of the boy, he could not get him out of his mind. Having got the information he needed he made his way to a small hutment, which had mud walls and a galvanised iron sheet for a roof. It had two small rooms and a rear portion of one of them served as a kitchen. He found the boy sitting cross-legged on the floor and having lunch. He also found a middle-aged man reclining on the cot in the centre of the main room, fanning himself with a handheld fan.

When Seth bent down and went into the hut a ripple of fear ran through everyone. The middle-aged man, obviously the boy's father, reacted first. "What's the trouble this time?" he asked as if he was expecting nothing but trouble. "What has he done? Has he damaged your car or something? He's always getting me into trouble and God knows how I put up with the boy."

"No trouble at all. In fact he's been good and I like him."

This surprised the man and his demeanour changed. He got up from the cot, arranged a makeshift seat for Seth and asked him to sit and make himself comfortable. Meanwhile a small girl came from outside, looked at Seth in bewilderment and took a seat in her father's lap. "What has he done this time?" the girl repeated the same old question.

"The boy has done nothing wrong and you don't need to worry about him. I want to know about the boy and if you will allow me, to speak to him."

"There's nothing much to say about the boy. In fact, I don't know anything about him myself. One day I found a baby abandoned on the outskirts of the village. I brought the baby home and raised him. I'm a schoolteacher in this village and I've been looking after him with the little I have. Unfortunately, he has an uncanny knack of getting into trouble too often. He keeps breaking something or fighting with someone almost everyday. I keep getting numerous complaints about him. Since I'm the teacher of the local school, I command a little respect and the boy has been spared punishment many times."

"How is he at school?"

"At school I keep a close eye on him and he behaves well, giving no cause for concern. He's not a bright student but he minds his own business. However, he likes this girl, his sister, and looks after her like a doting brother. He doesn't let any boy do any harm whatsoever to her. I've asked many a wealthy family to take care of the boy but no one wants to touch a child whose parentage is not known. They have plenty of money and acres and acres of land but their hearts are very small," he said with anguish written across his face. Obviously he was finding it difficult to provide for the boy.

Seth thought that the situation suited his plan. "What if I propose to take full care of him from now onwards?"

"Obviously I would love that. You seem to be a prosperous man and the boy will get a better deal in life, but why do you want to do so? Are you the father of this boy by any chance?"

"Not at all. I'm not even from these parts. I'm Colonel Seth, a retired Army Officer, and I like the boy mainly for his passion for cricket."

"What is cricket? I don't think he knows about it."

"It's a game and everybody knows about it! Your boy plays a good game and I want to train him."

The boy, who had finished his meal by then, jumped with joy when he heard that. "You want to teach me cricket! That's wonderful. Am I dreaming?" he said with childish glee.

"I'll look after the boy, provide him with everything he needs including his education and treat him as my son. You see I have two daughters but they live in America. I lost my wife and I'm all by myself. I promise to look after him as my own son if you allow me to take him with me."

"I'd be a fool if I didn't. If luck comes his way, why should I object? You may take him anytime you want."

"I'll take him home with me now. I'll give you my address and you and your family can come and visit him anytime you want."

"This makes me very happy for several reasons. Firstly, the boy will get a better deal. Secondly, the girl will get a better deal too, as I will have one less mouth to feed. Thirdly, I don't have to answer to any more complaints! Take him whenever you want."

When Seth took the boy to his car no one shed a tear except the little girl. She was obviously close to him, she hugged the lad and held his hand and shook it for sometime, showing her love for her brother in her own way.

The boy looked at the car with its plush interior and could not believe his luck. He was getting out of this village, this godforsaken piece of land. He did not even know what existed beyond the village but soon he would find out. He was sitting in a car for the first time and when the car started moving he felt a blissful feeling as though he was being taken to heaven, although he had no idea of heaven but had heard about it in passing. In a village, word spreads fast and, as the car was leaving the outskirts, all the boys were waiting near the cricket field so the Colonel stopped the car.

"Where are you taking Raju, sir?" they asked in unison.

"I'm taking him to the city, to my place."

"Why are you taking him, sir?"

"To teach him cricket."

"Why him, sir?"

"Because he plays a good game of cricket."

"Do you know that he has no parents, sir?"

"That doesn't bother me."

"Does that mean you will not be returning to this village to teach us cricket anymore?"

"No! I will keep coming. I love cricket and those who play the game."

"We all wish him good luck, sir." They cleared the way for the car and waved them off.

When he had left the village, the Colonel asked the lad next to him, "What's your name?"

"Raju."

"Yes, but what's your full name?"

"Everyone just calls me Raju. I have no other name."

"What's your name on the school register?"

"As I said, I'm known as Raju. I have no other name as I don't know about my parents."

"Don't worry. I'll give you a full name and I'll not allow anyone to trouble you."

"Why are you doing all this for me?"

"I'll tell you in time."

"What should I do to thank you?"

"Play cricket. Play it well."

"Oh, thank you! I love to play cricket."

"That's what I want you to do, play cricket and play it exceedingly well. I'll do the rest."

Soon the car reached Seth's bungalow. The boy looked at his new home, which had a spacious compound and flowery trees around the perimeter. He had not known that such buildings existed, as he had never left the village until then. The Colonel took him to a spacious room and called his servant. " Fix this room up for the lad."

The servant looked at the half-clad youngster and wondered what had got into his boss to bring this unkempt village boy home.

Raju started his voyage that day into the unknown, a new life, a new frontier and a dream destination. He thanked his stars and uttered a silent prayer to some unknown God.

GROUND

Cricket is played on a ground that is normally round. The Oval at Kennington, London is one of the few exceptions. The boundary of the ground is marked by a rope. When the ball, either hit by a batsman or missed by a fielder crosses this it is called a boundary and the batting team gets four runs. If the ball crosses the boundary rope via the aerial route without pitching on the ground, it is called a 'sixer', which means six runs. It is akin to a homerun in baseball

The centre of the ground is the main part where the pitch is prepared carefully. The grass is shaved off and the creases are marked. A set of three stumps is placed at either end of the pitch. The batsman who is the striker takes his stance on one side and the bowler, who hurls the ball like the pitcher in baseball, bowls from the opposite end. The second batsman who stands at the bowler's end is the non-striker and takes a keen interest in how the pitch and the bowler behave and prepares himself to face the ball when he goes to the striker's end. In between the pitch and the boundary is the field, which is nicely carpeted grass. Some of the cricket grounds have a well cut and manicured grassy field and provide an ideal surface for the players to dive, fall and execute different forms of acrobatics, all to prevent the ball going past them. The grass provides a cushion. The cricket adage is that a run saved is like a run scored as at the end of the game the team that scores the most runs wins the day.

The grounds are prepared by specially trained curators and great care is taken to provide proper drainage in order to let them dry quickly even after a heavy downpour. Some outfields are very fast and the ball races to the boundary line, while the slower outfields, heavy with dew or more grass, slacken the speed of the ball. Scoring fours or boundaries in such slow outfields becomes a difficult task. The outfield does not behave the same all the time. Although the pitch proper is covered with thick waterproof covers to prevent any seepage of rainwater onto it, such luxury is not provided to the outfield, which becomes soggy and works to the disadvantage of the team batting at that time.

The cricket grounds at Lords in England, the Sydney Cricket Ground a.k.a SCG in Australia and the Mohali cricket ground in India are fine examples of what a cricket arena ought to be. The Eden Gardens at Calcutta, Lords and SCG at Sydney also have an added mystic around them. Playing a Test at Lords, still regarded as the home of cricket, remains to many cricketers the pinnacle of their career. Any batsman or bowler who achieves a remarkable feat at these grounds finds his name permanently etched in the annals of the game. A century at Lords is every batsman's dream and the few who score a 'ton' here find their names in the hallowed Hall of Fame at Lords.

The ground at 'Gara', the village where Raju had grown up, had none of these facilities. In fact, the village had no facilities, not even the basic necessities like running water and sanitation. The village did have a small school albeit without a proper roof. Whenever the sun rose up in the sky and became unbearable, the few teachers present invariably shifted the classrooms outdoors under the spreading trees that provided some semblance of shade. If the heat became intense, they took a siesta and asked the students to fend for themselves. If it rained, a holiday was declared and the children enjoyed soaking themselves in the downpour as it provided a free bath with plenty of pure water.

The teachers in the school run by the local government were

few and attended the school whenever it pleased them. The writ of the Government does not run large in the villages. Far removed from the seat of the District administration the teachers flout the rules with impunity. They are completely unconcerned by the results produced as the powerful union of the schoolteachers protects them from any disciplinary action that might be contemplated by the District Educational Officer. The parents of the children do not mind this situation for the young students can be gainfully employed when the teachers play truant or abandon them. The parents, not educated themselves, equate schooling with unproductive work and want to wean their wards away from the school at the first opportunity. The only incentive for the students not to bunk classes is the midday meal scheme in which the Government provides a somewhat sumptuous lunch to keep the children at school. Some of the youngsters partake of the lunch and then quietly slip away whereas some, after a heavy meal, slip into deep slumber under the shade of a banyan tree. However, the scheme, originally conceived by the late MG Ramachandran, an actor turned politician like Ronald Reagan, was a huge success and reduced the school dropouts considerably. Thus, it was adopted quickly throughout the country in all villages.

In sharp contrast, the towns and cities had plenty of private schools. The competition to get into good schools, which provide quality education, was immense. This competition puts a heavy burden on the students in the form of heavy backpacks and intensive study to get good grades and seats in prestigious colleges. Finally obtaining a seat either in any of the renowned IITs, Indian Institute of Technologies, or a prestigious medical college is the ultimate aim of the students and their parents. Instances of students not meeting the expectations of their parents and ending their lives happen with morbid frequency.

The schoolteacher was different from the run of the mill villagers and ensured that Raju attended all classes. He himself carried out his duties diligently and took immense pains to teach whatever little he knew to his pupils. He wanted his daughter to study well and become a renowned teacher and headmistress of a school, the boundary of his imagination. He also wanted Raju to study and make a name in whatever field he liked. The teacher in fact was the only altruist in the entire village.

The village head, called Sarpanch, was the richest farmer as he was the first to start farming with new seeds that had been developed and introduced by the Agricultural College in the state. He was the forerunner of a small agrarian revolution in the village. As he got more yield and better profits from his small farm he bought more land and soon formed the *nouveau riche* of the village. With his newly acquired wealth, he developed new contacts, acquired some political clout and became the kingpin of the village. He also acquired new habits like drinking whisky and became increasingly arrogant.

He had enough means to improve the village and the lot of other farmers but, being a tight-fisted fellow, made hardly any attempt to look after the needs of the village like primary education and primary health. Wealth brings in its wake greed and he learnt ways and means to gobble up public funds meant for the development schemes initiated by the well-meaning government. He brooked no opposition and thought that all the other villagers were his vassals and treated them with contempt and disdain. He had a firm grip over the village and controlled every aspect of life in it. He followed a dictum, 'democracy as long as others do what I say'. Unfettered by the district officials who made rare appearance in the village, Sarpanch ruled the roost and feathered his nest.

"Where are you going?" Sarpanch had shouted at Raju some weeks earlier to Seth's visit to the village.

"I'm going home as school's over." He did not want to tell him that he was going to the makeshift ground to play cricket.

"Come and work in my house for two hours as we're expecting guests."

"I'll ask the teacher and then come," Raju had answered politely.

"Why should you go to his house?" the teacher said with a certain steel in his voice. "You're not his slave, he has no hold over you. You need not go, for that matter you need not obey his orders." Although a teacher of a primary school with little education, he had a gritty determination, more so than many of his peers. He was well aware that Sarpanch was well above him both in class and caste, the two domineering factors in the village, but was always ready to stand up to the bullies and fight for the rights of the common village folk. He had become their undisputed leader in some unknown way.

This invoked the ire of Sarpanch, who took every opportunity to torment him and trouble him in whatever way he could. He sent for the teacher who initially refused but later complied when others persuaded him to try and find out what Sarpanch wanted. "Why didn't you send the orphan boy to my house to work?" the irate man bellowed immediately.

The teacher was unruffled. "Why should he work in your house? What right do you have over him?"

"He's an orphan and not your son. Why are you so possessive about him?" demanded Sarpanch.

"He's in my care. He's not obliged to work in your house. So what if he is an orphan? Orphans also are human beings and have their rights," countered the teacher.

"You're being impertinent and will pay a heavy price!"

"I'm not going to be cowed down by your threats. I can't stand injustice."

"Don't you ever forget that I'm the headman and I call the shots in the village!"

"You may do as you please. If you were so interested in him, you could've taken care of him. You've been making plenty of money of late."

"Yes, but not for spending on bastards," he said with

contempt and dismissed the teacher as if he was brushing a fly off his shirt.

"You don't look after the school. You eat up the funds meant for it and you want the schoolchildren to work in your house like slaves. What type of headman are you? You got elected mainly because of the clout of your money and your caste. This state of affairs isn't going to continue for long. The day is not far off when you will be made more accountable for all the funds provided for the school, and you will learn to rue that day."

The encounter with Sarpanch left a bad taste in the mouth of the teacher who rushed home. He started worrying about the safety of his daughter and Raju but steeled himself.

Next day he found Raju loitering in the school premises aimlessly. "Why are you roaming round? Why don't you study? Remember that in the final analysis your studies alone will fetch you three square meals a day."

"What can I do? Our teacher hasn't come. When I sit in the classroom, the other children just torment me. They don't want to play with me and they don't let me read. I'm fed up."

"Go over to the banyan tree and read whatever you have been studying. Take a slate and learn to write the English alphabet that I have taught you."

"Why the English alphabet? The other teachers aren't teaching it and no other child is learning it."

"I know that, but I feel the future lies in learning English. Please do as I say."

"Yes, sir," he said with great respect. Whatever the teacher said was the gospel truth as far as Raju was concerned and he complied with the request.

The teacher, although no Anglophile and who knew little or no English, believed that a good knowledge of the language would stand Raju in good stead. When he was a student, he had learnt English but the politicians, in their regional fervour, decided to dispense with English and directed all government schools to teach all subjects in the regional language; in his state it was Telugu.

The politicians themselves sent their offspring to expensive public schools where the medium of instruction was English while making sure that the children in all government schools learnt their subjects in their regional language. This policy caused a two-tier structure to develop and put the children who studied in English at a considerable advantage. Those who spoke good English, with a proper accent, ruled the roost and those who wrote good English sailed through competitive examinations with ease and got the cushy jobs in the country.

Pratap, Sarpanch's son, was a chip off the old block and inherited all the qualities of his father, including the arrogance. He made frequent trips to the city where he found some of his cousins playing cricket in the school and college. The game caught his fancy and he got hooked on to it. It takes two to tango but at least a half a dozen to play cricket. He acquired a few items to play the game but he had few or no friends in the school. He quickly made amends and put forth a charade of friendship, distributed sweets and called on a few boys to come and play cricket with him. He provided the ground on his father's land, a bat and ball, and explained the rudiments of the game to the other children who were fed up of playing soccer. Football was an easy game to play and needed no special gear but the ball. When kicked hard though, it often used to land in the thorny bushes, deflate and put an end to the game for the day. The frequent stoppages infuriated the kids who wanted to play a game with a ball that needed no inflating.

The game of cricket, as explained by Sarpanch's son, also resembled a local game called *Gulli-danda* where the bat was a stick and the ball was a small piece of wood that tapered around the edges at both ends. It needed strength and skill to hit the *gulli,* as the ball was called, over a long distance and so make the opponents run more. Cricket also involved hitting the ball as hard as one was able and dispatching it as far as possible. The kids adapted themselves to the game very quickly and Pratap found to his surprise that the other boys whom he taught started playing better than he did. He was especially peeved at Raju who showed rare talent at hurling the ball very fast. He wondered how Raju, a thin emaciated fellow with hardly any flesh on him, could hurl the ball at such a speed. He hated his guts but not many kids were willing to join his group and play with him so, left with no alternative, he allowed Raju to continue.

THE STANCE

The stance, or the way a batsman stands in front of the wicket when facing the bowler is very important. He bends from the waist, placing the bat firmly on the ground. He keeps his body parallel to the line of the stumps and turns his head to watch the bowler, particularly the bowler's hand and the seam of the ball. His stance should first provide a good balance and allow him to take a clear view of the bowler, his bowling arm, the seam and the shine on the ball. All these play an extremely vital role in the direction the ball moves after delivery. Since his reaction time is very short, the batsman's mental calculator and the years of practice and training should guide him to predict correctly the way the ball will behave and take appropriate action. He steps onto the front foot to execute his stroke or onto the back foot to defend his wicket and sometimes stays put to wait for the ball to come to him. He has to decide his course of action in a split second and if he is caught on the wrong foot, he will meet his Waterloo. Footwork, then, is a very important aspect of batting, as it will enable him to select the right shot and position himself to execute it properly. The stance should also permit him to flex his muscles whenever the ball provides enough width and length to execute a shot firmly and send the ball racing along the carpet to the ropes.

The batsmen take their stance with the help of the umpire. They will indicate their preference to stand on the line of the leg or middle stump. The umpire will indicate when the batsman is in line with the stump that he prefers and the batsman then marks that position by drawing a line on the batting crease with his bat. Once the position is established the batsman places his feet on the spot and the bat close to his legs. Some batsmen mark the position by taking the bails from the stump and making a hole in the ground with the help of the bat. Each batsman takes his stance according to his own preference, technique and the type of bowler he is facing. While most take their stance on the crease, some prefer to stand outside it giving them a millisecond extra to meet the ball or to attempt to put the bowler off in terms of length. While most batsmen crouch, some exceptional few stand erect with the bat half raised and ready to hit the ball.

When Raju started his new school he did not know where to stand or sit. The Colonel believed that he should let the boy solve his problems by himself in his own way. He completed the formalities and after enrolling the lad in the English speaking school, quietly left. A bewildered Raju found himself quite at a loss as he found everything so different. Here the classroom had chairs and desks. He had never sat in a chair and did not now how to sit correctly on one. However, he quickly noticed out of the corner of his eye the way the other boys sat and so went and seated himself in an unoccupied chair.

"Oh no, that is Sunil's seat. You take the last seat," someone shouted more to help him and without any malice.

Raju felt reassured that someone had guided and not chided him but did not really understand. He took the seat, diffidently placing his backpack on the table. The classroom also had a raised dais with a large blackboard and an ornate chair for the teacher. A small pile of books on one side and notebooks on the other stood on the table.

As Raju sat down, one boy quietly came up to him and asked him in English, "What's your name?" When it was obvious that Raju did not understand the question someone else translated it into Telugu and he muttered his response. He sounded quite apologetic, for the word Raju meant a king and he hardly looked the part. Some boys laughed while the more cultured controlled themselves.

One tall, well-built lad approached menacingly but before he could ask anything someone shouted, "He's the Colonel's son so you'd better be careful!"

This dampened the spirits of the class bully who quietly retreated to his seat.

Meanwhile the teacher arrived and the whole class stood up. She was a young lady, smartly dressed in a sari with a matching blouse and with a crowning glory of a beautiful coiffure. She exuded confidence and commanded respect instantly. All the students wished her, "Good morning, madam" and she responded with a beaming smile. Thereafter she proceeded to teach arithmetic, in English.

Raju felt completely lost. He could count up to six, for an over in cricket meant six balls, but he had had no occasion to use the word seven in English. Even the numbers up to six had never been spoken so fast and repeatedly. He sat in a trance not knowing what was happening around him and what the teacher was saying. Luckily he soon caught her attention and she took pity on him and came to his desk. She put her hand out and patted him on the shoulder. "What's your name and why are you looking lost?"

"He doesn't understand English, madam," somebody kindly mentioned.

"Don't you worry! You'll learn English quickly enough; it's not a very difficult language. Hey boys, you must all help him to overcome this problem."

"Yes, madam," they shouted in unison and someone remarked that Raju was the Colonel's ward.

"You're the Colonel's son and you don't understand English. Very strange indeed!" she muttered to herself, but the boys nearby heard her and they also looked quizzically at Raju.

The morning passed in a similar fashion. At lunchtime, every student opened his backpack and took out his lunch box and Raju followed suit not knowing what lurked inside. He found a stainless steel box in which he discovered some rice, lentils and some vegetables. The lunch was more than what he used to get at the village school and tastier. He remembered the Colonel's manservant cooking and packing the lunch box.

"Let's see what you've got to eat!" said the boy next to him as he helped himself to a couple of morsels with his spoon. Raju found most of the boys were eating with the alien utensils and not with their hands. He had never known how to eat in any manner other than using his fingers. When he was about to do so another boy wagged his finger at him and pointed to the spoon. Slowly Raju ate his lunch for the first time with the strange implement; he found it difficult. The boy at the next seat pulled out a boiled egg and another produced a piece of chicken from his box. Both offered their food to the young, village lad. Raju had never eaten an egg or chicken before and yet did not refuse. He ate both items with great trepidation but found them really delicious. He realised that food could be very tasty and relished his meal immensely. He was also moved by the kind thoughts shown by the two boys who had added to his lunch box. He looked at them gratefully, his eyes saying what his lips could not utter.

In the evening, the boys trooped out into the playground and played several different games. Raju found many new ones that he had not seen before. He also discovered a few boys playing cricket but, at school, it was an entirely different ball game. The boys practised at the nets where the batsmen took turns at facing six bowlers. They all shouted with unbridled enthusiasm every time the ball hit the stumps or when the batsman executed a good shot. The spirit shown by the boys was infectious. Raju also wanted to run and join the group but some unknown fear held him back. He watched the boys really enjoying all the games and running around the field without a care in the world and he experienced for the first time the joy of childhood.

After school, Raju had to find his way back to the Colonel's house. Although Seth had explained in his broken Telugu, Raju had not understood much. There was a definite language barrier between him and the Colonel who was originally from Punjab, a northwestern state close to the Pakistan border. Only later had he settled down in the peace and quiet of Visakhapatnam in the southeast corner. Consequently, the Colonel spoke Punjabi, Hindi and English fluently but only knew a smattering of Telugu. As Raju was looking lost, a boy who had helped him at lunchtime again approached him and spoke to him in Telugu. The moment he heard the other boy, Raju could not control himself anymore and broke down completely and cried like a four-year-old kid. All his feelings of helplessness, which he had controlled for the whole day, flowed out in torrents and tears cascaded down his cheeks like an immense waterfall.

He hugged the other boy as if he was a saviour. He kept crying until he ran out of tears while the lad gently rubbed his head reassuringly and promised to help. When Raju regained his composure, which was quite some time after, the other boy introduced himself as Mathew and took him to a quiet corner of the school playground. He made Raju comfortable and asked him what the problem was.

"I don't know anything. I don't belong here. I don't know what to do. I am like a fish out of water. How am I going to survive?" He started crying again.

Mathew calmed him and slowly got the whole story out of the grief-stricken boy. "It's a good thing you told me but promise me not to tell these things to the other boys. Some of them can be very cruel you know. They will torment you all the time. I'll teach you all the things you need to know. You can trust me; Jesus would support that."

"Who is Jesus?"

"Jesus is my god like Ramah and Krishna for you."

"I don't know my god. I told you there're so many things that I don't know."

"Don't you worry, I'm here to help you. First things first; I'll teach you how to cross a road and to find your way to the Colonel's house."

"Do we have so many vehicles on the road all the time?"

"At this time of day most people are returning home after school or work and that's the reason for the heavy traffic."

Mathew left Raju at the Colonel's house and took his leave. The Colonel was sitting on the lawn at the front, taking his evening tea and called him over. Raju stood meekly bending from his waist with his arms folded.

"Why don't you sit down and tell me how your first day went at school?" He spoke in English. "I know that you probably didn't understand anything that I've just said. Nevertheless, I will speak to you in English only so you'll learn more quickly. That's the practical way of teaching you English. Remember though, if you make a mistake I'm not going to harm you anyway. I won't even scold you but correct your speech. So take courage and speak to me in English from today."

Raju, not understanding a jot of what the Colonel had said, just nodded his head and rushed inside. He found the manservant, with whom he could communicate in Telugu, and spoke to him non-stop for half an hour all about his experiences of the first day at school and how he had found his way back to the house. The manservant, who was not given much opportunity to speak, listened with rapt attention and wished him well in the days to come. What Raju did not know was that the Colonel had come inside the house and had stood behind the door listening the best he could to the long lament of his ward and managed to get the general drift of the situation.

As he retired to his own room, the Colonel's thoughts wandered down memory lane. As a young schoolboy he had been sent to a public school, an expensive one at that, as his father had been a major. A major's salary before the independence of the country had been a small fortune compared to many others. The lifestyle of the officers in the services before independence had been excellent.

They had had large, well-furnished bungalows with huge lawns laid out in the front, a kitchen garden at the rear and a great number of servants to tend to the gardens and maintain the house. There had always been a well-prepared spread of chicken and mutton and other curries on the table and the closets had been full of splendid clothes. Sending their children to one of the reputable public schools located in the valleys, which provided a salubrious climate and all-round education, was the ultimate aim of most parents in those days and indeed continues to be so to the present day. These schools had a tie and blazer outfit and an established old boy network. They were run on the British model and the young schoolboys could even learn equestrian sports which the other children in India could not even dream of.

Seth senior took his son to one of the schools in the valley where they were received by one of the teachers. He took great pains to take the boy on a guided tour of the school and showed him his dormitory. When the formalities of admission were over Seth senior had left, leaving the boy to fend for himself. The senior boys watching the proceedings from different corners pounced on the new entrant and started ragging him.

"What do you think is the distance from here to the school gate?" asked one burly senior boy.

"About three hundred yards."

"Here, we want exact answers. You've got to be precise so no guessing!" the same lad said before asking, "What is the best way to determine the distance?"

"By measuring it."

"Why don't you start then?" He tossed a foot rule at the new boy.

Seth junior all dressed up in jacket and tie specially tailored for the occasion took the foot rule and started measuring. He had no problem for the first fifty feet. Thereafter he started feeling the pain, which increased with every yard. By the time he finished at the school gate, he had lost count of the distance he had measured and fell flat on the ground. He woke up only next morning in his dormitory upper bunk still dressed in the same clothes but now thoroughly crumpled and soiled.

In the next three months Seth scaled the school clock tower, took a dunking in the school swimming pool, polished the shoes of his seniors and paraded naked in the dormitory all at the bullying orders of his seniors. He heaved a sigh of relief when fresher's day was celebrated and all the seniors who had ragged him to their heart's content hugged him, declared the end of the ragging and started treating him as a friend. His life started afresh that day and, until he joined the NDA at his father's behest, he enjoyed his schooling. He played games, established long-lasting friendships with his classmates and picked up an excellent English accent. Above all, he developed an interest in the game of cricket. This interest slowly grew into love and thereafter an addiction. He could not sleep the days that he did not play cricket. He won a place in the school cricket team and started making a name for himself. He also decided to pursue his career in cricket and make a name for himself at the national level.

"Those were the days," he sighed to himself that night after Raju's first day at school.

He was about to retire to bed, with a smile on his face recalling his past dreams, when the telephone began to ring. Although initially annoyed, his mood improved rapidly when he heard Aparna, his daughter, on the line.

"Hi, Dad!" Aparna said.

She was his elder daughter and she could always take great liberties with her dad. Seth liked the buoyant spirit and enthusiasm of his daughter and had given her full freedom to blossom in the way she had wanted. He had not wanted to be like his father, and so had let her have her way in everything. He had developed the father daughter relationship in sharp contrast to what he had had with his father.

"I was about to go to bed. Anyway, what news have you? How are you doing?"

"Fine, Dad. I'm having a great time at the university. I've been offered a good job in the campus interviews and I'm going to join a firm as soon as I finish my course. "

"I thought that you wanted to do a doctorate."

"My friends here told me that doctorate is not a very good idea. It seems when things get bad in a company the fellows with the doctorate get laid off first. I don't want to be in such a situation. The American economy is booming and jobs are a plenty. I want to earn dollars and start enjoying life. I've been studying for too long."

"Whatever you say, my dear girl, it is your life. You make it or mar it."

"With an MS degree from Berkley University there's no way I can mar it, Dad. It'll take me places."

"Do you need anything?"

"Nothing, particularly money, as I am getting a full scholarship. I'm even saving money to buy myself a used car."

"You are? Now I was thirty before I could afford to buy a car. You're not even twenty-three and buying a car! What news have you about your sister?"

"I call her every weekend and she seems to have got over the teething problems in the first semester. She's doing pretty good."

"I keep reading about crime in the USA and worry about the safety of both of you."

"Since when did you become the worrying type? Anyway, we confine ourselves to the campus and our apartment, which is close to the University. At night when we're late, the University provides an escort, so don't worry. Relax and enjoy your retirement."

She spoke for another few minutes and hung up. Seth felt snug as a bug in a rug. Both his daughters were at university abroad. They were doing well in their studies and were confident of good futures. This added to his feel-good factor.

He felt happy, contented. He got out of bed and went to the adjacent room, unlocked his wine cabinet, picked up the best bottle of whisky and helped himself to a good drink. Relishing the taste and recollecting the happy memories of the days that he had spent with his family, he returned to bed and quickly fell asleep.

VISAKHAPATNAM

Visakhapatnam is a second tier city in Andhra Pradesh on the east coast of India. With no fortresses and ramparts from which the guns boomed earlier, the municipality had no place in Indian history, not even in the struggle for independence. It was hailed as a city of destiny but showed no significant progress until the eighties. The only thing worth mentioning about the place was the various educational institutions, which provided academic learning in almost all subjects including engineering and medicine.

It provided a somewhat salubrious climate, with the summers not suffering the extreme heat and the winters being almost nonexistent. The Bay of Bengal adjacent to the city provided it with a cool breeze, which helped calm the tempers of the inhabitants. The city never witnessed either communal rights or political turmoil. The Maoist revolution was still in the nascent stage and was nothing more than an occasional nuisance. Therefore, when the central government offered a plot of land to Seth in recognition of his gallantry award, the Vir Chakra, an equivalent of the Victoria Cross in the erstwhile British Empire, he selected the aforementioned city, much to the surprise of his family.

"You're becoming like your father and taking decisions unilaterally. You never mentioned this to us before you gave your decision." His whole family, the wife and two daughters, attacked as one voice.

"I want to get as far as possible from Punjab and the Indo-Pakistan border; there are too many memories, bad ones, and they depress me. I want to start life afresh, devoid of the ghosts that have been haunting me. Besides, the city has an excellent medical college, engineering college and a good university, and it is quite cosmopolitan as there is a sprawling naval base and many public sector companies. It's also, in case of another war with Pakistan, well beyond the range of their missiles."

He did not tell them that the primary reason was to get as far away as possible from his father's place and his desire to dispense with the property that he had inherited. He had held a lifelong grudge against his father who had compelled him to join the NDA and had prevented him from joining college and playing cricket. He thought that his dream of playing for the country had been nipped in the bud by none other than his own father. Ever since he had joined the NDA there had been an uneasiness between father and son and Seth had never been able to look his father straight in the eye.

"Oh, I forgot to mention, at the naval base we can be members of the Officers' Club and continue our social life as before. Just think of it as another posting, but this time permanent. It also has a good stadium and is on the cricketing map of the country. I can see some international cricket matches there," he added happily.

The children did not understand the logic behind the decision but Priya could read her husband's feelings without much effort and let it pass without any comment. The daughters, who by then were very keen to study engineering and wanted to go abroad for further studies, also believed that the city would suit their plans. They thought that in case they did not get seats in the IIT, they could study in the local engineering college as day scholars, so they also consented happily.

When Seth disposed of his father's house, he made a complete job of it. He sold every item in it including his father's favourite golf clubs as though he wanted to erase the memory of his father once and for all. He did not want to keep the smallest trace of his memory in the new house. Finally, Seth called his manservant to him. The loyal man, and his family before him, had served for many long years. Now he was told to pack.

"I'm sorry I have to say goodbye to you and your family, but I'll definitely make it worth your while," Seth explained.

"We've served your family since your grandfather's days. You grew up in my arms. How can you dismiss us?" The servant was very upset.

"I'm not dismissing you. Would I be so ungrateful after the excellent service that you and your family have given us for so many years? I've a good compensation package for you. We're going to a far-off place. You'd be like a fish out of water and would find it hard to adjust there. I leave you with a heavy heart but leave I must. Please try to understand."

The servant understood the ways of Seth. Once he had made up his mind there was no way that a servant, despite his long years of service, could change it. He was resigned to his fate and left with tears rolling down his sunken cheeks. The relationship between Seth and his servant was beyond words for he had spent many years in the care and company of the older man. Seth had always shunned the company of his father and had found solace in the love and affection that the servant and his entire family had shown him. Some things had to be done though and he decided to do so, no matter what inconvenience or heartache they might cause.

He moved lock, stock and barrel to Visakhapatnam and his new bungalow, which he constructed with great care. He made new friends and got his daughters into good schools and settled down in his new life. Both girls studied well and thanks to the Vir Chakra and the government policy of reserving seats in the colleges for armed forces personnel, he got them admitted to the best engineering college in the city. They would have got seats on their own merit but his gallantry award enabled them to get the branch of their choice and at the place of their choice. The daughters excelled in their studies, as was their wont, and went abroad according to plan. Visakhapatnam has been kind to him, he thought, but providence proved him wrong.

When the children flew the coop, the parents were left alone. Priya started missing her daughters badly. The heart rules the body in many ways. When she started missing her daughters, she also started picking up ailments as though she was shopping in a supermarket and soon her bag was full. Seth made frequent rounds to the naval and civil hospitals. Tragically, after a minor operation for a knee complaint, she developed complications and breathed her last, leaving Seth in unmitigated grief. The daughters rushed home but could not console their father. They were unable to stay long as they were halfway through their education abroad. As they approached the end of their studies and began to seek well paid jobs they asked their father to shift his base to the USA and stay with them.

"Why do you want to stay all by yourself, Dad?" they asked.

"I've some work to do here. I'll come when you settle down and have huge houses and loads of kids."

He did not ask them to return to India and provide him with their company as that would have been tantamount to putting fetters on them. He had all along given them their freedom and was not going to change now. He prided himself as a champion of women's rights. He had brought up his daughters as sons and, unlike other fathers in the country, he had been determined that his daughters would have the education they wanted and pursue jobs of their choice. He promised that he would not interfere even in their selection of life partners. He thought that he was a liberal and was not going to change his perspective under any circumstances.

"You must promise to visit us often then."

"Fine, we'll settle on a formula. I'll come to the USA during the odd years and you come in every even year."

"That's a deal!" the daughters said in one voice during a conference call.

Seth slowly got into the habit of managing his loneliness and waited for the annual reunion with his daughters. One had finally settled down in San Francisco and the other in Philadelphia. Every alternate year he went and spent time with both daughters while the other years they came home together. Their presence made him very happy during each short stay of three weeks. He appointed a local man as his servant, who understood some Hindi, and gradually adapted to retired life.

Raju found Visakhapatnam a complete paradise. He had of course had no real concept of paradise but he thought, if there was a paradise, it ought to be the city of Visakhapatnam. He had never stepped out of the village until the Colonel had brought him home to the city. Raju's village had one small road made of mud, which used to soak up the water and become terribly soggy in the monsoons. The village had mostly thatched huts and the few, slightly richer villagers had buildings made of brick walls. The very rich, like Sarpanch, had concrete houses. The teacher's thatched house was in a remote corner, reserved for people of lower castes, who were never welcome in the better part of the village.

Here in the city, Raju found many concrete buildings neatly arranged in rows and streets that were well laid out, with wide roads covered with bitumen. Above all, he found many vehicles, whereas only bullock carts plied the mud tracks in his village. A ride in the bullock cart was almost painful and had rattled all his bones but the ride in the Colonel's car had been so smooth, giving him a feeling as though he was floating on air. The Colonel's car was good but Raju found many cars of different sizes and shapes, shining brightly and rolling down the streets at amazing speeds.

In the village the people always tormented him in every respect as the teacher, who had taken him in, was poor and from a lower caste. He was the worst dressed in the village as all he had were a few pairs of shorts and no shirts. In the city, no one asked him his caste and he found many people dressed more shabbily than himself. Thanks to the clothing that the Colonel had arranged for him, he found himself well dressed when compared to many others. The city had plenty of shops that stocked a wide variety of goods of different colours and designs, whereas the village had only one or two shops and the shopkeeper had always kept him waiting until he had finished with all the other customers.

Raju found that in the city everybody minded their own business but they were always in a hurry and tearing around at great speed. In the village, time passed so slowly and often he had not known what to do with himself. His main problem in the city however was he did not know his way about. He was scared of getting lost and losing the Colonel. Seth was his lifeline and he desperately wanted to hang onto him at any cost. He spoke to few people as he was scared of showing his ignorance and could talk freely only with the manservant in the house and Mathew at the school. His communication with the Colonel was also sketchy as the latter was not fluent in the local language and mixed in many words of English, which was all Latin and Greek to Raju.

One evening, when the Colonel left for a party and the manservant had retired to his quarters, the telephone in the hall started ringing. He had heard the Colonel talking to someone on the telephone before but Raju had no idea how to use it. He had not yet learnt the role and importance of telephone in daily life. As the telephone continued to ring for sometime, he plucked up enough courage to pick the instrument up. He heard someone saying, "Hello." He took that part of the instrument from which the voice was heard and placed it next to his ear to hear more clearly.

"Hello, who's speaking?" he heard the voice say from the other end. He mustered up all the courage that he could find and said that he did not understand English.

Unfortunately the Colonel's daughters spoke little or no Telugu. "Where's my dad? Where's his servant,

Simhachalam?" a girl's voice shouted.

The young lad could not even decipher this little bit of conversation and put the instrument down helplessly. He then decided that the only way to manage in the Colonel's house was to learn English and learn it quickly. He decided to confide in Mathew regarding his latest troubles.

After some time the Colonel returned from the party in a good mood. Normally jovial and exuberant he was feeling even better as he had enjoyed the party and had met some old colleagues from the NDA. As he was changing, the telephone rang and Aparna was on the line.

"Who answered the telephone last? It wasn't Simhachalam but some strange boy who didn't understand a word of what I said. Who is he?" The Colonel explained the circumstances under which he had found Raju and his plans for the boy. "I know that despite all your assertions to the contrary, you've always yearned for a son, like any Indian father, and you want him to be your son."

"Don't be silly. I've never craved or cared for a son. If you recollect your upbringing, I have always groomed you as a son. I don't miss a son and I'm not going to make him my son. I brought him home with me to improve his talent for cricket. You know my love of the game and how I feel about it."

"Dad, you're perhaps cheating yourself. You wanted a son badly and since you never had one you're now taking this boy under your roof. Why don't you admit that you are fulfilling your dream of having a son?"

"You're partly correct. I brought him to fulfil one of my dreams but not about a son. In fact I never dreamt about a son."

"I am not convinced, Dad. Anyway it's your problem. At least teach the fellow how to answer the phone and convey messages."

"I'll certainly do that. Give me some time; remember that Rome wasn't built in a day. I don't know why he picked up the telephone, he doesn't even know how to use the thing."

Next morning Raju told Mathew the whole incident in graphic detail and how bad it had made him feel.

"I'll teach you a couple of words and sentences everyday. You'll have to practise them and then repeat them to me the next day," Mathew told him and then assured Raju that he would make him proficient in English and on a par with other boys before the end of the year. He also presented his friend with a Telugu/English dictionary.

"Why are you giving me this present?"

"I told my father about you and he asked me to help you out. He gave me the money to buy the book."

At this point Raju learnt to say thank you.

OFF STUMP

The off stump plays a pivotal role in cricket. A ball pitched on the off stump has immense possibilities. It may proceed straight and, unless the batsman is a novice, connect with the meat of the bat and drop dead like an unsung hero. However the pitch, the grass, or lack of it, the humidity, the wind along with seam, pace, swing, spin, the bowler's action and a host of diverse factors produce many interesting variations.

A ball swinging into the batsman may crash into the stumps or knock the pads in its way sending the batsman back to the pavilion. Equally, a ball swinging away from the batsman may find the edge of the bat and end up in the safe hands of a slip fielder. A ball spinning and turning into the batsman may end up in the hands of a leg slip or a ball spinning away from the batsman may end up in the wicket keeper's gloves. It may bounce, surprise the batsman and hit the handle of the bat and fly into the hands of any of the close fielders.

However, the delivery may also be hit if it is of a short length and soon find itself kissing the ropes on the covers or mid-on. Sometimes it may get hit hard and fly over the head of the third man for a six. It may also bounce very high, sail over the batsman and the wicket keeper and speed away to the boundary line. So is life. It swings, bounces and takes many curious turns in an altogether unpredictable way at times and springs many surprises on everyone, including the spectators, Seth thought. He was always prone to delve into his past and recall the various googlies and flippers that life had delivered and, at times, bowled him all ends up.

Seth initially had no inclination to join the army or any of the services for that matter despite continuous prodding from his father who had served as a major in the army before independence. Seth liked cricket and wanted to play cricket in school and college. He was good at the game and mediocre in his studies. His father, Major Seth, had a different mindset and ideas of his own. Like most Indian males, he ran his house like a mini dictator but his service in the army had made him worse. Tall, ramrod straight and unbending he was unbending in life too. His word was law in his house and he brooked no dissent. "NDA for you!" he told his son and that decided the matter once and for all.

Accordingly he put his son into a reputable public school which, although expensive, had a reputation for sending many students as cadets into the National Defence Academy at Khadakavasla. His father also paid special fees for extra coaching to ensure his objective and soon Seth found himself as a cadet in the famous NDA, which provided the bulk of officers to the three services in the country. Seth's father dragged his reluctant son to the Academy and left only when he had satisfied himself that his son was well ensconced in the portals of the hallowed institution.

Seth's first reaction at the sight of the imposing buildings and the smartly marching cadets was outright fear. He felt intimidated and thought that he would never fit into the organisation. He wanted to protest or run away back to the railway station and get home. However, before he could think of a real plan of action, one of the senior cadets literally caught him and started ragging him. The ragging, although hard, was without malice and was a process of breaking in the newcomers, fitting them into the routine and the way of life in NDA, which is unique even today. His seniors noticed his reluctance, intensified their efforts, gave him no time to think for himself and kept him on his toes all the time. Seth found life rushing past him and, before he could comprehend what was happening, was well and truly into the process of training and was halfway through his first term. One evening out of desperation during the games period, he went to the playing grounds and found the cricket nets. He stood in a corner watching his seniors go through their paces of a regular practice session.

A senior approached him. "What? You think you can play cricket? It's not a game for sissies, you know? What's happened? Has the cat got your tongue? Why don't you answer? Do you want to bowl?" he asked all in one breath.

Seth, speechless out of fear for the senior, simply nodded his head. The older lad tossed a ball, a fairly new one, at him and pointed towards the bowling end in a contemptuous way. He made Seth feel small by implying that he should ask no favours and earn his place to play cricket with such 'outstanding players'.

Infuriated and insulted, Seth bowled the first ball with all the speed that he could muster. The batsman in the nets, obviously a senior from the last term, confidently drove it away with ease and everyone had a good laugh. "We have a Hall in NDA from now on!" someone joked and everyone had a hearty laugh at the expense of Seth. This made him mad and he bowled the next ball with real venom in it. The ball sped at a very fast pace and crashed into the woodwork behind the batsman who looked surprised and puzzled.

He was the captain of the NDA cricket team and he had earned his Blazer in the second term. He had made a name for himself for his batting technique and prowess and did not like it one bit when a novice, a cadet in his first term, knocked his stumps flying with his second ball. "What's your name, boy?" he asked with all the contempt at his disposal although he was senior to Seth only by a couple of years.

"Seth, sir," he murmured.

"Okay, they say one swallow doesn't make a summer. Come on, let's see whether you can bowl me out again."

This time he threw the ball mockingly at Seth and challenged him to bowl his best. Soon it was a contest between Seth and the captain of the team. Although there were six other bowlers bowling at the same time the batsman paid particular attention when Seth bowled. His ego, already hurt, made him play with caution. The way he showed respect for the bowling of Seth made others take notice of the bowler. Seth did not win the contest but he did win their acceptance and was admitted into the NDA fraternity of cricket players on his first day of playing. He also picked up a nickname 'Hall'.

Playing cricket provided great relief and good motivation to continue in the NDA and Seth started taking more interest in his studies. He slowly moved up in his class and improved his grades. At the end of the first term, he was presented the NDA Blazer in cricket and he felt proud wearing it. It was indeed a rare honour for no first term cadet had ever received the Blazer until then. He caressed the NDA emblem with 'cricket' underneath affixed to the pocket of his blazer and felt immensely happy as he now formed part of the first string team of the Academy. That moment remained permanently etched in his memory, as that was the moment his dream started and a new idea began to germinate in his young mind, the idea of playing cricket at higher levels and for the country. Thereafter he played cricket with great passion, taking advice from the coach and his seniors. Whenever he had spare time he went to the ground and honed his skills in bowling, bending his back and trying to generate as much pace as possible.

During the late fifties, the Indian cricket team was still in its embryonic stage and had few or no pace bowlers at all. Indeed the majority of bowlers concentrated on spin of both varieties. Ramakant Desai was the lone player who relished bowling with the new ball and generated some medium pace, which was way below the speed of bowlers of other countries. Indian spinners earned a good name for themselves and the Indian batsman also mastered the art of thumping the spinners for fours and sixes. However, the same batsmen fared poorly when they faced fast bowlers. They used to feel terrorised, intimidated and got out cheaply. Although cricket was confined only to the educated lot and was played in the good schools and colleges in the fifties, the game had a good following and all the cricket lovers felt the need for good fast bowlers.

It was during Seth's last term in the Academy that 'Hall', of the NDA, had the chance to meet the original Hall in flesh and blood. The West Indies team that had fast bowlers Wesley Hall and Roy Gilchrist, the two most feared bowlers in the world at that time, visited India. The Board of Control for Cricket in India, BCCI, in its wisdom and to everyone's surprise, scheduled a three-day match between the visiting team and the NDA. The team consisted of mainly cadets from the Academy with a few players from the services team. The joint team had neither any standing in the country nor any chance against the visitors.

Seth, one of the frontline bowlers for the NDA, got his chance to play his first international match without having played any match of true importance. The young cadets, with hardly any experience in domestic cricket let alone international cricket and all of them only in their late teens, put up a very spirited display of guts and determination against the world-renowned West Indies; particularly against the fast bowlers who put the fear of God into the batsmen of many countries.

The young Academy captain, a cadet by the name of Sengupta, scored a flawless century braving the fast bowlers. When Seth got his chance, he bowled with all the energy and reserves at his command and generated what he thought was a very good pace but the West Indian batsmen made mincemeat of him and smashed his bowling and confidence to smithereens. When he bowled fast the visiting batsmen did not even bat an eyelid and hit him hard, sending the ball crashing to the ropes. The NDA team lost and lost badly but won the hearts of the cricket loving public in the country. The young cadets showed rare courage in facing the fast bowlers. They proved that the West Indians were, after all, not invincible and with grit and determination they also could be made to bite the dust. When the game ended there was a spontaneous round of applause from all the spectators for the young cadets. The NDA stadium, although small, was jampacked with discerning cricket fans and even the visiting team joined in the applause. The touring captain complimented the young cadets on their enthusiasm and talent. He had a special word for the batsman who had scored a century against them and finally added a word about the bowling of Seth for whom he predicted a good future in cricket.

Although demoralised, Seth found renewed hope in those words and continued to play with greater passion. Sengupta, the batsman who scored a century, was picked by the national selectors to play at number three position in the next Test against the visiting team. He scored only a four and later drifted into oblivion.

On completion of his training at the NDA Seth was posted to an infantry battalion. His reputation as a fast bowler preceded him. Although his battalion and the entire army gave him much encouragement and provided many opportunities to hone his skills in cricket, he could never attain the heights he hoped for. He remained as the star player for the services team, which was one of the best teams in the country at that time but made no progress worth mentioning. One of the principal reasons for his failure to make progress was his father's apathy towards the game.

Major Seth had always thought that he had not achieved his true potential and that he had been poorly treated by one of his superiors, an Englishman, while writing the Annual Confidential Report, the ACR. He had always believed, and the Major's colleagues confirmed it time and again, that he had the potential to be a general, and was bound to rise through the ranks, but his career stopped short at a mere major. He did not even make it to the rank of lieutenant colonel.

Disappointed and disgusted by his treatment, Seth's father left the army and retired to his country home to look after his ancestral property. He thought that his son, who had successfully completed his training at the NDA and had fared really quite well, would blossom and then rise through the ranks to be a general. He truly thought that it was within his family's ability to produce such an officer and possibly even a Chief of the Army Staff, COAS. When he found his son was concentrating more on cricket and less on his career he vented his fury on him. He emphasised that cricket would get him nowhere in life whereas the rank of general was worth something to strive for and achieve.

"But I like playing cricket, Dad!" Seth protested.

"What good will cricket do you? It won't get you even two square meals a day when you retire."

"But I get a great thrill from it and I've many admirers. My heart's truly in the game. When I become too old for it then I'll shift my attention to my career."

"You can't build a career overnight. You have to work hard for it from day one. Playing cricket in my opinion is a waste of time."

"But I've got a good name playing cricket and I am sure that this will pay good dividends in my career too."

"You've never been brilliant and you've never listened to me. I can only hope that good sense will prevail." He dismissed his son with disdain.

Seth's passion for the game took a severe beating with his father's comments and he could never put his heart and soul into the sport again. Although he continued to play cricket and made headlines in the newspapers with his bowling figures against several teams, he missed something. He lacked the fire in his soul and the passion in his heart, which had been doused by his father.

Cricket in the fifties and sixties was more a gentleman's

game and professionalism had not yet set in. Most of the cricket players all over the world were amateurs, who played not for money but for the sheer joy of playing the game. They had good jobs or other incomes to sustain them and the few professionals were financed by the not yet extinct Maharajahs and other business tycoons.

The cricket players of repute were popular in society circles and became what we now term celebrities. They were invariably invited to all the important parties and hosts took great pride in having the star cricketers on their guest lists. No second thought was given before placing a glass of spirits of the very best variety before the players. Neither the hosts, nor the players, realised that alcohol and cricket do not mix. Scotch whisky was difficult to get due to the policies of the government at that time but, at the parties of these celebrities, not only Scotch but also a wide variety of imported wines and exotic liquors adorned the tables. The cricketers slowly got into the habit of imbibing liquor, even on the eve of an important match or Test, as physical fitness was not considered an issue. India's opening batsman, Pankaj Roy, who established a record for the first wicket partnership with Vinoo Mankad against New Zealand and showed good technique and temperament in batting, was a great liability as a fielder.

Seth followed this pattern. Slowly the drink and the advancing years took their toll and his pace slackened quickly. Although he played the game with the same ardour, the results slowly and steadily declined until they mattered no more. It was the saddest day in his life when he was omitted from the services team. His dream of playing for the country died on that day and he gave it a decent burial with a fine bottle of whisky. He drowned himself in liquor for quite some time until his commanding officer took charge of him and weaned him away from the bottle and put him on the right track for progress in his career. However, by then, the drink and defeatism had taken their toll and undermined his confidence and progress. His dream of playing for India played on his mind time and again and whenever he slept, he dreamt of the day that had never arrived, a goal that he had never achieved. He never dreamt of riches, high ranks or success in any other field than cricket.

THE NON-STRIKER

The non-striker, who occupies the crease opposite the batsman, is not a *horse de combat*. His role, apart from helping the batsman taking a run, is to keep the strike rotating all the time in order to destabilise the bowler, who otherwise would bowl to the same batsman and quickly find chinks in his armour. When the strike is rotated, the bowler has to adjust his line and length to the new batsman and his rhythm is upset.

A combination of a left-handed and a right-handed batsman is best as the bowler and the entire set of fielders will have to adjust their positions and the captain will have to adapt his tactics. The non-striker also helps in calling for quick singles, especially when the ball goes behind the wicket and out of sight of the striker; these quick singles keep the scoreboard ticking over. He also helps in watching the shine of the ball and gives indications to the facing batsman of the likely reverse swing the ball may take when the fast bowlers bowl with an old ball. The non-striker at times provides caution and advice when he finds the striker getting carried away after executing some audacious strokes. He keeps a track of the scoreboard and advises the striker either to step on the gas or to slow down to adjust the run rate.

Mathew proved to be a Good Samaritan, a non-striker, to Raju. He taught the country boy the most common words in English, their usage and pronunciation. Above all, he kept Raju away from the class bully and other boys who were prone to make fun of him and treat Raju like a country bumpkin. Mathew's theory, which he kept repeating, was that it was not Raju's fault that he did not know any English and that the entire class should help him to become one of them. Soon Raju graduated to learning to speak full sentences and since Mathew was a bright student and commanded the respect of his peers, he was able to pressurise the other boys into accepting the village lad.

Before long, he took Raju back to his house and introduced him to his parents. Mathew's father was a Deputy General Manager of a public sector company and always looked worried.

"He's always anxious about labour troubles," Mathew explained.

One evening, after several visits, Mathew's mother produced some beefsteaks. "Do you eat beef?" she asked.

Raju became anxious, he had never heard of beef and desperately wanted to find out from the Colonel if it was right for him to eat it or not.

Eventually Raju took Mathew to the Colonel's house and his friend introduced himself. He found the Colonel to be an affable gentleman and made a point of visiting his home regularly. After a few visits Mathew plucked up courage and asked the Colonel whether Raju could eat beef. The Colonel told him that beef was not used in his house and so Raju also should conform to that policy.

"But he says that he doesn't know who his god is," Mathew said politely.

"He's in my care and so he'll follow my practices. It has nothing to do with his religion."

Raju explained to Mathew that as far as he was concerned the Colonel's words were law and he would never do anything not approved of by his mentor.

The next month the monsoon set in in India while the months of June to September were ideal for visiting the USA. The Colonel always made certain that he left early in June to avoid the monsoon and to spend the summer with his daughters. While the Colonel was away, Mathew would come to see Raju every day and they played in the grounds and practised cricket together. The boys had the run of the whole house, except the study, and Mathew was taken by the neatness and order of the place. He was particularly impressed by the trophies in one cupboard and decided to increase the pace of his lessons with Raju.

The Colonel called from the USA once a week to check on the welfare of the boy and issue instructions to his manservant. During the three months of the Colonel's foreign tour, Raju visited the village and found out how his sister and the teacher were. He took cookies and trinkets for the girl he thought of as his little sister. The villagers noted the change in him and all the boys who he had played cricket with saw the rapid alterations in the village lad, his new clothes, his manner of speaking and his ever-increasing fluency in English.

When the Colonel finally returned from the USA he noticed a huge improvement in Raju and, by the year-end, he found the lad was speaking broken English. He complimented Mathew and asked him to continue the good work.

On one occasion, when the Colonel was out, the telephone rang. This time Raju picked it up with confidence. By then he had learnt which was the mouthpiece and held the telephone properly.

"Hello, who is speaking?" He heard a girl's voice and he realised that the girl must be one of the Colonel's daughters. "I'm Raju, sister," he replied without any hesitation.

"Don't call me sister! My name's Aparna. Where's my dad?" she spoke with a twang of an American accent and a certain irritation in her voice.

However, Raju found no problem in understanding her and looked heavenwards and thanked Mathew in his mind. "Not home," he managed to say although he could not understand the slight anger in his sister's voice.

"Tell him to call me when he comes home," she said rather haughtily and disconnected.

The Colonel rang his daughter back on his return.

"So your ward could understand part of what I told him. I am glad he's making some progress. Is that all your own effort?" Aparna asked.

"No, it was all the effort of one of his classmates, Mathew. He seems to be doing a good job."

"Let the boy learn some Hindi too. That would make our problem of communication with him a little easier."

"Let's not overburden him with too many languages all at once. As it is, the Government is trying to do this and ruining young minds by trying to stuff the kids with too many subjects and languages."

Suparna, the younger daughter, was more supportive of Raju. Whenever she spoke to her dad she asked to speak to him too and spoke endearingly, using simple words and explaining their meanings. She had spent a longer period in Visakhapatnam and could speak a smattering of Telugu which made her task easier. When Raju spoke to Suparna on the telephone, he felt very happy. Unlike the elder daughter, she had accepted him as part of the family and always spoke to him softly. He had only seen her photograph in the main living room but she looked kind and compassionate compared to the older girl who appeared more beautiful but a bit self-centred, if not arrogant. He compared the two girls with his poor sister in the village and could not accept that they should have such different lives. He resolved in his young mind that he would strive to get his younger sister to the same level as his newfound ones.

Twenty-two languages are spoken in India and many more dialects exist. The communication between Indians is very strange. Even people from the same state and speaking in the same tongue but hailing from different parts of the state cannot understand each other. This is because the language spoken in the border districts is so often corrupted by the language of the next state. Consequently, Indians meeting abroad invariably converse in English.

When the central government tried to impose Hindi as a national language, there was a revolt and the government was forced to retract. Where the government failed however, Bollywood succeeded and, through the Hindi films and songs which gained popularity, the following for the language increased. The Hindi used in the films is a peculiar combination of many languages and liberally sprinkled with English words too. It is now widely used and understood by a good percentage of the population but Hindi can never be the sole official language as it would deprive a large section of people of their jobs. Language was one of the principal divisive forces, which dissolved by itself without help from the government. However, there are still so many other undercurrents lurking in Indian society.

Raju wanted to sort out the issue of eating beef so he asked Mathew, "How come you eat beef and the Colonel says not to?"

"In our country some people don't eat beef, some don't eat pork, some don't eat any meat at all. And you won't believe it but some don't even eat onions! It all depends on one's religion and caste."

"What is this religion and caste?" demanded a confused Raju.

Mathew, although a young boy of nine, knew much more than many of his peers thanks to his mother, who took pains to teach him several things not connected with their class work. "Even I don't know really, but I do know that Hindus don't eat beef which is cow's meat because for them the cow is a sacred animal. The Muslims don't eat pork which is pig's meat; the pig in their eyes is a dirty animal. The Brahmins do not eat meat at all as they think it is a sin to kill animals for food. So you see, in our class we have people of all religions and different castes."

"What's a country?"

"You keep asking so many questions for which I don't know

the answers yet. We'll have to learn together as we go along."
He sounded a bit annoyed and Raju did not want to offend him
and anyway, by then, the teacher had entered the classroom
and a sudden hush descended.

The young Mathew did not know that country, religion and
caste were closely linked. He did not understand yet that
religion was one of the dominant divisive forces in his country
and that the caste system divided the Hindus and caused
avoidable damage to the society and body politic.

MIDDLE STUMP

The middle stump is the centrepiece of cricket, like the King in chess and the Prince of Denmark in Hamlet. Every bowler dreams of knocking the middle stump out and most batsmen take guard on it; in fact, they protect it with great care as their pride takes a severe beating when the bowler uproots it. A ball pitched on the middle stump is a bowler's delight and is treated with great respect by most of the batsmen for it can knock out any of the three stumps with little or no deviation.

Even the umpires respect a ball pitched on the middle stump as it helps them in arriving at a decision for LBW, leg before wicket, and makes their decisions less open to criticism. It can also be a batsman's delight when pitched either full or short of a length as it enables him to turn the ball to the square leg boundary with a mere flick of the wrists. It can easily be worked out for a single by a simple shot of turning the blade of the bat a wee bit. Such a shot became almost the bread and butter stroke for the Indian batsmen, who endearingly named it a *chapatti* shot.

Raju felt that he had been pitched into the position of a middle stump. He was a nobody, not even a player, and nowhere in the field when the Colonel took him away from his village. All his life he had been subjected to ridicule mainly because of his unknown parentage. All his schoolmates and the other villagers had taunted him continuously. Only the schoolteacher, who had found him abandoned outside the village, took care of him and he never mentioned anything about his parents. He alone assured Raju time and time again that the latter could not be faulted if his parents abandoned him. Therefore, the schoolteacher had taken care of him and provided whatever little he could without any prejudice. He had treated Raju and his own daughter equally.

When the Colonel took the young lad to a store and bought him trousers, shirts and a couple of pairs of shoes, it was the first time that Raju had worn such things. He had never seen a full-length mirror before so he could not believe his reflection and preened in front of the mirror in his new clothing. He was delighted with what he saw and did not know how to thank the Colonel. In fact, he did not even know that his benefactor was a Colonel and was at a loss as to how to address him.

"What should I call you, sir?"

"Call me Dad from now on."

Raju wanted to call him 'God' as he had heard about 'Him' but not the word 'Dad'. "What does Dad mean, sir?"

"It means Father."

"Are you my father, sir?"

"No! Not at all! Not even by a long shot. In the absence of any other suitable word I thought it best for you to call me Dad."

Raju did not fully understand the word Dad even when he had joined the school and started lessons; it was an unknown concept for the lad. The Colonel's house, the school, school uniform and a room all to himself; it all seemed like a dream to him. He did not know why the gentleman was doing all this. He tried to believe that it was not his fault that his biological parents had abandoned him outside the village and he did feel he deserved a better deal than he had been getting in the village. He thought perhaps that some angel must have visited him, taken pity on his plight and finally placed him under the Colonel's protection. He did not know whom to pray for, the schoolteacher was an atheist and had never mentioned about God. He did not know his religion, caste or such other things which played an important role in the life of any individual in India.

"Whom should I thank for all this, sir?" he asked quietly.

"You thank yourself," was the reply.

"Why not God?"

"Who is your god?" the Colonel asked him gently.

"Right now you're my god. I don't know of any other."

"Don't elevate me to that status. At best I am your godfather." Seth was horrified.

"What does that mean?"

"You'll learn when you grow up."

"What should I do to thank you for all these things that you are providing me with?"

"You play cricket, play it well and play to my satisfaction. In between you also learn your lessons in school and the school of life."

"I love playing cricket and I'll do as you ask happily."

Seth chalked out a programme for Raju in his mind. He began his programme with good food; Raju, half starved all his life, started having three square meals a day. He went to sleep not on an empty stomach, as was his wont, but as a happy and contented boy. He had a bed all for himself and the bed included a mattress and sheets to cover him up when required and he had a bathroom attached to his bedroom. Raju started to fill out and grew quickly. His lean frame, which had been nothing but bones, began to take on a more normal appearance and he started to have more energy. He went to a school which had proper classrooms and a well-dressed teacher who did not wield a cane and turned up for lessons. Slowly he started to assimilate his new world and began understanding the people around him. Above all, he felt a great relief as no one taunted or teased him about his parentage. The other boys now readily accepted him in their set and even talked to him with respect as they took him as a ward of the Colonel.

Raju often rambled around the large spacious house feeling

very happy that he had became part of a dream home, the like of which he had never seen before. He was always particularly impressed by the living room, which had a special cupboard with several trophies and shields that were all kept gleaming with polish and neatly arranged. He often asked Seth about the trophies and learnt that the collection signified the latter's success in cricket. Looking at the vast collection he began to understand his benefactor's passion for the game.

His young fertile brain, devoid of preconceptions, thought for the first time that he should somehow make Seth proud. He did not really know how to repay the kindness of his benefactor but a small notion of succeeding in cricket and winning trophies like the ones in the cupboard took root. It was a small root but it provided him with some goal, some purpose in his young life, which until then had been drifting along without any point or meaning. He often looked at the family portraits and found the two daughters of Colonel Seth beautiful. He wanted to do something in order to give his sister a chance to grow up and be beautiful like them.

Seth's house, located in the centre of a huge plot of land gifted to him for his gallantry award, looked a picture of order and cleanliness. He made sure that everything in it was put in its correct place and maintained in typical army fashion, always spic and span. So he wasted no time in getting the area next to the bedrooms cleared up and levelled. With help from his army friends and advice from the right people he got a good cricket pitch prepared and arranged a serviceable net and half mat.

Seth started the programme proper when Raju was eleven. The first step consisted of running, and running fast. He made his ward run everyday and made it a part of his own morning routine. The second step was developing a stride suitable for fast bowling. Raju took to all this training like a duck takes to water. Then, finally, the Colonel started teaching him about bowling. Soon a daily routine developed for the pair; the retired Colonel and his ward would get up well before sunrise, practise running and then have the bowling lessons. Raju picked up the art and craft of fast bowling easily and made good progress. Seth, satisfied with his ward's development, found his own dream also taking some sort of shape.

Cricket is a mind game and full of dreams. A man without a dream cannot be a successful cricketer. Some may acquire the technique, some may have the intrinsic skills but they cannot succeed without dreams, dreams of name and fame and making it big in the game. A vision, coupled with determination and belief in one's self, constitutes the main ingredient of success in cricket.

One day a young boy of the same age as Raju approached Seth. He looked well dressed and well behaved. He also had a sparkle in his eye which promised a good future and much confidence. After paying his respects to Seth, he said that he also loved to play cricket and wanted to join them in the mornings for practice. He had a simple proposal that he would stand between the bowler and the stumps, provide a target for the bowler, wield his bat and learn the art of batting if possible.

"Are you also poor?" asked Seth.

"No, is that an essential requirement to join your group?" the lad asked politely.

Seth was fascinated with the young lad for asking the question and also appreciated his guts in facing up to him and posing it. Normally boys of his age tended to be meek and obsequious to their elders who have a standing in the society.

"No, that's not essential at all! What is essential is a love for the game. What's your name and who are you?"

"My name's Ramu, I'm the son of the Professor in Psychology at the university and I love to play cricket. I can get my own bat and other gear."

Seth could find no reason to deny the simple request of the young lad. Soon the three of them formed a cohesive team. Under the guidance of Seth, Raju bowled and Ramu batted. He set the goals for the two young lads, one to bowl out the other and the other to defend his wicket and, if possible, hit the ball as hard as possible. He taught the basics to both the boys and, as days progressed, the several different techniques in batting and bowling. He bought them books on cricket, which showed the correct skills involved in bowling and batting and the boys, quick on the uptake, learnt quickly and made good progress.

Sometime after Ramu had joined them, Seth had a visitor who introduced himself as Professor Deb; it was Ramu's father. "I wanted to thank you for including my son in your small cricket team."

"Don't mention it. The boy must be really interested in the game as he took the initiative and asked me to join us."

"I'm a Professor of Psychology at the local university. My son is quite good at his studies, yet he wants to play cricket. I don't know what to advise him. I believe in letting the children do what they want and not force our ideas down their throats."

"I couldn't agree with you more. Sometimes the parents want their children to do what they themselves wanted to do but couldn't. They want to achieve success vicariously."

"My wife is a lecturer in psychology too and we give great importance to child psychology. We decided not to interfere in Ramu's interest in cricket although cricket doesn't provide a decent living these days."

"I live alone as I lost my wife and my two daughters are in the USA. Ramu is always welcome here and I'd be happy to have your company at any time."

"Thank you, Colonel. We'll take your offer up now we've met." Thereafter Professor Deb and his gracious wife Latha visited the Colonel regularly and became his firm friends.

Seth, despite the intervening years, had not lost his knowledge of the game and taught the finer points of it to the two boys. He was a fatherly figure, friend, mentor, guide and a dedicated coach all rolled into one for them. Under his guidance, the two boys improved their game slowly and steadily. Ramu started showing signs of natural instincts and a flair for batting, he took enormous pains to practise each shot as given in the book. Soon both the boys attracted the attention of the sports master at the school and they were included in the school cricket team. Thanks to the coaching of Seth, the boys started making a name and winning matches for their school. When their team won the interschool trophy for the first time the cricket fraternity of the state started taking a keen interest in the two boys.

VIR CHAKRA

When Seth returned from his morning walk and run, he found his house bathed in bright sunlight and shimmering in the heat. The red tiles on the roof, the jutting out French windows, painted green, and the pastel colours of the exterior paintwork gave the house a continental look. The Gulmohor tree, in full bloom in the left corner, added a riot of colour to the whole scene. The green and well-manicured lawns on one side and the cricket pitch on the right helped create an attractive picture. The bougainvilleas planted around the perimeter wall were in full bloom and added a fine mosaic of different hues to the picturesque scene. Seth felt proud of his house. After all, it was the only tangible thing that he had salvaged out of his life, which had been ruined by several factors beyond his control.

The house had been made possible by the grant of the huge plot of land gifted to him by a grateful nation for his gallantry. The government had awarded him the Vir Chakra, one of the highest gallantry awards bestowed for valour in battle. In recognition of the award, he had received a very large plot in the best area of the city. When he looked at the house, he felt both proud and at the same time heartsick. The memories of the battle that gained him the coveted award, Vir Chakra, came into sharp focus and played before him, unrolling his career in the army and the way it swerved and swung.

During his cricket playing days, Seth had served as a captain in the army, but this had had its problems. After the 1962 war with the Chinese, the Indian army underwent a massive expansion and raised many battalions to guard the country on three fronts. It recruited a large number of officers from the civilian population, giving them emergency commissions and inducting them into the army after a condensed form of training. The young officers, plucked out of civilian life and given a semblance of training, were very different from the hard trained lot from the NDA. The army also provided an opportunity for the more educated amongst the common soldiers. They took educational tests and those that passed were sent on a short training course and then commissioned as officers.

The Officer Corps, especially the younger bunch, consisted then of three classes: the hard core from the NDA & IMA; the emergency commissioned officers with college degrees, some of them having good educational qualifications and academic minds; and the ones who rose from the ranks. This division rattled the budding officers from the NDA who only earned their pips after three years of hard training in the Academy and later in the IMA. They had to rub shoulders with other officers who had won their promotion with little or no effort and had had hardly any training worth its name. No wonder they looked down on all categories of officers other than the products of the hallowed institution of the NDA. Only a few of the more discerning soldiers and those directly affected could see this fissure in the Officer Corps of the army.

As Seth spent many months touring with the cricket team and less on operational training, he found that he had to catch up on many aspects to make good progress in his career. He started taking more interest in his work when he began to feel that his dream of playing for the country was nowhere near turning into a reality and he studied the various manuals diligently.

The 1965 Indo-Pak war changed Seth's life completely. In September 1965, Pakistan attacked India without any warning. Sri Lal Bahadur Shastri, the then Prime Minister of India, declared in parliament in no uncertain terms that "India had the right to select a time and place to attack" in retaliation. The army chose Seth's battalion, then stationed on the Punjab border, to attack immediately and deliver a blow to the flanks of the enemy. The commanding officer summoned his entire battalion and issued instructions for a surprise attack on the very same night.

The plans were made in haste and the troops were issued with full-scale ammunition. At the stroke of midnight, the battalion stealthily advanced and pounced upon the enemy battalion on the other side of the border taking them by surprise. Seth, commander of Alpha Company, was entrusted with the task of seizing the enemy's ammunition dump and so disarming them.

A surprise attack always has many inherent advantages and his battalion enjoyed all those. When they stealthily approached the enemy lines and the fighting started, the battle was mostly 'close encounter', the range hardly being sufficient to use even their rifles at times. Mostly it was hand-to-hand combat and bayonet charging. Seth, while advancing, charged and drove his bayonet into a soldier behind the defensive sandbags and when the next one turned towards him, he took out his *kukri*, a short but deadly dagger, and slashed the other's throat. When he found his way clear he advanced towards the headquarters tent where he met with stiff resistance. He killed two soldiers with his rifle and bayoneted another one.

Finally, when he reached the headquarters tent, he took out a grenade to lob in. "Watch out!" he heard someone shout from behind. He swung round to find an enemy soldier almost on him with his dagger drawn. Seth turned on the balls of his feet and, with all the agility that he had acquired during his cricket playing days, sidestepped and brought the butt of his rifle heavily down on the attacker's head. As the enemy reeled under the blow, Seth took out his *kukri* and slit his throat in one rapid swing of his arm. He then lobbed the grenades into the tents and wrought havoc. Soon after the entire enemy was wiped out and Seth's battalion celebrated with battle cries and shouting. The second in command of the battalion had watched Seth at close quarters during the entire operation.

During the next few days, Seth's battalion advanced quite some distance, earned a great name for itself and put the fear of God into the enemy battalions in that sector. They seized quite a chunk of the enemy's territory and were quickly reinforced so they could stay on and fight further. The battalion received orders to advance deeper and capture two important towns on its way ahead but as they prepared to move forward, a ceasefire was ordered and the war came to an end after a short period of twenty-one days.

Seth felt very disappointed as his battalion was advancing rapidly and, given half a chance, would have easily seized all the objectives that it had been set. No doubt covering itself in glory and a flurry of gallantry awards, which form the pride of any battalion. When the ceasefire took effect and peace prevailed, Seth found that he had won the battle but lost his personal peace. A short while later, while recollecting the events of the attack, he realised that he had killed not one but six soldiers in hand-to-hand combat either with his bayonet or the *kukri*. He had no idea how many died due to the rifle fire or the grenades he had used, not that that figure bothered him ever, but killing six soldiers using hand-held weapons of ancient times truly disturbed him. It would have been unqualified murder in other circumstances but, in this case, won him recognition for his courage, agility of mind and body, leadership and, above all, his devotion to duty with little or no care for personal safety.

The second in command of the battalion who reported the matter to the commanding officer sang paeans of praise about Seth and made sure that his name was sent up for the highest gallantry award. Seth received a Vir Chakra, which was presented to him at a glittering ceremonial parade a year later but, by then, Seth had lost his mental balance. He abhorred the very thought that he had killed six men although they had been his enemy. He had never thought of himself as a savage, but killing those six men in close combat with antique weapons like bayonets and *kukris* began to make him think otherwise. Firing machine guns, rapid firing guns and killing even hundreds was par for the course in warfare. Killing many while advancing into towns and other areas or shooting down snipers was also considered normal and he would not have given a second thought to it. However, killing six soldiers all in a matter of half an hour in close combat was something that had affected his psyche very badly and he never came to terms with it.

Often he would withdraw into his room or tent and sit crouched in the chair like a wounded animal. He would switch off all the lights and keep his room in total darkness. He used to suffer with bouts of depression, self-doubt, and then question his own actions during such periods. When his commanding officer learnt about his mental condition, he repeatedly assured him that his action was all in the course of duty and perfectly normal. He also told him that any other officer or soldier in his position would have either acted in a similar fashion or failed to live through the day. When his counselling did not produce the desired results, he sent Seth to the Command Hospital, Lucknow, for further counselling and psychiatric treatment.

Seth became a difficult patient for the doctors who took some time and effort to put him back on an even keel. Although they declared him fit, Seth knew full well that he was far from cured. He had many devils within him and he battled them constantly. He would sink into bouts of depression or unprovoked violence and aggression when alone. He felt many a time that his behaviour was far from normal but managed to keep his feelings and inadequacies to himself.

The Chinese debacle, the quick expansion of the army and the 1965 War brought quick promotions and he found himself a major while still very young. Even the emergency commissioned officers who served in the forward areas with the operational battalions became majors in double quick time. Earlier, such a rank used to be the second in command of a battalion and was entrusted with responsible jobs. Seth discovered that many young officers without even five years experience were made majors and given responsibilities which they could not discharge without difficulty. He also found that some of the emergency commissioned officers were in a position to give him orders and he resented the situation. He felt frustrated with life on many counts. What he did not realise was that his frustration mainly stemmed from the fact that he made no mentionable progress in cricket. He found great relief in his family life as his wife provided a shoulder to cry on, gave sensible advice and steadied the rocking boat on many occasions.

As Seth advanced in life, he found that his advance in the army was not keeping pace. His psyche, once badly damaged, prevented him from being a normal human being and he often displayed some peculiar characteristics in his behavioural patterns. He was termed 'unpredictable and unreliable'. He also found it difficult to get along with the emergency commissioned officers as he considered them as usurpers, as men who had stolen his rights.

The emergency commissioned (EC) officers were later put through severe tests and those found fit were given permanent commissions. Some of them later rose to higher ranks and excelled both on the battlefront and in administration. The government gave an option to all the EC officers to take a condensed version of the civil services UPSC examination. The academically bent officers successfully passed the exam and later rose to high positions in the government. Some in fact became senior to their erstwhile commanding officers. A few of them left the army and found some positions in the civilian world but spent their remaining life with a hurt psyche and branded themselves as failures.

Seth could have retired as a major because of his medical

history. While the ACRs spoke of him as a cricket player of great repute, a battle-scarred officer, who had won the coveted gallantry award, Vir Chakra, the medical reports declared him unpredictable and the army was hard-pressed to make a decision about his future.

Fortunately for him, the 1971 war with Pakistan found him on the eastern front and his battalion advanced again very rapidly and took everyone by surprise. The Indian army stormed to Dhaka within twenty days and the Pakistani troops surrendered. Seth's battalion was in the forefront in this rapid advance and he won many laurels again, although not on the same scale as in the 1965 war. In the 1971 war the Indian army avoided the places well defended by the enemy, outflanked and encircled them and cut off their supply lines leaving the enemy with no option but to lay down their arms.

When Seth's turn came for promotion the army found it difficult but decided to take a chance and promoted him to the rank of lieutenant colonel. The promotion committee recorded in bold letters that he had been 'given the benefit of the doubt' and should be watched carefully before any further promotion. That remark in his dossier put paid to his career but Seth was unaware of it. During the peace that followed, he found an urgent need to find his own peace and mental balance. He took to hunting as a sport and, in those days when the national consciousness about preserving wild life was yet to take shape, he became an expert hunter and won several trophies to his credit.

Meanwhile the government slowly started enacting laws to protect wild life and began to enforce them. Seth then only answered calls from the civil administration to hunt when wild animals threatened the tribes or people living in and around the forests. He enjoyed the time he spent in the wild when he was all by himself. He wanted to pit himself against the wild animal and play a game in which both the hunter and the hunted had an equal chance. It was his way of silencing the devils within him.

This attitude of providing a level playing field slowly spread around his thinking process and thereafter he insisted on a level playing field in any activity that he was connected with. This became part of his nature and he found himself waging a one-man fight against several ills that were gaining ground in both the army and the country in the seventies and eighties.

MAN OF THE MATCH

In every cricket match, whether it is a full five-day Test or the shorter version of One Day International, the player who makes an outstanding performance is declared the Man of the Match and is awarded a special prize. He is selected either by the commentators, who have a ringside view of the entire proceedings and the expertise to follow the turns and twists of the game, or the match referee. It is difficult to make this decision until the last ball has been bowled and the outcome of the match has been decided as the action swings from one side to the other many times.

A single session of two hours or the contribution of a single player can change the complexion of the game and fortunes of either team. The player selected could either be a batsman, who wielded his willow to great effect and changed the final outcome, or a bowler who took a good number of wickets and thus caused the downfall of the opponents. The Man of the Match is normally selected from the winning team but occasionally he could be from the losing side that puts up a valiant fight against all the odds and brings a match to the wire. It is the dream of every player to be selected the Man of the Match, as he not only gets a cash award but also recognition of his valuable contribution to the game. He is the equivalent of the most valuable player of the NBA league.

When Seth's name was called at the Republic Day Parade in New Delhi for the presentation of the gallantry award, Vir Chakra, he marched smartly from his place and once in line with the President turned right, clicked his heels and presented a salute with his sword to the President of India. The spokesperson from the army read the citation, which described in short but glorious terms his valiant effort on the battlefield and declared that, for his services that were in the best traditions of the Indian Army, he was awarded the Vir Chakra. The ADC to the President produced the medal on a velvet cushion that was decorated very ornately. The President took the medal and pinned it to Seth's chest and shook hands with him.

"Well done, son!" the President exclaimed and disregarding protocol patted him on the shoulder with affection. His pat signified the 'pat' of the entire nation for his act of bravery and acted as an exhortation to all personnel in the three services to emulate the feat of the soldier.

Seth said, "Thank you, sir," saluted, turned right and marched off to his appointed seat.

On that Republic Day he was the Man of the Match and the cynosure of all eyes. Tall, fair, handsome and smartly attired in his ceremonial uniform, Seth presented a picture of a suave and sophisticated officer. All the spectators clapped and nodded their heads in approval. As he took his seat, a slight breeze blew from behind and with it a fragrance, which he had never experienced before. He quickly turned round and found a girl sitting behind him next to a brigadier. One look at her and his body and soul suddenly came alive. He thought that the whole world had stopped, the earth was held motionless in its orbit and his heart missed a beat. The winter morning sun, which broke out of the foggy weather, spread a glossy shine on her face, her captivating smile and sparkling teeth. He quickly turned round for sake of propriety but wished he could see the lovely girl behind him again.

Cupid has no respect for place or occasion. He strikes at any time or place of his choosing, irrespective of the solemnity of the situation. Republic Day Parade was all about ceremony, hardly the place to start a love affair. Seth wished that Cupid had selected a more appropriate setting to fire his arrows, igniting the spark of love. When the parade was finished, he stood up taking his time before leaving and stole a glance at the girl behind him. He could not believe it when she came up to him, extended her hand, congratulated him for the award and shook his hand. For a few seconds Seth floated on air and felt a surge of happiness well up from within. He felt speechless and tongue-tied for she seemed to cast a spell over him.

He managed to mutter, "Thank you."

"I'm Brigadier Darshan Lal and this is Priya, my daughter," the Brigadier was kind enough to introduce himself.

"You killed so many all by yourself!" Priya exclaimed. She also looked lost in admiration. "Fantastic. You're a real hero, and your tale should go in the text books for kids."

Seth continued his silent wonder and savoured the beauty of the girl. She was dressed in a light blue *salwar kameez* with artistic embroidery work from the shoulders to the waist and a matching *dupatta*. Slim and slender with a sharp nip at the waist and a smile that would melt icebergs, she looked the ideal girl to spend one's life with. Captain Seth checked himself for she was the daughter of a brigadier and well above his position. The rank structure played strange games in the army and his feel-good factor suddenly took a nosedive. Undaunted he decided to pursue the girl. He felt like a batsman, clean bowled, but appreciated the beauty of the delivery and acknowledged the clever bowling of the bowler by a nod of the head and a look of approval.

During the next few days he tried to find out about the brigadier and meet the girl again. He was pleasantly surprised when the brigadier invited him for tea at his house. Thanking such providence from heaven, he turned up at the officer's house dressed in his best and all set to impress the girl who had captured his imagination. He found her very responsive to his attention and with ready smiles and warmth throughout the conversation.

Over the course of a short time, Seth took Priya for several sightseeing trips round the picturesque and historic place of New Delhi. Conquered several times by the ambitious warlords, the city was devastated many times and rebuilt by each new set of rulers. Most of the beautiful structures were mercifully left intact. The monuments and the gardens set up by the Moghuls, the modern buildings constructed by the British, and the architectural marvels created by the Indian planners provided several interesting sites. New Delhi had many romantic places where the winter chill and the sprawling gardens, laid out neatly with grassy lawns and well laid out beds of flowers in full bloom, provided ideal settings for cooing sweet nothings.

He took her to Agra and the Taj Mahal, the most graceful symbol of love in the world. Sitting on the lawns in front of the beautiful monument and holding hands with the girl one loves is the ultimate experience for any young man and the moment remained permanently etched in his memory. It was at this historic site that Seth decided to take the plunge. Priya had been in Delhi for three years before that and she had been through this circuit before but she enjoyed every minute of the company of her magnificent hero. After saying all the sweet nothings he could think of, Seth thought that it was time to get down to the business of spending a life together.

"Since I love you," he began, "I want to tell you some things now lest you be disappointed in life later."

"Go on, I'm listening!"

"I have a greatly coveted gallantry award but I have not been a career minded army officer so far. I have been spending most of my time playing cricket for which my passion is immense. I would rather play for India than become a general. This may be against the scheme of your thinking."

"No one is certain of becoming a general. Every officer doesn't make it to such a rank. You do your best and leave the rest to Almighty or the Lord High Commissioners as you call them in the army."

"I have been passionate about cricket all along and I made

my decision to concentrate on the game. I may not progress much in my career and I don't want you to be disappointed later when others supersede me."

"You do what you like best. I'll be supportive. You've stolen my heart and I can't find a place for another man. It is you, despite whatever rank you attain, that matters to me." She left no doubt in his mind.

"Another important thing, I've another two to three years still to achieve my ambition and I am afraid we'll have to wait until I get a cap for India or hang up my cricket boots."

"That suits me fine as I can finish my post graduation course by then. Go ahead and win your cap and achieve your ambition. I'll wait for you."

Everyone was happy with that decision; even Seth senior approved of it. He thought that the brigadier was knocking at the doors of the generals' club and he would have the satisfaction of having a general's daughter as his daughter-in-law. Although normally reticent and prone to speaking in a peremptory tone, he appreciated his son's choice and even half approved his son's wish to concentrate on his game. However, he could not help saying, "For God's sake, hurry up and don't keep the girl waiting for too long."

For the next three years, Seth tried his best but got nowhere near the coveted India Cap, which eluded even some young and well deserving candidates. Priya's father did not make it to the rank of general and Seth senior, disappointed on many fronts, suffered a stroke from which he never recovered fully for the rest of his life.

When the time came, Seth formally proposed and Priya accepted without any hesitation. The marriage was celebrated in a low-key style as Seth senior was not in good health and the brigadier had not got over his disappointment of being passed over for promotion.

The only place where the marriage was truly celebrated was in the battalion. Seth's commanding officer arranged a gala party. The picturesque lawns in front of the Officers' Mess were decorated with lights of many different hues, arranged in helical patterns around the Ashoka trees that grew along the perimeter. There were also several colourful lamps strategically placed on the lawns. The lounge in the mess was converted into a dance floor and the regimental band, dressed in their best, played wonderful music. After a couple of turns, the commanding officer, or CO as he is called, proposed a toast to the new couple and welcomed Priya to the battalion. The CO also presented the couple with a huge package, gift-wrapped in an attractive way, and the young officers asked Seth to open it. Beneath the layers of wrapping paper, he found a cricket ball nestling on a rich velvet cloth on a throne. The ball had been inlaid with colourful semi-precious stones and the entire throne had been covered in gold. There were several different engravings on it, signifying the records that he had established while playing for the services. Seth felt immensely happy and passed the gift to Priya who almost cried with joy.

Finally, the band started up and the CO asked the new bride for the first dance. Priya danced the quickstep very gracefully and everyone applauded. Seth then partnered her and felt incredibly happy when she rested her head on his shoulder as they danced the slow step. The other officers took their turns with the new bride as the party went on into the early hours of the morning. It was the first of many such happy occasions in Seth's life with Priya.

PRIYA

Priya grew up in several of the cantonments close to where the brigadier was stationed. She studied in convents as the Sainik schools, which were meant for children of frequently transferred personnel in the armed forces, were yet to come. She managed her schooling without giving any concern to her parents and although she was not academically bent, she hoped to become a teacher in a higher grade school. While she was in the process of graduating, she met Seth and took the long engagement as an opportunity to complete her post graduation and teachers' training. When she got married she was fully qualified to be either a teacher or a lecturer in college.

During her stay in Delhi she took immense interest in cricket and attended all the matches in which Seth played. She found that her presence with the few spectators gave an extra spring to his run up and bounce in his bowling. His performance whenever she was present in the stadium had been excellent. This prompted him to ask her to accompany him to all the outlying matches. However, an unmarried girl accompanying a player was not only impractical but also improper, as Priya's character would have been sullied.

Marriage was a respectful institution and any contact between the boy and the girl before marriage was not encouraged. In the higher echelons of society, it was permitted to go to a movie or at best out to dinner. Restrained by social niceties she confined herself to New Delhi and pined for him. Whenever the full moon bathed the front lawns of her house, she used to sit alone in a wicker chair and imagine her future with the handsome but cricket-loving beau. She also prayed for his success in matches at other grounds. The Hindu Gods must get millions of prayers from many people at or below the poverty line in India and find it hard to keep track of all such prayers. Perhaps her prayers were lost in the multitude and left unanswered as Seth's performances at far-flung grounds remained lacklustre and nothing to write home about.

When Seth finally hung up his cricket boots, he returned straightaway to Priya and arrived feeling downcast. He wept in her arms. "I failed, Priya," he cried inconsolably. "Now I've nothing much to offer as I'm just an acting major in the Indian army. I've nothing to show except the trophies that I've won and a scrapbook recording my performances. I've money, which has come through my father's family but I won't touch it with a bargepole because I've a longstanding feud with him so I can't even promise you riches. In short I can't promise you anything except my unswerving love."

"You needn't be a great man. I understand how much you tried. Success depends upon many factors and sometimes eludes even the most deserving."

"Will you marry me despite my failure?"

"Yes! Yes! Yes! What do you think I've been waiting for for the last three years?"

She jumped into his arms and kissed him. She told him how she had spent all three years pining for him and had spent many sleepless nights. "I even had a tiff with my father, who discovered the details of your career. He wanted to find a more suitable boy for me, but I lost my heart to you on the day you received the Vir Chakra and I've never entertained any thoughts about any other than you. Many of the smart boys from St Stephen's College have been after me and it was quite a job shaking them off. I've been waiting for this day. Let's get married once you're ready, but for my part let's make it as soon as possible. I can't wait any longer."

Meanwhile things changed on the home front of both

families. The brigadier had checked out Seth's career prospects and found that, with his psychiatric problems, he had little or no chance of making it to the rank of general.

Every officer who joins any of the three services: the army, navy or air force, dreams of making it to this rank or its equivalent and this dream almost turns into an obsession. To achieve this dream and win the rat race some work very hard and some employ devious means. The politicians and the top-level bureaucrats also play their cards at the time of selection of officers for higher ranks. The brigadier, who himself did not make it to general, felt very disappointed that his daughter had decided to marry Seth who had no chance of making it even to the rank of brigadier. He tried to stop her from taking the plunge but when she reminded him that he had encouraged her in the initial stages and all along had approved of their courtship for three years he found his options had narrowed down to only one and finally gave his consent, albeit reluctantly.

After their marriage, Seth encouraged Priya to take up a job as he wanted them to be economically independent of his father. The lot of the services' officers at the end of the sixties started to deteriorate while at the same time inflation raced skywards due to the burgeoning population and the profligacy of the socialist government. The new bunch of IAS and Officers of the Central Services manoeuvred the files cleverly to get themselves additional allowances in some form or another leaving the officers of the armed forces to fend for themselves. Fortunately, Priya to begin with found a job in the local school and, with her growing experience, she also picked up a job as a teacher in one of the best schools with ease. The two pay packets kept the home fires burning brightly.

Priya found that Seth loved her and made love to her with the same passion that he had shown on the cricket ground and the couple was immensely happy when she became pregnant. They did not want to know the sex of the child and swore to give the baby all their love irrespective of its gender.

The technology of ultrasound and determining the sex of the unborn baby had not appeared in India by this point. When the technology arrived, it brought in its wake complete havoc. The Indian male, obsessed with the idea of a son and heir, and a society which was despoiled with the dowry system, considered a girl child a liability and in many cases the female foetuses were aborted. This caused uproar and the government, quite rightly, banned any tests to determine the sex of the baby.

Priya's first born was a bonny girl who took the physique of her father and the features of her mother. She was a bundle of joy and the cynosure of all eyes at functions that the couple attended. As Seth had married late, he wanted to have a second child early so that he could raise them before his retirement and then relax once he gave up work. They fervently hoped for a boy and prayed regularly as a boy would make a complete family. they even selected the name for the boy to be born. Alas, it was not to be and a second girl was born.

"What shall we do now, Priya?" Seth asked.

"Nothing, we may get a boy with the third attempt."

"But the Government has been on about limiting the population and allowing only two children per family."

"Bah! What rubbish. It's none of their business."

"I want a boy too but what's the guarantee that we'll get one?" Seth was most concerned about having another child.

"We'll take a chance."

"What if it's a girl again? Will we be able to look after the third girl with the same love and affection as the first two? Won't she be the subject of our disappointment and frustration?"

"Can't you see it from my position? Everyone will fault me for not producing a boy," Priya countered.

"If they know their beans they should know that it's my fault not yours," muttered Seth.

"Unfortunately many people don't know the scientific facts

and will blame me. I could never look your father in the eye. As it is, he's mightily disappointed that my dad didn't get promoted to general. With this as well, he'll never like me."

"Let society and my father think what they want. I couldn't care less. It's our family and our life. We should decide matters between us and care less for the opinions of others."

The couple however did not have to wait long to make the final decision. Seth took his family to the swimming pool in the Officers' Institute regularly as he was teaching his elder daughter, Aparna, to swim. Priya, with the young daughter, Suparna, sat on a poolside deck chair. As he finished his lesson and was about to come out, a lady asked him to pull her daughter out of the shallow end. When he had done so, she asked him to repeat the exercise with another girl. Seth readily obliged and thought that the job was over but the lady looked apologetically at him and asked for a third girl also to be helped out. She looked at him sheepishly and was obviously desperately trying to avoid embarrassment.

"We tried for a boy, the third time," she said sounding very awkward while looking like she had committed a cardinal sin. That one incident dispelled whatever little doubt Seth had left in his mind. The next morning he went to the doctor, was quickly furnished with a date to go under the surgeon's knife and had the necessary operation.

The central government, in order to control the burgeoning population, announced several incentives to males and females of productive age to have their reproductive abilities curtailed. These included a cash award of 180 Rupees and a lucky dip for a transistor radio, which was a valuable item in the early seventies in India. Seth was declared the winner of the lucky dip and the Formation Headquarters announced his name across the airwaves, which was sent to all units. This provided him with an opportunity to tell all the ladies that he was the safest man in the Formation for flirting with!

Unlike other Indian males, Seth did not run a tight house. He never insisted on his ideas. He always consulted Priya and respected her opinions. The family as a whole unit took the all-important decisions only after obtaining a consensus. This process was a reaction due to his upbringing. He learnt from his father what a father ought not to be. He gave full freedom to his wife and children from the word go and wanted their creative abilities to grow without any let or hindrance. This freedom and the teaching experience of Priya helped the children to excel in studies and they used to harvest most of the awards in their schools much to the happiness of the couple.

In the initial stages however, the family suffered for want of proper accommodation. They used to share with other officers and live mostly out of suitcases. When they got proper housing, they used to get transfer orders all too soon. This constant movement of the home, transfers of schools for the children and job for Priya left them wondering when their troubles would end.

Despite this, the family enjoyed life to the hilt when Seth was sent to the DSSC, the Defence Services Staff College, located in the hills of Ooty in South India. The salubrious climate, the picturesque landscape, comfortable quarters and the camaraderie of the officers of the three services of the same seniority provided a wonderful ambience for a peaceful life. Their social life was a whirlwind of birthday bashes, wedding anniversary celebrations, regimental days and parties for every important occasion. It provided a great relief from the normal hurried life in the battalion. Priya, with her good looks and academic qualifications was drafted into several ladies' committees and she enjoyed interacting with other women of her age and thinking. There were many happy reunions of batch mates from the NDA where they indulged in nostalgia and backslapping. The officers relived their lives of younger days and recycled their old jokes.

As the children grew up, Priya became the main pillar of the family. Seth was frequently transferred to some frontline area where no family accommodation was provided. She managed the house, looked after the children and their schooling and, above all, kept reassuring them about the safety of their father. When Seth went to the eastern front the kids were small and their perception of the situation was low. However, when Seth was posted to Kashmir in counterinsurgency operations, the casualties of the army officers and other security personnel were very high and his daughters used to get up in the middle of the night after nightmares.

"Don't you worry, kids; your dad is very smart and agile. He can get out of any tricky situation easily," Priya used to say with conviction.

"Everyday we see many casualties on the TV, Mummy."

"The army has a job to do and in the process is prepared to suffer some casualties. It's part of a soldier's life."

"Why are the terrorists so bad?"

"It's difficult for you to understand now. Wait till you grow up."

Priya and the kids enjoyed life most when Seth was appointed the commanding officer of the battalion. They had a house provided for them with all the best furnishings and amenities. Priya had a cook and other servants to look after the daily chores of the house and she kept a very neat and tidy home. The officers and their ladies treated her with great respect and called on her for advice on many matters ranging from professional to marital. The men of the battalion worshipped her almost like a goddess and acted very deferentially whenever she was present. Some considered her as their mother, some as their sister and the older lot as their daughter or *bahu*, but they all showered her with affection. She was the first lady of the battalion and she played her role with care and dignity. The children also enjoyed the attention being paid to them and revelled in it. This provided added motivation to them to excel in their studies, as they had to set an example to others. The battalion commanders are supposed to lead from the front and their families liked to follow the same path.

Even when the battalion was posted to the eastern front for counterinsurgency operations and the family was left behind at the peace station, the family never felt insecure. After seeing the dedication of the jawans and their unswerving loyalty to their commanding officer, Priya and her daughters were thoroughly convinced that no harm would come to Seth. Thankfully, they were never disappointed.

Priya always felt happy and had no occasion to cry or shed tears. She often read that the Indian male dominated and suppressed the female under his jackboots but she never felt that she was suppressed in anyway. She did not realise that she was an exception as she was from the upper echelons of society.

However, she was inconsolable when Aparna, the elder daughter, was leaving for the USA. She had won a seat at Berkley University and her I-20 showed a huge amount for annual expenditure. Although brilliant, she did not get the scholarship as the GRE examination was cancelled thrice due to some leakage of the paper. Leakage of question papers for important examinations was a common practice in India but the authorities in the USA did not take kindly to it. When the exam was finally held amidst tight security she performed well and obtained a very high score but the results reached the university too late and the scholarships had already been distributed. Consequently Seth was required to show a huge bank balance to convince the consular officer in the US consulate at New Delhi that he could support his daughter during her studies. Fortunately, he had invested the money which he had saved while serving in the frontline units in real estate wisely. Thanks to the boom in property in New Delhi, he could get more than the required amount to show in his bank balance.

When the entire family went to the airport to see Aparna off, Priya for the first time felt very apprehensive, as Seth and his family had neither friends nor relatives in the USA. She thought that someone was wrenching her daughter away from her and started sobbing at the airport. There was no way Seth could control her. He was sure that the girl, having been brought up under his care, would look after herself and make him proud. His efforts to console Priya failed, so he left the mother and daughter to cry their hearts out and comfort each other. When the security check was called, Aparna picked up her bag along with her courage and walked away without looking back.

On the way home Priya rested her head on Seth's broad shoulder and started crying again. Seth continued to drive in an impassive manner. When they reached home, Priya regained her composure and promised Suparna that she would not cry at the time of her departure to the USA.

SILLY MID-ON

Silly mid-on is a position in the field very close to the batsman on his leg side. A fielder is placed here only when the bowler and his captain feel certain of getting a batsman out with a bat and pad catch. It is a position that calls for a fielder with quick reflexes as the player is expected to catch the ball low when the batsman defends a turning ball. A ball pitched on the middle stump that can turn either way is normally defended by the batsman with an inclined bat to ensure that it does not rise to give a catch to any of the close in fielders. If the bowler gets any purchase from the pitch and the ball turns effectively, the batsman is hard put to keep it on the turf. The fielder at silly mid-on then comes into the picture and literally plucks the ball inches from the ground and takes a catch much to the delight of the bowler.

Players like Eknath Solkar excelled themselves in taking many catches in this position. However, the fielder at silly mid-on puts himself at considerable risk as the spinners sometimes bowl a full toss or a short-pitched ball. In such cases, the batsman uses the full blade of his bat and pulls the ball with full force endangering the life or limb of the fielder so close in. The most junior player in the team is normally employed in this precarious position and many have started wearing protection such as shin guards and helmets.

Raju's first test came when he attended the selection trials of the state Under-13 team. The Colonel took both his wards, Raju and Ramu, to the selection trials, which were held in a reputable stadium in the state. The selection committee, consisting of players who had hung up their boots, came to the nets in full strength and put the players through a rigorous practice. All the members stood next to the nets, watched the boys at close quarters, observed the technique and deficiencies of each of them and took copious notes. After watching the young lads for a couple of days they made up their minds; well, almost made up their minds.

The selection of any team should be the exclusive right of the selection committee, but it hardly remains so in India. Several external factors come into play before the final list is announced. The officials of the State Cricket Association, drawn from different walks of life with little or no knowledge of the game, have a greater say than the cricketers on the selection committee. Their clout, either due to their wealth or their positions in the Government hierarchy, is enormous and the selection committee is often rendered no more than mere mute spectators before these players of a different game.

As Raju was relaxing after a tough practice session, one well-wisher brought him a soft drink and plate of eats, which contained some meat products. "What's this dish?" Raju asked and, when his admirer explained, the lad ate it with great relish.

What Raju did not know was that he was being put through a test to ascertain his religion and caste, as people pertaining to some religions or castes do not eat the offered dish. It seems ludicrous that players were put through such ridiculous tests to determine their religion and caste, which unfortunately then played a large part in the selection process. Raju and Ramu passed them all and were finally selected for the state team. Since the two players had come with the Colonel, his standing meant the selection committee could not deny them their rightful place. Although the secretary of the State Association wanted to slot in a couple of his candidates of doubtful talent the selection committee prevailed upon him and told him about the Colonel and the chances of him creating a ruckus later.

Being selected for the final sixteen was only the first trial of many that the players had to negotiate. The captain and coach formed the second hurdle; although they should normally select the best players and those in form for the actual playing eleven this was not always the case. Some players even played cricket for the country for many years and yet only served as the twelfth man, their 'playing' confined to the role of a substitute or drinks carrier for their state side. Even in the Under-13s, the pressures and pulls exerted by different outside influences on the captain and the coach were enormous. To begin with, they preferred the locals, but over the years the presence of players from other regions in the state teams slowly increased and the selectors could not deny a place to the talented ones. The same machinations ruled the matches of the seniors too.

When Raju and Ramu played their first match the Colonel was more excited than the boys. He turned up for the game in his services blazer and Professor Deb and his wife, both also suitably attired, accompanied him. The few cricket lovers who were present to witness the match recalled the daredevil deeds of the Colonel right from his playing days in the NDA and they recollected how he used to work up a decent pace. The captain of the team had also heard about the Colonel and the Professor had his own standing in society. So, all said and done, both Raju and Ramu showed a lot of promise and potential to be the eventual match winners.

The captain, a young lad with hardly any powers of decision-making, preferred another bowler to Raju. However, the coach, who was streetwise and knew which side of his bread the butter lay, made no mistake and made sure that both the boys were included in the first eleven. He also instructed the captain to open the bowling with Raju. It was an Under-13 match of hardly any consequence except for the players but the Colonel and the Professor attached a lot of importance to it and felt excited for their own reasons. The Professor wanted to decide once and for all whether his son should pursue the game or continue his studies. The Colonel, on the other hand, wished desperately that his ward would strike gold and start his career in cricket on the right note.

When the match started in earnest, the captain threw the new ball to Raju and set the field. The Colonel felt really quite nostalgic; he was back in the NDA playing against the West Indies team. The West Indies began the batting and their openers made mincemeat of the opening bowlers and sent them on a leather hunt. The morale of the young lads had started to sag when the captain called Seth and handed him the ball. The captain, another young lad senior by one term, stood next to him full of confidence and said, "Just believe in yourself and bowl your guts out. Remember they are not supermen."

Seth measured up his bowling run and started his career in cricket. His head was awhirl with stormy thoughts. Firstly, he had never bowled against batsmen who played international cricket. Secondly, he did not know whether he would be able to live up to the expectations of his captain. Thirdly, he knew that his superiors, including the commandant of the NDA and his own divisional officers, were out in the stadium watching him. Lastly, many cricket lovers from the adjacent cities of Bombay and Pune had turned up and filled the tiny stadium. Above all, he felt the presence of his dad weighing heavily upon him.

He desperately wanted to succeed, not to impress the commandant or other officers but mainly to show his dad that cricket was his first love in life and that he would, one day, be the frontline bowler of the country. He wanted to convince his dad that he had a will of his own and would like to plough his own furrow. It was his chance to settle some sort of score with his dad, who forever bullied and badgered him. He wanted to succeed, to throw away the yoke that his dad had put on his young shoulders for too long. He wanted to break free from his dad's control and go ahead, under his own steam. The only way to get his point across to his dad was by getting the batsmen out. It was more a game between him and his dad; the visiting team was only incidental. He did not bother about the name of the batsman and his reputation. All that was important to him was to get him out and fast.

With all these thoughts buzzing around his brain like a swarm of bees, he bowled the first ball with all the energy and skill at his command. He bent his back as much as possible and generated the maximum pace. The ball pitched on the off stump and at a good length. He thought that he had a winner but the West Indian batsman, who was tall and almost giant-like compared to the young cadets, stepped a wee bit forward, converted it into a half volley and hit hard. Before Seth finished his follow through, the ball crashed into the ropes. He felt disappointed and disheartened but remembered his captain's words and continued to bowl, putting his heart into it. All the remaining balls pitched on the off and middle stumps and the batsman negotiated them easily by playing defensive shots, which yielded no runs.

The next few overs were almost a repetition of the first. The batsman played defensively but occasionally scored a four. Encouraged with the results, Seth bowled maintaining his line and length. No one spoke of swing in those days and the pace of the bowlers was hardly adequate to cause any lateral movement of the ball either in the air or off the pitch. The batsman showed respect to the balls pitched correctly and took some risks to hit him to the ropes. When one batsman tried once too often he missed the ball and found his off stump uprooted. Seth tasted blood on the cricket field for the first time in an international game, if it could be called that. He looked towards his dad and almost said aloud, "Howzat!" In the remaining overs that he bowled, he achieved moderate success and the captain rested him and promised a second spell soon.

Seth relived that glorious day when the entire nation applauded the grit and gumption of the young cadets for it was in sharp contrast to the meek and spineless spirit showed by the senior and more experienced players who represented the cream of talent in the country. The senior team particularly dreaded two bowlers, Hall and Gilchrist, whom the NDA cadets thrashed with gay abandon. At the end of the match when the visiting team paid compliments to the young cadets and made a special mention of one batsman and Seth's bowling, Seth thought that he had finally won the battle against his dad. He did not know that his dad was like the Rock of Gibraltar and not susceptible to change.

As Seth was reliving those memories Raju started his own cricketing career. He also desperately wanted to achieve success but for different reasons. He wanted to succeed more for the sake of his benefactor, who had pulled him out of the rut of the village and a veritable hell in which he had little to live for and was subjected to constant ridicule. Here was a chance to satisfy his benefactor and get a nod of approval from him. Until then, nobody had said even a kind word to him but now he had a chance to get appreciation from the Colonel. He also feared that any failure on his part would mean a return to the village and the living hell. He bowled with all the energy that his developing frame could provide. He used all the techniques he had learnt up to then and hoped for the best. He prayed to some indeterminate god to help him succeed or make the batsman commit some mistake. Unfortunately, for him, neither the god nor the batsmen obliged and, on the contrary, the latter thrashed him all over the field.

He finished his first spell which was totally uneventful. He had bowled a good line and length and also managed to swing the ball a bit but his bowling action gave a clear indication of the likely movement of the ball and the batsmen found no difficulty in negotiating him. Whenever he erred slightly, either in line or length, the batsmen punished him without mercy and scored freely off him. At the end of the first spell, Raju gave away as many as fifty runs in eight overs and the captain rested him for some time. The story ran the same way throughout the first innings and Raju returned without any wicket to his credit. Seth, fresh from his memories by then, felt very disappointed but told his ward during the interval that it was not the end of the world and that the latter should try his best in the second innings.

Ramu's story ran to a different script. The captain put him down as third in the batting order, almost the pride of the place in the team and given to the best batsman. With Ramu hardly padded up and ready, one of the openers nicked the ball into the gloves of the wicketkeeper and returned to the pavilion in the first over itself. Ramu hurriedly made his way to the middle still adjusting his gear. Once he took guard he forgot about his parents, the Colonel who had trained him and everything else. He had no scores to settle, no demons within to be exorcised. He was by himself and enjoying playing. He focussed only on the bowler and kept the field setting in the back of his mind. The rest of the world around him did not matter at all and for the first few overs he concentrated on defending his wicket dourly and making sure that the bowler did not get any psychological advantage over him. When he thought that he could read the bowler's action and the likely movement of the ball, he opened up and started playing shots that he had learnt.

Once started, he gained confidence with every delivery and executed his shots with a carefree attitude. He hit the ball with the meat of the bat and a turn of the wrists; the noise of the bat meeting the ball was sweet music to him and to the few spectators. Seeing Ramu play with confidence, the batsman at the non-striker's end also started playing his shots. Soon both the batsmen helped themselves to a feast of runs and kept the scoreboard racing. Before he could say presto, Ramu found that his score had reached the nineties and he was within range of the coveted figure of a century, which is a dream for all batsmen and particularly for debutants. He decided not to look at the scoreboard and continued playing his shots without any circumspection. In fact, he played with a rare abandon and only realised that he had scored a century when everyone started clapping.

Having crossed the coveted mark, he threw caution to the winds and hit the bowlers at will. However, his partner had some ghosts within him still to be exorcised. Although buoyed up by Ramu's batting skills, he could not execute all the strokes that he had learnt and gave away his wicket trying an audacious shot. The other batsmen followed but no one could match Ramu's brilliance and technique. Even Raju tried to copy Ramu but failed. At the end of the first innings, Ramu stood 'not out' like a colossus amidst ruins and joined the ranks of the select batsmen who had made a century in their maiden appearance in an important match.

The few spectators and pressmen present took note of his skills and above all his carefree attitude. The second innings was almost a replay of the first innings but thanks to the huge score of Ramu, the opposition found it difficult to post a respectable total and caved in. The team won and Ramu was hailed as a hero much to the satisfaction of the Professor. The Colonel did not know whether to feel happy that Ramu, one of his wards, had succeeded beyond anybody's expectations or to swallow the failure of Raju. The Colonel though was not given to throwing in the towel easily and decided to intensify his efforts. Raju, despite his wicketless performance, attracted the attention of the team management for his ardour and the lively pace that he had generated. The general consensus was that he had the potential to be a very good fast bowler but his bowling needed further honing to smooth out the rough edges, so the team decided to persist with him in the next few matches.

"Are you disappointed with my performance, sir?" Raju asked the Colonel.

"No, not at all. Fast bowlers are not made in a day and failure can be a stepping-stone for success. You have to intensify your efforts to get better results."

"But Ramu fared very well and made a name for himself in the very first match."

"I'm very happy that he tasted success but I want you both to succeed."

"I'll try my best, sir."

"That's good enough for me. We should always try our best. The results will follow automatically."

Raju felt encouraged and continued his efforts. However, the results in the next few matches were not commensurate with these efforts, although he did start picking up wickets in twos and threes. He did not lose his place in the team but there was nothing to write home about, whereas Ramu progressed from match to match and posted some fantastic scores which attracted the attention of the press and the cricket lovers in the country.

THE UMPIRES

The two umpires play an important role in the game of cricket as they are required to give the all important decisions about leg before wicket, (LBW), catches, stumping, run outs and such like. In the earlier days, the umpires were provided by the host country and they were often accused of being biased towards the home team. The ICC, after long deliberations, adopted neutral umpires for Test matches and one foreign umpire and one local umpire for the One Day International matches.

With the advent of TV and technology to view the game frame by frame, the third umpire was brought in to decide close call situations. The services of the third umpire may be called upon whenever the field umpires feel the need to refer a matter to him for his decision. It was hoped that this third umpire would put an end to the acrimonious debate over some umpiring decisions and provide a level playing field for all the teams. The technology progressed further and the commentators, with the help of the new software, could judge whether the field umpire's decision was right or wrong. This technology is advancing so fast that the day is not far off when the field umpires could be declared redundant and an umpire sitting in the pavilion with all the technical gadgets will be the one and only arbiter of the proceedings of the match.

Suparna, Seth's younger daughter, had grown up under the careful guidance of her parents, especially her mother. Both Seth and Priya wanted to ensure that she was no less loved than their first daughter and their disappointment of not producing a boy was never felt by her. They paid much attention to her and made it a point not to give her hand-me-downs from the elder girl. They also instilled in the elder daughter that it was part of her duty to look after her younger sibling. At first Aparna never used to take her sister with her when she went to play with her friends but, as the time progressed, she included the younger girl in her close circle of friends. This gave Suparna an exposure to girls older than herself and she matured rapidly. She excelled in her studies and made her parents proud as her name was inscribed in the hall of fame in all the schools at which she studied.

Sibling rivalry reared its head sometimes in their lives but they, for the main, kept it under wraps. Unfortunately, once grown up and studying at the engineering college it came out into the open and they fought for an equal share, whether it was a matter of clothes, jewellery or any goodies bought by the parents.

The older daughter went abroad to study at Berkley University but Suparna, equally as ambitious, decided she did not want to stay in India either. She made up her mind on the day that Aparna was going abroad that she too would go and study for a MS degree in a prestigious university in the USA.

"Won't you change your mind for our sake? When we get old we'll be alone with no one to look after us," Priya appealed to her daughter.

"I feel uncomfortable working in India and I've some reservations about Indian boys for husbands. They're too self-centred and don't look after their wives no matter how clever and qualified they are."

"Where did you pick up this prejudice against the Indian male?" Her mother was surprised. "Your father never ill-treated me. You've seen how he adores all of us. All Indian males do not confirm to your notions."

"If I study abroad and get a good job then a suitable boy will come and ask for my hand and treat me as an equal. I'll marry only such a boy who will share all the tasks in the house and look after me properly." Suparna was adamant.

"You may have to wait quite some time to find such a boy!" Priya pointed out.

"You told me, Mum, that you waited three long years for Dad and it paid off for you, so I'll follow in your footsteps."

"It's your life, lead it the way you like," was Seth's comment about the situation.

When it was time for her to apply for a seat she wrote to several universities making sure to leave Berkley off her list. She wanted to grow up on her own and out of the shadow of her elder sister, Aparna. She finally selected the Rensselaer Polytechnic Unit at Troy to study. This gave her independence from her parents and her elder sister. She wanted to develop under her own steam and wished to make something of her life. Priya supported her as usual and Seth contained his disappointment at his second daughter leaving to himself. When Suparna left for New York, Priya went to the airport and as promised did not cry as she wished her *bon voyage* with a smile.

Suparna was an archetypal Indian girl shaking off historical shackles and fighting to be liberated. When the Indian team won the Cricket World Cup in 1983 another revolution had begun to take place but which almost went unnoticed.

Firstly, the Indian market started producing a moped of 50cc, which had no gears and started with a small kick. The revolution was spearheaded by a south Indian company called TVS. The small motorcycle was easy to handle, manoeuvrable and easy to put on its stand. The girls of the growing middle class loved it as it provided them with mobility for the first time. Up to this point, the young girls had always had to depend upon their parents or brothers to take them anywhere. The public transport system was overcrowded, irregular and full of 'Eve teasers', who used to take every opportunity to pinch and touch the girls, much to their chagrin. The moped gave them liberation from the 'Eve teasers' and mobility to go wherever they pleased.

Secondly, the new breed of politicians like NT Rama Rao of Andhra Pradesh, a south Indian state, recognised the importance of the role of women in society and empowered them. He gave them the right to succession and an equal share in their father's property. He also reserved thirty per cent of seats in all professional colleges in the state for women and reduced the capitation fee in these colleges. His argument, which was widely acclaimed, was that the woman was the central pillar of the family. She provided the sustenance and support for the whole unit against the all too often wayward man who squandered away the family income on unproductive things like alcohol and women.

With these changes, the girls flocked to the professional colleges and soon started nursing greater ambitions to go abroad for further studies. The scholarships provided by the American universities were adequate for the girls of the middle class to survive and pursue their studies and ultimately get good jobs. The booming economy of the USA and the nascent IT sector provided the ideal ambience for the Indian girls to grow and grow. An exposure to the American way of life and the freedom enjoyed by the girls in the USA enabled them to throw off the shackles that Indian society had fettered them with for thousands of years. They abandoned the idea of arranged marriages and started looking for life partners on their own. Economic considerations told them that two pay packets were always better than one and they selected their mates from the boys studying or working with them.

The boys responded too; no longer would they be shackled to some uneducated girl back home with a large dowry and with a bride whom they had never seen before. By the time the Indian economic reforms were introduced the professions like doctors, engineers, architects, chartered accountants and management consultants included a good percentage of women, and competent ones at that. This prompted a prominent rock singer, Remo Fernandez, to sing a song "Indian woman, you have come a long way, baby."

When Suparna was in the final year of her engineering course, a tall handsome boy in her class proposed to her. "What's your aim in life?" she asked outright.

"I want to take up a good job and settle down in India and look after my parents. I've some property and I can live comfortably."

"Your ambition's too limited. You've no vision whereas I want to go places and make a life for myself. You can't afford my ambition or me. Thanks for proposing but the answer is no and a resounding no," she said dispassionately.

She was equally firm with her parents.

"Why don't you join the civil services? If you try I know you'll succeed," Seth suggested.

"Dad, I've set my goals to stay in the USA and that's what I'm going to do. Please do not try and stop me." Her parents did not discuss the matter further and provided her with their full support thereafter.

She pursued her goals with a single-minded purpose and got a good job. With her education, her vision broadened and she became increasingly compassionate and so helped many a girl who had studied at her college to come to the USA and pursue further studies. She provided financial help to those students who did not merit scholarships in the form of loans or grants and helped many a girl succeed. When India played a full series of Tests and ODIs in Australia, Suparna organised a live telecast of the matches in the Indian temple in Philadelphia and charged an entrance fee. She found that she was making enormous profits and so donated the money to the temple for its upkeep. The late 1980s had heralded a new era for the girls of the Indian middle class and it soon began to spread to those of the lower classes too.

Finally, Suparna met Raju during one of her visits home. She found him meek, diffident and unsure how to address her.

"You can call me *Akka* (sister in Telugu) from now on and treat me as such, remember that's what I am, your elder sister." She took him to English movies, explained the dialogues and taught him many things about life. Above all, she took pains to instil confidence in him and helped him to grow through his adolescence. Raju was bemused by the vast difference between the two sisters and wondered when or if he would be accepted by the elder girl.

THE WRONG ONE

When a ball is bowled, the batsman watches the bowler's action, predicts the likely direction of the ball and plays his shot having estimated the future position of the ball after pitching. It is like hitting an aircraft with an anti-aircraft gun. The aircraft moving at speeds of Mach 2 or more are traced by radar and the guns are then locked onto the radar that has a computer. This accurately predicts the future position of the target. It takes into consideration various inputs like the speed of the projectile, the wind speed, the movement of the gun platform, whether it is mounted on a ship or aircraft, and a host of other factors. Finally, the computer instructs the gun to shoot at a particular second.

The fire control solution is achieved with the sole aim of hitting the aircraft. The computers and the radars so employed are the end products of extensive research carried out by brilliant scientists and engineers and are very expensive. The situation with the batsman hitting the ball is similar except that bowlers bowling at supersonic speeds have yet to come. The tiny computer in the batsman's brain calculates the future position of the ball and directs the hand to execute the shot. More often than not, the computer is right and the bat meets the ball and sends it crashing into the ropes.

The aircraft pilot, knowing the abilities of the computer, tries several methods to confuse the computer and manoeuvres his plane to dodge the guns and attack the target. So does the bowler, who sometimes deceives the batsman by bowling a 'wrong one'. Basically, a 'wrong 'un' is a ball bowled with one action but producing a ball turning in a direction opposite to what is expected. A leg break bowler bowls a googly and an off spinner bowls what is nowadays called a *doosara*. When the batsman meets this 'wrong 'un' he more often than not is duped and falls prey to the guile of the bowler unless he reads the bowler's action in good time. Life can also bowl a 'wrong 'un' and produces results the opposite of what the mortals desire.

Raju failed to make any progress in the next two years. He could not be faulted for not trying or putting in sufficient effort. In fact, he tried very hard to taste success. He got up everyday earlier than the Colonel and went for a run achieving a speed that would qualify him for sprints. He pursued his cricket single-mindedly and put in all his efforts to the satisfaction of the Colonel, who was a hard taskmaster, but to no avail. His results were never more than mediocre, which surprised everyone. He always found a place in the state team for Under-19s and played matches with great fervour but achieved little to write home about. Even the Colonel failed to understand Raju's lack of success. He found that the lad had enough self-motivation and a burning desire to succeed and needed no further goading to intensify his efforts.

Ramu continued to stroke the ball well and played his shots with great aplomb. His good run of form continued and he achieved fantastic results. He scored many centuries and soon attracted the attention of the selectors at all levels. When he was barely sixteen, he was selected for the state team and given the pride of place as the one down batsman. He did not disappoint his selectors, scored a flawless century and established a name for himself. Soon the cricket legends of yesteryears started speaking of his immaculate technique, temperament, and carefree attitude to playing his shots coupled with his determination to succeed. The cricket scribes started seeing signs of another Sachin Tendulkar in the making so Ramu obliged his admirers by continuing to score heavily in all his matches.

One day the Professor came running to the Colonel with the unbelievably exciting news. He said that the President of the Selection Committee of the national team had rung him up personally to inform him that Ramu was selected to represent the country and asked him to send the boy to attend the camp at Bombay. Ramu, who followed a few steps behind his dad, gave Seth a military salute, which he had learnt as a NCC cadet and thanked the Colonel for everything that he had achieved. Seth exulted in his ward's success; he felt as if it was his own success, but success has many fathers and failure is always an orphan. The Professor thought that it was solely down to him as he had allowed Ramu to pursue cricket and had not insisted on him sticking to his studies but, even so, he graciously thanked his friend.

"It's all due to you. I don't know how to thank you," the Professor said. "My wife and I weren't at all in favour of him playing cricket, but the coaching and encouragement that you've provided have been of immense value. We're very much indebted to you but this is only the beginning and we ask that you continue your efforts," he added sounding very grateful.

"Please, don't embarrass me. It's all your son's effort and talent. He joined our practice sessions of his own volition and practised very hard without much help from me. I might have given him some tips at the most. The credit goes entirely to the young lad, he has natural talent."

The Professor arranged a grand party to celebrate his son's selection for the Indian team and, during the party, in a short and touching speech, said that it was all due to the efforts of the Colonel. Soon Seth found his name in all the leading newspapers of the country as the mentor and guide to Ramu and overnight he became a celebrity. He could not ignore the comments of several sportswriters about his old cricket playing days and the dash and guts that he used to display on and off the field. His army career, which at best was chequered, also came into focus and for great praise. Most of it, Seth believed, was unwarranted. A few discerning columnists however caused a chord of discontent to ring and commented about the failure of Raju who was also being groomed by Seth.

OVERSEAS TOUR

An overseas tour is one of the many attractions for the players of Team India as they get to stay in the best of hotels abroad, are provided with tight security and treated like VIPs. In countries like Pakistan, where the anti-Indian sentiment persists in some pockets, they are given more security than a visiting Prime Minister. The Indian Diaspora, present in every country that the team tours, invites them to many parties and showers them with plenty of gifts. Apart from the additional money they earn, they also get a chance to do some sightseeing in some of the most wonderful cities in the world and have time to shop for goodies and souvenirs. The members of Team India, whose place is never in doubt, have had chances to see most of the world, even the USA, which although it is not a cricket playing country does host cricket matches especially for the team.

An overseas tour is also a difficult proposition as the conditions in other countries are quite different from home grounds. The climate, the unpredictable weather, the pitches, which are totally different from the flat Indian pitches, and less supporters are some of the many factors that provide unique challenges to the players on such a tour. Several good players who have performed very well in India have failed in overseas tours and consequently lost their places.

The players of the host country, who are normally on their best behaviour when on tour themselves, tend at home to be boisterous and indulge in 'sledging' to upset the members of Team India. The players then need to show guts and grit in playing under such conditions when facing the hostile opposition. During the tour of South Africa, Alan Donald, the quick bowler, was despatched to the boundary by Rahul Dravid who revels in the cover drive. The enraged bowler could not control his temper and told Dravid what he thought of him in no uncertain terms. An unruffled Dravid had the gumption to tell him, "Let's see what you've got." Needless to say, the bowler definitely found that he had met his match, both in talent and use of expletives and walked back to his run up with his tail tucked neatly between his legs.

The Colonel decided to take Raju along with him on one of his trips to the USA. When he told Raju to pack up his clothes and some woollies that had been specially bought for the purpose, Raju could not contain his excitement. He straightaway ran to his friend Mathew. "You'll never guess what I'm doing! I am going to the USA."

"How? It is very expensive for a lad like you."

"The Colonel is taking me with him this year."

"You're a lucky fellow! I'll have to wait for many years to make such a trip. Congratulations and good luck."

"Why do you say that I'm lucky? I'm failing repeatedly; success seems to be a distant dream."

"Don't despair, you'll get your chance. Until then count your blessings."

The news of Raju's impending trip to the USA spread like wild fire in both the school and college. Suddenly Raju jumped several notches up in their estimation. Everyone offered him advice, some taught him the finer points of the American accent and others displayed their knowledge of the country. A few asked him to bring some unusual items back but without risking the ire of the customs officers.

The Colonel's main objective was to impress upon Raju that he was completely accepted as part of the family and to remove any traces of reservation his elder daughter still had towards the lad. He also wanted the trip to act as a 'carrot' and provide an incentive to the young player.

When Raju boarded the plane at Visakhapatnam for his outward journey, he could not believe it and pinched himself. He had never dreamt that he would fly and, as the aircraft took off and started to cruise through the sky, he felt that he was floating not only on air but also on several beds of roses and other exotic flowers. His imagination took wings and flew skyward taking him to cloud nine. When he looked down through the porthole all the villages and the agricultural farms looked so very tiny. The houses appeared like matchboxes and the fields as though they had been carved into some great geometrical pattern on the ground. He felt that he joined the elite crowd that are fortunate and rich enough to fly.

That flight was the beginning of many as they changed planes at Bombay, then Heathrow en route to Philadelphia where they were met by Suparna, the younger daughter. She hugged her dad and then extended her hand gracefully to Raju, who felt her touch to be so reassuring. It was more soothing than the Colonel's, who on rare occasions patted his shoulder while telling him not to get disappointed.

"Good to see you, Raju! Fancy you being here in the USA!" Suparna said, "You look well and I guess you're feeling excited."

"I don't know what to say. I'm still dreaming, I'm waiting for it all to sink in."

"You look really smart, and your English has improved and soon no doubt you'll be a celebrity. I'm glad that Dad decided to bring you along. Welcome to the USA, Philadelphia and my home."

Her house turned out to be far larger than the Colonel's with five bedrooms, two living rooms, one formal and the other for the family, and two dining rooms, again one for formal use and the other for daily use. All of it was furnished and arranged with great aesthetic sense. He found several photos featuring the Colonel and his wife. The photos showed clearly how Suparna adored her parents. He also found the photos of Suparna's family with Sekhar, her husband, who was obviously tall and handsome. They looked like a couple made for each other and the look on Suparna's face showed how much she loved him.

"Sekhar had an important meeting and couldn't come to the airport; he sends his apologies. He should be home soon."

As if on cue, a car entered the garage and shortly after in walked Sekhar, apologising for his inability to receive them.

The next two days, Suparna looked after her dad and her new brother with great love and affection. She took them round the downtown area; they visited the malls in several places, the Iskon temple and various other tourist attractions.

When she explained the history of the broken Liberty Bell and the room where the first constitution of the USA was drafted and passed, Raju was awestruck. By this point in his life, he fully understood the significance of liberty. He felt that the Colonel had rescued him from poverty and had provided him with his freedom so it was fitting that the Liberty Bell had been the first item on his itinerary. However, the historic bell had a large crack all along one side and Raju fervently hoped that his own liberty would not crack in the same way. Once more, he looked heavenwards and sent an extra prayer to the almighty, whoever He was.

Raju visited the Valley Forge where George Washington had conducted his campaign successfully and was amazed to see the General's bedroom preserved in excellent condition and the quarters of the troops who had successfully fought the British. On a trip to New York by road he had the good fortune to see the fine network of roads and freeways, the fast moving cars and the amazing skyline of Manhattan. He was astounded by the beauty of the Hudson River, the history of Ellis Island and the size of the Statue of Liberty. The well laid out, furnished and stocked malls amazed him; he had not known that any place could be so vast. Suparna told him that there were many such places throughout the USA and a visit to such places would be not only a great treat but also widen his knowledge. She took them to the university where she did her

Master's and showed them the single bedroomed flat where she lived initially. This was to emphasise that she too had begun her life in the USA in far more humble circumstances.

After visiting Washington, Baltimore and Pittsburgh, the Colonel took Raju to San José where they were received by Aparna, the elder daughter.

"Good to see you, Dumbo. Welcome to 'Frisco'," she said smiling. Raju thought that Aparna still did not like him; she was certainly more flamboyant and had a different way of speaking. She took them to Berkley University where she had studied and showed them round Silicon Valley, where Raju heard many people speaking Telugu in the malls and cine theatres. She also contacted some of her friends who were members of the local cricket clubs but, for some reason, she always introduced Raju to them as Dumbo.

There were many such clubs and the young cricketer received several invitations to play in matches which were played on baseball grounds with the diamond suitably adapted. The pitches were different but the passion for cricket was the same as in India. Several ladies and children attended the matches and filled the improvised stadiums. Strangely, the attendance at these matches was much better than the attendance for many first-class matches back home.

The players themselves had entered the high-tech world, maintaining websites of their clubs and posting the pictures and profiles of their players, the programme of league fixtures throughout the USA and scorecards of every match on it. They wore special jerseys marked with exotic names akin to those that baseball and basketball teams use. The league matches were televised and they were in fact better than the television programmes back home. All this showed the passion of Indians in all parts of the world for the game of cricket. The converts are more zealous than the faithful and all the software engineers in San José who played cricket during their college days in India pursued the game with renewed vigour. Raju was given the opportunity to bowl in several matches and they all recognised his talent and predicted that his inclusion in Team India must be just around the corner.

"But he's dumb," Aparna scoffed.

When Raju could not stand it any longer he blurted out, "You're dumber!"

"Goodness me! You've showed some spine. I have been waiting for this day." So saying she hugged him and said, "Now I can take you as my brother because that is how a brother talks to his sister."

Raju now did feel really dumb. It had needed an outburst of pent-up anger to win the acceptance of his sister. Thereafter his relationship with both of the girls changed completely. They taught him to call them *Didi* in Hindi and showered him with presents, love and affection. They could now take liberties with him and tease him and did not mind when he teased them back. Their behaviour showed that they had missed a brother all along and now wanted to make full use of their newfound sibling and started revelling in his company. In the pre-family planning days, each family had many brothers and sisters and the affection between them was always cherished until the end of their lives. Even the normal sibling rivalry took a back seat when the situation demanded.

Aparna took Raju on a tour to Hollywood, the Grand Canyon, Los Angeles, Disneyland and several other theme parks in California. She sat next to him when they went for roller-coaster rides and a panic-stricken Raju gripped tight hold of Aparna. "Don't be a scared puppy. Life is like a roller-coaster ride. It takes you through hope and despair with the same speed and ease. You've got to take it all."

"Now you're speaking like a philosopher."

"No, just your elder *didi*! But I can teach you a thing or two about life!"

When Raju left the USA, both his sisters felt truly sad. They were close to tears and wished him good luck and God speed. Raju returned to India a much changed boy; he had suddenly grown up in many ways, his confidence had increased and he felt more satisfied with life. He had made many friends in the USA and had gained the love of his sisters, which at one stage looked far beyond his reach.

On their return to India, the Colonel and his ward continued their efforts and Raju continued to float in his pool of mediocrity. He could not go break through some barrier so the Colonel consulted the Professor.

"Why is Raju not succeeding in spite of his best efforts?"

"Success is not always guaranteed. Everyone who tries hard doesn't necessarily make it, such triumph is given only to a few."

"But I don't believe in luck nor do I believe in any supernatural force. There must be some reason for his failure to make it big or something I can do to make him achieve his potential."

"Why don't you try the carrot and stick policy?"

"I tried the carrot already. I took him to the USA and instructed my daughters to treat him as if he was their biological younger brother and they did without any reservation. I could see that the trip to the USA made him very happy and intensified his resolve to succeed."

"Perhaps it is time to try the stick."

"I can't be harsh towards the lad! I've my own problems. If I act tough I become engulfed in memories from my past and I get submerged in a host of mixed feelings, some pleasant but most are things I'd sooner forget."

"You have to forget your past and wield the stick at him. You have to de-link your experiences with his treatment."

"But I can't be two people at the same time. I'm spending my retired life peacefully forgetting several unpleasant memories. I don't want to get into the old rut again."

"Then be satisfied with what you've achieved. After all, your effort is extraordinary. It's very commendable. You've taken a neglected orphan into your care, given him food, shelter, education and made him a good cricketer who plays for his state Under-19 team. That's no mean achievement."

"I don't want to give up so easily."

"Didn't you give up in your own life? Do you think that you achieved success?"

The Professor's question touched a raw nerve. Every cadet who joins the NDA aspires to be a Chief of the Army Staff or its equivalent; failing that at least a general, but very few achieve such success. There is a high attrition rate at every stage of promotion in all the services and many officers meet their Waterloo for several reasons, some of their own making but mostly due to factors beyond their control. Seth, like his father, thought that he had all that it takes to make a general but never reached his goal. He always regretted the pyramid-like structure of the armed forces and the filtration at every level. He believed that officers in the civil services reached the higher echelons automatically unless they did something drastically wrong or got on the wrong side of the law or some politician.

As he was thinking of his army career, the Professor continued, "Didn't you dream of playing for India?"

"Of course I did, but I failed because of reasons known to me. I didn't know that alcohol and cricket do not mix."

"It's not that simple. You didn't have enough motivation. You didn't have some compelling reason to succeed. You had it easy in your life. Your dad provided most of what you needed and the army took care of the rest."

"What compelling reason did Ramu have to succeed at a very young age?

"I don't think he has succeeded as of yet. He shows great talent and he has some motivation because he wants to prove me wrong. He doesn't want to follow my path and wants to plough his own furrow. He wants to assert himself and move away from the career that I had chosen for him. It is his way of throwing off the yoke that I had put on his shoulders for so long."

"So what do you think I should do with Raju?"

"As I said try the stick method first."

The Colonel returned home and summoned Raju to his study. When the servant told him about it, and the way he told him, Raju sensed immediately that something was amiss. He had never entered the Colonel's study, which the latter guarded zealously and kept all intruders at bay. He knew that the Colonel spent time in the room only when he wanted to relive his past, recollecting the pleasant times he had spent with his wife and family or whenever he got into his depressions thinking of his earlier days in the army. The Colonel had declared many years earlier in a stern tone that the study was always 'out of bounds'.

When Raju entered, the Colonel wanted to let him have it. He wanted to go hammer and tongs at the young lad and sever all connections with him. He set himself in an angry posture, ready to spew fire and brimstone but he heard a faint cry from the labyrinths of his heart. The cry became louder by the second and he could no longer ignore it. He had taken the young lad under his care out of his own volition and nurtured him for seven long years. During this time some bond of an indeterminate nature had slowly developed between them. The bond had become stronger as the years had rolled by. Now, just because the boy had failed to deliver, he was not going to sever it in one step.

He also realised that he had no son and he was slowly starting to view Raju as his own child. Every Indian male would like to sire a son and the absence of such in the family leaves a void that is difficult to fill. He was alone in the rambling house and, although his daughters visited him every alternate year which filled him with joy and he visited them in the other years, it was during the remaining period that the only soul who provided him with company was Raju. He was definitely, slowly, filling the empty spot of a son. The Colonel could not deny that all said and done the boy never gave him concern in any matter and behaved himself very well, showing due respect and complete devotion to his training and playing of cricket. How on earth was he going to dismiss him to some unknown fate and leave him to the mercy of the uncaring public? Cricket players playing at state level hardly got any attention or suitable employment. They always needed either their parents or some patron to sustain them. Was he going to throw his ward to the wolves just because he fell short of his expectations? the Colonel asked himself.

When Raju entered the study, the demeanour of the Colonel changed in a flash. He recollected the days when his own father used to berate him and talk in a peremptory tone and how he used to resent his father. When he looked at Raju, he recollected the hard life that the latter had gone through initially and how a talented lad like him had been languishing in an unknown village and constantly berated by one and all. He had rescued Raju from such a wretched life and he was not going to consign him to the same scrapheap again, the Colonel told himself. His anger gave way to pity and the scowl on his face to a smile. He realised the lad was hardly eighteen and already playing first-class cricket; perhaps he would succeed in the future. With the crisis of conscience over, he became his normal affable self.

"What did you feel when Ramu was selected to play for the country?"

"I felt very happy for him. Of course, I also felt jealous. I should've got a chance too."

"But you had no excellent performances to show for yourself. How did you expect to be selected?"

"I know, but I'm working very hard and I don't know why I am not getting good results."

"Do you think that I've not provided something that you need?"

"Not at all. You're my hero, you've provided everything, more than what I deserve. It's my own failure that I'm not able to live up to your expectations."

The Colonel did not know what more to say and dismissed him. The idea of using a stick to motivate Raju did not appeal to him and he dismissed it. There must be some way to make him perform better though. When Raju left, he asked the servant to pour a stiff drink and he put his feet up on the table, reclined on the sofa, sipped his drink and lit a cigar. As the cigar fumes encircled the room in a misty haze, they took him down memory lane. He was back on the cricket ground in the NDA and the whole film replayed once again.

THE GENERAL

During 1977 Seth won command of a battalion. He gained his promotion to the rank of lieutenant colonel thanks to both his gallantry awards and his very good cricket record. He had also excelled at the Staff College and everyone predicted a good future for him. The battalion that he was given to command was one of the elite in the Indian army and it looked as though Seth was on a roll as far as his career was concerned. He decided to put aside his disappointment on the cricket field by making good in the army. He also felt that he was at last on the road to fulfilling his father's expectations if not his own.

By then the old man had become feeble and an invalid. The news that his son had been promoted to the rank of lieutenant colonel, which had eluded him, and was commanding an elite battalion seemed to improve his health. For the first time, he wrote a congratulatory letter to his son and wished him further success in his career. Seth felt rejuvenated. On taking charge, he put his battalion through its paces meticulously and trained it to a very high standard. He commanded immense respect from both his officers and men for his straightforward dealings and no-nonsense approach towards everything in life. He earned the nickname 'Straight Bat' within the army.

What Seth was unaware of was that there was more to a successful career in the army than just professionalism and that 'straight bat' shots got an officer no runs. His boss, the officer commanding the division, was a major general with whom he initially got along with very well. The general liked professionals and appreciated Seth's professional attitude or so it seemed to begin with. However, he also had a darker shade to his persona as he was rather parochial in his attitude. He always thought that officers drawn from his own region were the best and deserved to get ahead of the others at any cost.

Although the three services in India were touted as great symbols of national integration, strong undercurrents of parochialism prevailed. These surfaced during the selection of officers for the choicest postings and promotions. The senior officers cleverly covered their bias with management jargon or other army 'slang' and made sure that officers of their regions advanced at the expense of other more deserving candidates. These officers, left with few or no chances of seeking redress, pocketed this ill treatment or denial of promotion. Barring a few who protested and went to court many quietly swallowed their pride and left the army with battered egos to seek greener pastures. These talented people however could never be put down for long and they usually made good in Civvy Street and later often thanked the generals for providing them with the freedom from the straitjacket of an army career.

Seth did not want to be such a casualty and handled his boss carefully and did everything as per his bidding right from the beginning. What he did not know was that his boss, apart from being a good professional, loved parties. There was nothing wrong with this; all officers in the services love parties. Unfortunately, they cost money and, as everyone appreciates, one should be prepared to shell out cash after giving a wonderful do. Many rich officers with incomes other than their salaries used to give plenty of parties particularly to the senior officers and thus gain promotions and upward mobility which they did not deserve. The senior officers were, after all, human and they could not ignore at the time of promotion board meetings those officers who had entertained them lavishly or showered them with expensive gifts. Most of the officers, barring the excellent and the markedly below average, were almost equal in their competence so nothing much differentiated the vast middle group. The senior officers in such cases could easily exercise their casting vote without any qualms of conscience.

Seth first tasted this unsavoury experience when the general gave a party for his personal friends in the battalion officers' mess. Later the battalion was asked to arrange another party for some civilian guests who contributed large amounts on Army Day. Seth realised the devious ways of the general when the latter's staff officer directed the battalion to combine the expenses for both the events and present one bill to headquarters. By a simple command, the general had skipped all the expenses that he had incurred for his party and made the headquarters pay for it. When Seth casually mentioned about this unfair handling of the matter, it somehow reached the general who, thereafter, slowly turned into an adversary. Hell hath no fury as a general scorned.

Seth recollected how the general later put him in several difficult situations and caused unnecessary harassment. When he fell out of the general's good books the latter took every opportunity to point out deficiencies, some real but mostly made up, and belittled him even in front of his own officers. The general, during his tour of inspection of the battalion, made some caustic remarks sprinkled with four letter words about the Colonel right in front of the junior officers, thereby undermining the latter's authority in the battalion. He pushed Seth right to the wall. When he had repeated this type of behaviour a good too many times, Seth could not stand it any longer and let the general have it.

He revealed publicly what his superior officer had been up to and his total lack of scruples. That single outburst put paid to Seth's career as the general proceeded to write some none too good things about him. The ACR, or the Annual Confidential Reports, are subjective assessments of the officers written by their superiors but they can make or mar the careers of the men. In one stroke, the general had signed off Seth's future career. However, the senior officers writing the reports are duty-bound to call the officer concerned and inform him whenever they make an adverse comment. Most of the senior officers do not have the guts to do so and therefore give average marks and an average report, which will still put the officer at a great disadvantage with his peers. Such average reports seal the careers of many and yet save the senior officers from the embarrassment and acrimony likely to ensue when informing about adverse reports.

Seth came to know through his friends that he had been done in. He thought that it was his misfortune to serve under a general who was both parochial and corrupt. Senior officers with such negative attitudes were few and far between but the few of his ilk did enough damage to the reputation of the army. Another officer in Seth's place would have resigned himself to his fate but he did not take it lying down. He put in a representation to see a superior authority on the ill-treatment meted out to him. A representation was not something that could be brushed under the carpet. The general was bound to forward it to his superiors or explain to the officer as to the reasons why it could not be forwarded. The latter action again needs confrontation with the junior and acrimony which the senior officers assiduously avoided.

When he forwarded Seth's representation, the general went to his boss, a lieutenant general, and explained in advance about Seth. The senior officers, once they become generals, form a club and support each other, except in their own rat race for promotion. They think that the discipline of the army would be undermined otherwise. At the same time, denying an interview to the officer who had put in representation also undermines the basic faith in the fairness of the army and its reporting system. The lieutenant general, left with no alternative, gave a patient hearing to Seth and promised to go into the matter which actually meant nothing. When Seth insisted that he be transferred to another battalion under a different reporting officer to get a fair chance, the general was hard put to deny the request.

When Seth was transferred, his name and courage to face the unjust senior officers preceded him. Tales from as far back as his NDA days when he faced the onslaught of the West Indies team and his heroic deeds in the 1965 war made the rounds once again. He took effective charge of the new battalion, which was involved in counter-insurgency operations in the northeast part of the country and acquitted himself creditably. Soon the media started glorifying him for his untiring efforts in tackling the menace of militancy. He soon became an expert in counterinsurgency operations.

One day, while he was returning from a reconnaissance, the insurgents almost ambushed his jeep and the small party with him. As soon as he realised the danger they were in he jumped out of the vehicle and hid his group under the thick bushes and undergrowth under the culvert. The militants waited for the jeep to come up to the roadblock but when it failed to approach the ambush point they emerged into the open, believing that they could easily outnumber and outgun the small party. What they did not realise was that the jeep had contained Colonel Seth who could be savage under pressure.

Seth in turn laid an ambush for the militants; he drew their fire to the wrong place and caused them to walk into the death trap. Yet again, it turned into a close encounter involving hand-to-hand combat and Seth and his small party took out a large group of militants against heavy odds. The Colonel went at them like a man possessed: he fired his pistol at point-blank range and slashed his *kukri* fiercely killing all but one of them. Just as the last one was about to fire, Seth's batman slashed at his throat with one single movement causing a gaping wound. The injured militant ran for his life and took shelter in the nearby village. Seth and his patrol chased him and quickly found the house in which he had taken refuge and the Colonel gave orders to open fire at the house. He shouted to the militant to come out and surrender but, when the latter did not obey, he continued the firing till the insurgent was dead and

135

the whole village became silent. Seth thought that the operation was a great success and returned to the battalion headquarters with his small troop unscathed.

The local media reported the case and praised the valour of the Colonel and his great achievement. That should have earned Seth another gallantry award and great fame but another section of the media, with a bias towards the insurgents, reported that when Seth fired at the militant's hideout he killed not only the target but also many villagers who were inside the house and nearby. They reported it as an avoidable and unnecessary massacre; they compared it to the My Lai massacre in Vietnam.

When one section of the press reported it in this manner, other sections followed suit and soon it became a full-size media event, a controversy. The human rights groups also got in on the act and reported it as a case of 'false encounter, military excess and gross violation of human rights'.

"Where were the human rights of the security forces when the ambush was laid for them? If the security forces were killed would the human rights groups cry hoarse about the rights of the security personnel?" the Colonel asked in anguish.

Meanwhile the international agencies also stepped in and made a hue and cry about the abuse of human rights. Seth argued that militants and human rights are mutually exclusive and militants who wanted to wreck the state and kill many innocent civilians should have no rights at all. He argued fiercely in the media that the militants forego their rights the moment they take up arms against the state. He disputed that several villagers were killed in the encounter and accused the media of falsifying the facts. He also said that if any civilians were killed in the process, which he disagreed with completely, it was only collateral damage and he could not be faulted for that. According to him, the only way to treat such militants was 'an eye for eye and a tooth for tooth'. He also pointed out that even civilians were given immunity and protection in matters of self-defence and that the same should not be denied to the security forces.

The army's top brass appreciated his arguments but bowed to pressure from the media and other international agencies. During the reporting of this incident the press unearthed the details about Seth's earlier record and his gallantry awards. They reported again how he had killed six enemy soldiers in hand-to-hand combat. What had earned him a gallantry award in the past had now become a subject of discussion and derision. The same media, which had glorified him earlier for his efficiency in counterinsurgency, went hammer and tongs at him for his lack of sensitivity and utter disregard of human rights.

"Imagine killing six militants with a *kukri* single-handedly," the headlines screamed in one of the local newspapers, despite the facts being inaccurate. Seth desperately wanted to point out to that particular newspaper that if he had not killed the militants in that way there would be no copy for them and he would have been part of the statistics of a large number of security forces that died in such operations.

The army reacted to the situation in typical fashion. First, it relieved him of command and shifted him to another station far away from the scene and out of the limelight. Bizarrely, they also decided to court-martial him. The army strongly felt that justice must not only be done but also be seen to be done. The 'straight bat' Colonel attended the court martial defending his own case. He cross-examined several civilian witnesses who testified about his brutality and proved them to be congenital liars. Fortunately for him, the senior officers who presided over the court martial appreciated his arguments and the way the civilian witnesses had falsified the facts. The court let Seth go scot-free but not without a mild reprimand. This reprimand, although symbolic, added one more stain to his dossier.

Seth's next posting was as a staff officer of a brigade. He started once again to try to prove himself and find his rightful place in the army. Alas, it was not to be so. While his brigade was taking part in an exercise, he slept in a rice field in his sleeping bag. The crop had been harvested and the field was bereft of anything except the stubs of the rice plants. To his misfortune, one of the drivers of a three-ton truck lost his way and drove the vehicle over him. A lesser mortal would have died instantaneously but Seth was made of sterner stuff. Despite many broken bones and torn cartilages, he survived and was taken to the military hospital. Since he was already a celebrity of sorts the doctors in the military hospital took every care to revive and put him back on his feet. Seth spent six long months in the hospital where he had to go through a series of operations. The doctors put steel rods into his broken bones and fixed many of the joints with surgical 'nuts and bolts'. They sustained him on a regular dose of Pathedrene injections to keep pain at bay and, thankfully, Seth showed remarkable resilience and recovered fast.

The regular dose of Pathedrene kept Seth free from pain but took their toll. Under their spell often he used to dream and sometimes have hallucinations. One particular day he kept shouting at the top of his voice that the demons were churning the sea and closing on him. This unnerved the other patients, who called the doctors. The patient kept shouting for sometime as though he was telling a tale. He stopped when Menaka arrived and calmed the turmoil but he kept calling for Priya before finally he fell into a deep slumber. The doctors felt relieved when they heard the name Priya; they knew it to be his wife's name but they noted this episode in the case notes in great detail although they did describe it as just a mere hallucination.

What was really painful was not his stay in hospital but his life after. He was rehabilitated into the army with a desk job and told to cool his heels and recuperate. First his life and health and then the career, they said. At last, when the moment of truth came, he was told in no uncertain terms that although the army appreciated his service his medical records had put him completely out of the reckoning for promotion as there was no way of disregarding the medical reports, both physical and mental.

"That is it," said the general who conveyed the bad news to him.

"That is it," Seth told himself and marked his time to earn his pension and retire to find greener pastures outside the army. Having lost on the cricket grounds and in the army, Seth often became depressed. The memories of his savage killing of enemy soldiers haunted him repeatedly and he became a broken man and would have resorted to violence but Priya provided the necessary moral support and kept reassuring him that there was life beyond the army. His two daughters, who were growing up quickly, provided great comfort and he made it a point to provide all the best that he could for them.

Seth, however, had more troubles in store for him when Priya fell sick with some minor ailment. She went on her own and got admitted to the army hospital as Seth was away from the base at the time. For reasons best known to them, the doctors decided that Mrs Seth needed a minor operation for which the good lady gave her consent. When she signed the consent form, she could hardly have anticipated what was going to happen. Due to some negligence or complication, the simple operation produced drastic results and she lapsed into a coma.

When Seth returned he found his wife in the ICU and the poor lady never recovered and passed away leaving him to lead a lonely life. With his wife in heaven and children now in the USA Seth felt like a soldier deserted by his own troops and left to fend for himself in the desert. To avoid spiralling into bouts of depression he took to hunting, at which he made a name for himself. Soon he started receiving calls from the civil administration to put an end to any menacing animal in the tribal areas.

The day he had discovered Raju he almost rediscovered himself. He thought of his old dreams in the cricket field and groomed Raju to realise the dreams that he had not achieved personally. He wanted to play for India albeit vicariously and spared no effort and expense so Raju's lack of success was very upsetting. The Professor advocated the use of the stick but somehow it was out of character for him to employ such a method in a case of failure. He reflected that he himself was such a case and his dad had never used the stick although he had showed his disappointment until his last days. There must be some way to make Raju perform to his true potential and achieve success so he continued searching for a way forward.

Seth decided to take Raju along with him for a dance performance. A noted danseuse, a celebrity in Bharatanatyam, was giving a performance in the city. Although the tickets were expensive, Seth bought two tickets for seats with a good vantage point. The dancer, an expert, both lithe and lissom went through her steps very gracefully. She enthralled the audience with her dance, which was like poetry in motion. Seth noted her excellent footwork, the perfect synchronisation of her steps with the beat of the music and her charming expressions.

"What do you see in the dance, Raju?" Seth asked.

"I see graceful movements."

"It's the coordination of the legs and the excellent way she moves them in perfect rhythm with the music. Does it make any sense to you?"

"I'm enjoying the dance and nothing else."

"But look closer; she has obviously spent many years of dedicated practice and, above all, she has mastered synchronisation of the movement of her legs. That's what is required of a good bowler. Perfect synchronisation of leg movements, which is called 'bowling action'."

"How does one perfect the synchronisation?"

"That's an art, and that's what separates the ordinary from the great. If you want to succeed as a bowler, you should strive to achieve perfection. Your legs should move like a machine at full speed and in good synch to form a good bowling action.

Your delivery and follow-through should also be equally good. You should achieve mastery over these to be a successful bowler."

Raju had no answer to that. How to achieve that perfection? he thought.

"Did you notice anything else in the dancer?"

"No."

"See the big smile on her face. It's not put on. She is enjoying what she is doing immensely. You should also enjoy your bowling. Cricket is after all a game and unless you enjoy playing it immensely you cannot thrive in it."

Seth took Raju to a military parade where the soldiers marched in perfect synchronisation with the music. The soldiers stepped to the beat of the music, each foot hitting the ground with the beat and they made it look very simple, as though they had been doing it for years.

"They must have been doing this for ages!" Raju said.

"Yes, but before each parade they rehearse many times to make sure that the final display is flawless."

"What's the lesson this time then?"

"You must practise everyday and even more so before a big event. You can never overdo your practise."

Seth continued to try several methods to motivate and propel Raju towards success. Finally, the lad was selected for the senior state team but his results were still not commensurate with his efforts.

THE TWELFTH MAN

The twelfth man is part of the team and yet not in the playing eleven. He stands on the threshold of success, waiting for the final moment to get his foothold into international cricket. He knows for certain that the day when he is included in the playing eleven is just around the corner. Although not allowed to bat or bowl, he still feels the thrill when he is called upon to field as a substitute to any injured player. He supports the batsmen in the middle by taking drinks or any items of cricket gear to them and he also assists his captain and coach by carrying important messages from the team management to the centre of play.

Some in the role of twelfth man, who come from rich backgrounds, resent the idea of carrying drinks to the senior players on the field and incur the displeasure of the entire team for their snobbish nature. Team India had a classic example of a batsman who resented this position and so was quickly dropped. However, a good man cannot be held down for long and, when given a second chance, he scored a century on his debut in a Test and cemented his place in the playing eleven. He blossomed and flourished into the most successful captain of the team in the annals of Indian cricket and a great hero for the cricket crazy youth of the country.

Raju found himself in the position of twelfth man. He stepped onto the threshold of his life as he first turned eighteen and then his physique changed dramatically. He grew taller and his shoulders broadened, his voice broke and he found strength flooding into various parts of his body. He was unaware though that he was in the difficult process of becoming a man. Above all, he was selected for the state team to play in the Ranji Trophy tournament. Suddenly, life seemed full of promise. He started dreaming and his dreams began to develop wings and he walked with an added spring in his step.

When Raju looked at the girls in his class he was aware of a strange feeling, a liking not experienced before and a sudden desire to be near them, talk to them and win their approbation. He wanted to share his newfound feelings and happiness with someone but he could hardly count anyone as his friend. He was constantly dogged by loneliness. The Colonel treated him like a son but he was not his son. There was a vast chasm between him and the Colonel despite the latter's efforts to put him at ease. Many a time the Colonel asked him to sit next to him on the sofa but he could never pluck up the courage to do so. At school, the other boys behaved in a standoffish way and never befriended him even when he won laurels on the cricket ground. His great friend and mentor, Mathew, had left the school as his father was transferred.

The girls Raju was so intrigued with were at best polite and nothing more. They constantly avoided him or invented some excuse or other to leave him. He always felt lonely despite having so much going for him. Loneliness is a great devil and plays tricks with one's mind. It dogs one continuously and causes torment; it is a formidable opponent and cannot be overcome easily. He tried several times to go out, seek friends and gain entry into their circle but his classmates showed little or no inclination to accept him into their crowd.

Unlike the villagers who had tormented him, his fellow pupils showed no resentment but showed no friendship either. The only person with whom Raju could relate to easily was his young sister from the village. He therefore decided to share his happiness with her and make a visit, taking her by surprise. Several years had passed since he had last seen her and he discovered a new girl. His sister, always playful, ever running around and full of mischief stood before him as a comely lass, now fully grown-up and dressed in a half sari, covering her form with more care. Her body had begun to blossom into that of a young woman and her skin was radiant with the delightful sheen of youth. Her eyes sparkled and she looked like a flower in full bloom. He thought that his sister could also grow up to be beautiful and smart like the Colonel's daughters. He went up to her and kissed her on the forehead. "You have grown, changed. I hadn't noticed all this time."

"So have you. Look at your arms and shoulders. You look strong, more like a man and less like a boy."

"Yes, I've grown up too. I'm so happy to see you again here. I've brought some presents for you."

"Thank you." She hugged him, opened the presents and jumped with delight. She also took the opportunity to tell him that the village headman's son had been teasing and troubling her. Incensed, Raju ran to he headman's house and shouted for the young lad to come out and face him. He sounded like a warrior, challenging the other to a fight. Pratap, once the village bully, appeared. He had also grown and filled out but not as much as Raju. He looked tall and lean but he stooped slightly and with one look at Raju, he shuddered.

"I understand that you have been troubling my sister. I've come to warn you that next time you trouble her you'll have to deal with me. So mind yourself!" he said in a strident, pointed tone that really unnerved the meek-looking fellow.

"You're speaking English and you've grown up," he said in his mother tongue. "I understand you're going to play cricket for our state as well."

"It's all true. Remember though, no more messing with my sister and tell all the other young fellows the same."

"Okay, boss," he said, in a cinematic fashion. "I used to be the boss of all the children when you were here but now everything seems to have changed forever." He continued as if he was reaffirming the truth.

Meanwhile all the other young lads with whom he used to

study and play cricket had gathered around in the centre of the village outside the headman's house. They gave him centre stage and congratulated him on his success in speaking English and being selected for the state cricket team. Most of them ungrudgingly acknowledged his good fortune and wished him success. They also bemoaned the lack of facilities in the village and how their own development had been stunted by the lack of good schools and playgrounds. Raju realised he felt much more at home in their company than at his school.

When Raju started his career in first-class cricket he was spared the agony of being the twelfth man and included in the playing eleven. His cup of joy was filled to the brim when the secretary of the State Association capped him and he walked on to the ground along with his team. He took to the pitch with a confident stride, stars in his eyes and heart full of hope. Unfortunately, the events of the match did not match his happiness. He had a bad day on the field and he had returned after the game with disappointment clearly etched across his young brow because his team lost badly by an innings and a few runs.

At the end of the match though, the captain had congratulated Raju for his excellent bowling and apologised for the lapses in the fielding. However, what good would the apology do? he thought. The result showed an abysmal loss and his bowling figures read pathetically, a mere two wickets for one hundred and twenty runs after three spells of ten overs each. He was supposed to be the spearhead of his team but his figures were nothing to write home about. What was he going to report to the Colonel who for some strange reason decided not to witness the match? As Raju continued to mull over his failure and to analyse his thoughts, he noticed the Colonel.

"A bad day in the field, I suppose?"

"How did you guess?" Raju replied downheartedly.

"One look at you and it is obvious."

"What should I do? I've been let down by the fielders three times."

"What was the result?"

"We lost by an innings and twenty runs. I took only two wickets for one hundred and twenty."

"Not something to be proud of," the Colonel commented.

"I know."

"Give me a brief account of it."

Raju sighed as he began, "We lost the toss and the opponents obviously elected to bat. I bowled two maiden overs and had the opening batsman as many as three times in those two overs. I had him beaten by sheer pace and I almost got him to edge the ball but unfortunately he survived. I had my chance finally in the third over and got the outer edge of his bat with an out swinger but the third slip spilled the catch, which was a sitter. Having got a life the batsman thanked his stars and threw his bat at everything with gay abandon. He scored freely and hammered all the bowlers like hell."

"What about the other batsmen?"

"I got the other batsman plumb before the wicket but the umpire ruled him not out."

"All bowlers think that the umpires are always in the wrong," Seth said with a wry smile.

"No, not in this case. The ball pitched right on the middle stump and the batsman played on the back foot and it hit him at knee height. I'd no doubt whatsoever."

"Why do you think the umpire ruled him not out?"

"It beats me. Even the batsman later acknowledged that it was a near thing, basically conceding that he had got away with it."

"What happened after that?"

"I lost heart somehow and I couldn't bowl with the same verve again in the rest of the match. The other bowlers didn't bowl well either. The batsman who got the reprieve made merry after that. He knew that he had got a life and thereafter threw caution to the wind and hit all of us all over the ground.

He made a century, whereas he should've been out on three."

"Don't you know it's not good to lose heart because of few reversals? You must press on regardless. That's the way to success. In fact, that strength to continue despite a few let-downs separates men from boys. As they say, when the going gets tough, the tough get going. You must be mentally tough to take some bad decisions and dropped catches."

"It is easier said than done. Anyway, I remembered your words and bowled with renewed vigour in the second spell but by then the batsman was well settled and full of confidence. He hit my good length balls without any problem. I should've got the other batsman though. I told the close in fielder that I would bowl a bouncer, rising up to the ribcage. True to my word, it did and the batsman hung his bat in midair to fend it off, the ball fell close, very close to the fielder at short square leg. He should've caught it easily but the fellow must've been daydreaming and didn't make a proper effort. Just my bad luck! The captain gave him a mouthful and replaced him. At that point the batsman was on twelve and he went on to make eighty-nine. I got two wickets but they were the tail enders and nothing to be proud off."

"How did your batsman fare?"

Raju shook his head as he told the tale, "It was another pathetic story. Thanks to the century scored by the batsman who slipped out of my fingers and the other who scored eighty-nine, the visiting team had piled up a total of four hundred and fifty runs which unnerved our chaps. They fell like ninepins. Their bowlers bowled with verve but their bowling was nothing more than mediocre. Our batsmen lost their nerve and confidence from the word 'play' and lost wickets at regular intervals. At the end of fifteen overs, we had lost three wickets for forty and never recovered after that. Our batsmen simply lined up, went in to bat and returned to the pavilion in quick succession. Not a single one of them troubled the scoreboard much. We were all out for a paltry one hundred and forty-five. We were asked to follow on and our performance in the second innings was no better. Our batsmen gave a repeat performance and showed that they were spineless. Once they had lost their confidence they never regained it and gifted away their wickets cheaply."

"How did you fare with the bat?"

"I went in at number eight and stayed at the crease for ten overs and scored twelve runs but, when I went in to bat in the second innings, it was all over bar the shouting. I was out for a duck. Anyway, nobody expected me to score runs. We all missed Ramu; his presence would have made a whale of difference."

"What did your captain say?"

"He made it a point to come to me and congratulated me for my excellent bowling. He also apologised for the fielding lapses of others but what good will those apologies do? My figures make a pathetic story, two for one hundred and twenty. After all the press and the selectors will look at the statistics so what chance do I have? All through no fault of mine."

The Colonel then explained why he had not attended. "I thought that if I didn't come to witness the match you might fare better."

"Why?" Raju was quite shocked.

"I thought that my presence was cramping your style and your bowling. I wanted to leave you on your own."

"On the contrary, your absence hurt me. You're like a protecting shield for me. As long as you are present, no one dares to make any comment about me but the moment you are out of my sight, well, they make snide remarks about my uncertain parentage. Some even call me a…bastard openly."

"I thought all of them were sportsmen and cricket, well it's a game for gentlemen!"

"Those days when cricket was for gentlemen are long gone. Today it's all professional and full of money. If you manage to get into Team India you make a fortune; everyone wants to get to that pot of gold first. In the process of getting there if they have to step on the toes of some, climb over the shoulders of others or slit someone's throat, they don't mind and do it without batting an eyelid. It's a rat race and dog eat dog out there."

"We used to have so much of camaraderie in our playing days," Seth commented.

"It may be there. In Team India however here, we all put up a show for the public but every fellow hates the other's guts and wants to get ahead of him. Team spirit is pushed to one side in order to get to the pot of gold."

"That sounds like a sad state of affairs. I don't believe you."

"It doesn't look sad on the surface but under the veneer and shine it's so."

"What do you want me to do to help you succeed?"

"I think no one could've done what you've done for me so far. I think I'm downright unlucky, unlucky in many ways right from my birth." Raju sounded miserable.

"Wrong! You must always learn to look at things positively. You were languishing in an unknown village and playing cricket in a rice field with an old hockey ball. You were bowling against the son of the village head who would never be given out anyway. Now you are playing first-class cricket. You've visited many places and even made a trip a to the USA. If you call this unlucky then I don't know what lucky would mean!" Seth spoke quite sharply to his protégé.

"I'm sorry." Raju realised he had sounded ungrateful. "I'll brush away such thoughts permanently. I'm just depressed; please don't take any notice. Thanks to you I'm the luckiest person in the world."

"Good. Now, if someone talks about your uncertain parentage, don't feel bad about it. Go up to him and tell him that it wasn't your fault; tell him that no one can choose one's parents. He'll never repeat the insult again but you must also keep telling yourself that it was not your fault. Keep saying this at least thirty times a day. That will do a lot of good to your psyche."

"I keep thinking positively but I'm waiting for a rainbow to appear on the horizon and all I see are dark clouds and nothing else. When will the skies clear and when will my star shine?"

"You've got to have patience. After all you are only eighteen and you've a lifetime ahead of you. Don't lose heart, keep at it, perseverance pays. This is the first state match that you've played in and you have many years of cricket ahead."

Unfortunately, Raju's bad run continued for the entire season. He always bowled his heart out but at the end of the day achieved little or nothing. The captain, the coach and the rest of the players in the team always acknowledged that he bowled very well but that was hardly any consolation to him. The team management assured Raju that he would definitely be picked up for the next season and asked him to hone his bowling further.

"It's the end of the season. I'll have to wait for one more year to see whether I can make any progress in my career," he told the Colonel despondently.

"You've at least six months to cut out the rough edges and polish your skills. Let me see what can be done in this time."

Seth went to meet the Professor, whose advice he respected very much. When he knocked, Latha, the Professor's good lady, opened the door and invited him in. She said her husband was expected in about half an hour and asked Seth to make himself comfortable. "You look very worried. What's bugging you?" she asked.

"Is it so obvious?"

"Yes, you look like a defeated soldier, who has lost everything."

"I am, a defeated soldier anyway."

"Today your defeat is not connected with your army career though."

Seth then explained his dreams, how they all lay shattered in ruins, how he had been trying to realise his own dream through Raju and all the effort that he had put in so far. "All I am getting out of this is frustration."

"You have a split personality. You keep telling Raju and

Ramu to think positively and see the brighter side of life but you yourself think just the opposite. You are a difficult man to understand."

"You seem to have put the finger right on the spot. What should I do?"

"First you should be glad that out of the two lads that you've trained one has made it into Team India and the other has been selected for the state team. By any standard, that's a great success. Your own children have also made you very proud, so, as far as I can see, you have everything going your way. So why the long face then?"

"I want Raju to play for our country. I'll not be happy until then. Tell me what more I should do?"

"Isn't it too early to think of Raju playing for the country?"

"Possibly, but in the NDA we used to believe in catching them young. Youth is a fleeting thing; before you say 'Jack Robinson', it's over. One cannot regain the spirit and splendour of one's youth. If he doesn't make his mark now soon it may be too late. Secondly, one has only a few playing years. The later he makes his debut, the shorter his playing life will be."

"But you can't jump the gun. He has to go through the mill and show consistent performance to merit selection. I think all your worries are unwarranted and premature."

"I can't disagree with you but I want quick results. You must strike while the iron's hot. I think Raju is hot now and he must succeed now."

"How do you think my husband can help?"

"I want him to tell me how to motivate the young lad further."

"That's interesting. Right now I'm doing research on a project about motivation. Perhaps Raju does need a stronger motivating force."

"What else could be more motivating than playing for India? You make a fortune and earn great name and fame."

"Perhaps money, name and fame are not enough in his case.

What is good for the goose is not essentially good for the gander."

"What other motivating force could be more effective?"

"My theory is 'love'. Love can make people move mountains. Have you tried that?"

"But he is only just eighteen or so. In fact I don't know his exact age but he couldn't even be close to twenty. He may not even know what love is! He's living with me under my watchful eye. Where's the chance for him to get to love someone?"

"You'd be surprised!" laughed Latha. "You don't know the youngsters of this generation. I suggest you find out if any girl is involved in his life and then we can work on him through her. If he has feelings for a girl then she might make our job easier. She can motivate him better than all of us put together."

Seth was far from convinced but said, "Thanks for your suggestion. Let me find out and I'll get back to you. But I also wanted to ask you what motivated Ramu to succeed at such young age?"

"You don't know? Well, as his mother I do know what drove him on. I'll share that knowledge with you at a later date because if I tell you now I'll incur the wrath of the Professor. Although my husband and I agree on many points I have some different ideas about psychology."

Having thanked her once again, Seth left with renewed hope. Waa it possible that Raju had met a girl somewhere and had developed a soft spot for her? he asked himself. He rephrased the question. "Is there a girl in town who can influence his mind more than I can?" He started to search both immediately and earnestly.

LEG STUMP

The role of leg stump in cricket is like that of a 'sidekick' in a movie. Although a main member of the woodwork, it is considered more as an appendage, although a very necessary appendage. The sidekick is essential for the progress of the movie and comes in very handy at crucial moments. Quite often, he provides the twists and turns of the tale but can also provide comic relief.

A ball pitched on the leg stump is like a free lunch for the batsman, who with a mere turn of the wrists can easily guide it to the ropes at square leg. If it is fast enough, he can execute a leg glance by turning the bat a fraction to send it crashing into the fence at fine leg or can also be easily manoeuvred to short square leg for at least a single without any problem. Such a delivery provides a staple diet to many a batsman.

It will, however, cause innumerable problems when bowled by a good leg spinner who can turn the ball or when the pitch provides a bounce and makes the ball rear viciously towards slips. The batsman in such cases is left guessing whether to leave it alone or hang his bat out to defend it with the possibility of only to end up giving a catch to the slips or short square leg. The delivery becomes unmanageable when the seamers bowl a leg cutter, as batsmen find it difficult to keep it away from the fielders crouching in the slips. One can go easy on a ball pitched on the leg stump but should never ignore it or treat it with disdain.

Seth asked his manservant to find out from Raju's room

whether the young lad was keeping any photographs of any girls. He did not want to spy on the young fellow and yet at the same time he thought that he must get his facts right before tackling the situation. True to his expectations, the manservant weeded out the photos of the cricket stars and brought a passport size photograph of a young girl. The photograph was a cut out from a school magazine or bulletin.

He made enquiries and found out that the girl, Usha, was from the same school and from a very good family. He talked to her and arranged to meet her in an ice cream parlour. The girl arrived right on time and she exuded class and confidence. One look at her and Seth felt that Raju had a good eye and appreciated his choice.

After exchanging pleasantries and getting the girl an ice cream of her choice, Seth got to the point without wasting time. "I understand you're a good friends with Raju."

"Not at all. We're from the same school but different sections and groups. I've seen him in a couple of cricket matches though."

"I thought he was…in love with you." Seth was confused.

"Maybe he is but that's news to me," Usha replied a little embarrassed.

"Do you like him?"

"I hardly know him. I've never spoken to him and know him only as a cricket player."

"Let me put it this way. Have you taken any special notice of him at all?" Seth was a bit unnerved by the conversation.

"I've seen him grow up; we're at the same school after all. He's grown into a tall and handsome fellow. He minds his own business and, although he's a good cricket player, he doesn't show off. That's all I know about him, nothing more."

"Would you be surprised if I tell you that he keeps your photo in his room and perhaps your image in his heart?" Seth pursued the delicate conversation.

"I'm certainly surprised, I've had very little contact with him!"

"Well, let me put it this way. Would you like to do something to help him?"

"In what way can I help him?" Usha was intrigued now.

"To achieve success."

"Success in what?"

"Success in cricket."

"That's strange, I don't know anything about cricket. How can I help him?"

"I'll tell you later. What I need to know is would you like to help him succeed?" Seth held his breath.

Finally, Usha nodded. "Okay, he's from my school. I guess if he succeeds I'd be happy to think I'd helped so I don't mind, but in what way can I help him?"

"I think you could be just what he needs."

"Go on, tell me more I'm curious now."

Seth then unveiled his plan and Usha readily agreed to it. The Colonel took Raju to the same parlour a few days later to give him a treat. As the lad was enjoying his ice cream, he noticed Usha alighting from a car with a few other girls. They occupied seats not far from where he was sitting.

Shy and diffident by nature, Raju was on his best behaviour since the Colonel was with him but the girls behaved in quite a boisterous manner. After sometime Usha walked up to Raju with an autograph book and asked him, politely, for his autograph.

"I'm a nobody. Why do you want my autograph?"

"You're a good cricketer and I love the game. I've autographs of many famous cricket players such as Tendulkar to the latest debutant. I'm sure that one day you will also play for our country."

"I'm delighted that you've so much confidence in me, here you are," he said as he signed his name with an extra flourish.

The Colonel looked the other way, pretending to be busy watching something with keen interest. In that short span of time, Raju had a good look at Usha and his heart missed a beat. He felt that he was in orbit in a strange world full of milk and honey. He took a glimpse into her eyes, just for a fraction of a second, and found a sparkle there. Before he could say anything, she had collected her book and left immediately. The Colonel also got up, paid the bill and proceeded to his car.

Waking the next day early in the morning Raju felt wonderful. When he drew the drapes of the window, he found that the sky was clear and the stars were winking out, one by one. The morning twilight was slowly fading, giving way to the dawn of another day. Somehow he felt that it was going to be a beautiful one, a heavenly one. He felt slightly light-headed and then he recollected the dreams he had had in the night.

He had dreamt of Usha, surrounded by flowers of myriad colours and he was holding her hands. He had dreamt of dancing with her, of dancing with such abandon across the Milky Way, hand in hand with Usha. He realised that for the first time in his life he had dreamt of something other than cricket, that he had dreamt of a girl and it had revolved around Usha entirely. He had seen her in several wonderful costumes, radiating like a fresh flower in full bloom and always smiling.

Her smile was captivating and mesmerising. He wished that the night had not ended and it had been able to provide him with the chance to go through the dream repeatedly. Such dreams are not like cinema, to be revisited again, he told himself and wished that Usha would visit him at least in his thoughts everyday. He also desperately hoped that he and Usha would have a dream run together. He wanted to skip his morning workout, sleep and replay his private thoughts once more but he accepted that the surest way to make his fantasy come true was through the cricket ground and success in the game. He put on his kit and found that the Colonel was waiting for him at the gate. He felt awful for keeping the Colonel waiting and apologised for the delay.

"Why are you late today? Have you been dreaming or what?"

"No, I was a trifle late because I overslept," Raju mumbled while blushing.

The Colonel smiled, a very thinly disguised smile, smug with the satisfaction that things were going according to plan. On that day he found Raju exercising with more vigour, a greater spring in his step and an increased zip in his bowling practice. From that day onwards Raju showed an intensified desire to succeed.

A few days later, the Colonel arranged a party at his house and invited several families who were close to him. When the guests arrived Raju found to his great delight Usha had come with her parents. She was dressed in a salwar kameez, which hugged her compact shape tightly and showed all her young and lissom figure to the full. She had both sequins and mirror work on the kameez and the sequins seemed to glow in the lights placed around the lawn. These, however, were eclipsed by her beautiful, bright eyes that glowed and her radiant smile that illuminated the entire lawn like a million watt bulb.

Raju's heart skipped a beat and he found himself drifting off into another dreamy world. Quickly he took control of himself and tried to behave normally so as not to upset the upright Colonel. Seth had a good chat with Usha's parents while the young woman stood next to her mum, wondering what she was doing at a party that was so obviously for adults The only other young soul in the group was Raju and she waited for him to make his move. Only after dinner did he pick up enough courage to speak to her. He hesitated, stammered and then stuttered before he spoke, "You look very beautiful in that dress."

"Thank you."

"I didn't know that your dad and the Colonel were good friends."

"I didn't know until today but look at the way they are hitting it off together."

Raju did not know how to continue with the conversation, he felt totally tongue-tied. The waxing moon bathed the entire lawns in a pale light and the gentle, cooling breeze provided a pleasant evening. The beautiful Usha completed the picture. It was almost like a dream sequence in a film. Raju just stood there in front of the girl that had filled his thoughts savouring every second; he did not want to spoil the wonderful sight with words. He thought that he would take his chance to speak to her later but wanted to make the most of the moment and take delight in her beauty and her captivating smile. He wanted time to stop and keep him with her frozen in that frame forever. Usha showed no special interest in him and kept looking around taking the scene in, appreciating the Colonel's house, the lawns and the flowers that surrounded it.

All too soon, it was time for the guests to leave and Usha's parents in fact were the first to go. As Usha left and got into the car, Raju felt that time had been a spoilsport and had shattered his dream. He realised later that he had not even mustered up enough courage to ask for her telephone number. He wanted to possess her somehow, even if it seemed an impossibility. He did not know that the first seeds of love had begun to germinate in his young heart.

Raju did not take long to find out that Usha was the only daughter of the leading advocate in the city. She had joined a different college to his, which took only the best of the students who all passed pre-degree course with flying colours. She was known to be both brilliant and ambitious. He felt that he compared very badly with her and stood no chance whatsoever in the fight to win her hand. However, he finally summoned up his courage and called her, having found out her telephone number via the Colonel.

When she answered, he bravely asked her out for a treat in the ice cream parlour. To his great surprise and delight, she accepted without much fuss.

On the appointed day Raju spruced himself up, wore the best of the clothes that he had and sported a big smile before meeting her. Usha came in her posh, chauffeur-driven car and made her way to his table in slow and graceful strides. Unlike other students, he stood up and behaved like a thorough gentleman taking cues from what he had seen the Colonel do in similar occasions. He enquired of her studies and plans for the future. When he learnt that she was planning to gain admission to one of the prestigious IITs in the country and then go to the USA for further studies, his spirits dampened. He did, however, find her full of enthusiasm and confidence. She had no doubt that she would excel in her studies and pursue them as per her plan. She kept talking of institutions of repute like the MIT and her chances of getting a seat in one of them. She said that she had no problem regarding funds as her father had plenty of money. He found her confidence very remarkable and realised it was something he should try and learn from her. The difference was she knew that she had everything and that things would definitely go her way. She had set her goals high, very high indeed, and had a determination to succeed and make a name for herself.

When she asked Raju to talk about himself, he had very little to say. He said he had nothing to boast of in his scholastic record or, for that matter, anything except his cricket. "I am just an average guy," he replied quietly.

"Why do you undersell yourself? You're a fine cricket player and at this young age you're already playing for the state and have a good chance to play for the country. I think that's an excellent record and something to be proud of. So, walk with your chin up and don't let things upset you. Set your goals and try hard, that's my motto. I'm sure that you'll succeed. Sometimes, there's more fun in trying than in actually achieving success."

"No, it's not so in cricket. Here you play for broke. Either you make it into the big league or languish on the sideline waiting for the golden opportunity. Soon age will catch up with me and I'll be fit for nothing. It's a make or break situation for me. I've another two to three years and then I must get into the big time if I'm to make a career in cricket. A lot depends on luck and lady luck is always fickle."

"You're sounding cynical for a young man. You just keep trying hard and leave the rest to God, if you believe in Him." She spoke with passion and tried to encourage him. She somehow seemed certain of the success of both of them and her enthusiasm was so infectious that Raju started believing in himself more than before.

During the off-season, Raju had a few opportunities to meet her and take her to the coffee house or ice cream parlour. She did not mind being seen in his company and she behaved very normally, as any young girl of her age would. She was not much interested in cinema, which was the popular subject amongst the students of her age group. Instead she spoke of big schemes and ambitious plans. She also realised that Raju did not have enough funds and made it a point to pay the bill on the few occasions that they went out. During their time together, she always took a couple of minutes to exhort him to work hard on his game and achieve his dream.

After every meeting, she moved a couple of notches higher up in Raju's estimation and he started believing her totally. He felt rejuvenated after seeing her and put extra effort into his practice sessions. He wanted to convert the sweetness of her smile into venom in his bowling. He wondered whether there was any magic formula for such a conversion. What he did not know was that the confidence she had shown in him had started working as a catalyst in his daily workouts.

Soon the season started again and Raju was selected for the state team. Fortunately for him, the first match of the Ranji Trophy for that region was slated to be played in his home town. He believed it was his lucky break because he could play before the home crowd and was sure that at least all the boys and the girls of his school and college would turn up for the game. He especially requested Usha to attend and watch him in action. She agreed without making any protest about her studies. In that first match, he played with newfound confidence. Whether it was his burning desire to succeed or his desperation to impress and to win the approval of his dream girl, or the driving force of the Colonel, something acted on him and made him bend his back yet more while bowling.

He sent the ball hurling at a faster pace than previously and surprised the batsmen and his own teammates. All of them acknowledged that he was a fine, fast bowler and destined to win laurels but they had never seen him bowl with such venom in his stride. The batsmen found him unplayable and often hung their bats out more in self-defence and less to score runs. Raju sent the stumps cartwheeling many times and achieved fantastic results. His performance drew good press and all the columnists stared wondering whether a new star was rising on the cricket horizon. The national selectors decided to take a look at him and made it a point to watch him bowl in the next match.

The end of summer brought the results of various examinations and entrance tests. Usha qualified for several engineering colleges, including the prestigious IIT. She had obtained a very good rank in the JEE, an entrance test for the IIT, and was brimming with confidence having gained a seat in the choicest faculty at the place she had opted for. She decided to treat all her friends and included Raju in the group. Her father, a rich advocate, spared no expense and it was a party that all the youngsters remembered for a long time. The girls who attended encircled Raju and lavished him with praise. They also wished him well and hoped that one day he would play for the country. Raju, feeling exulted, savoured the adulation of all the young women who turned out to be his fans.

The day he learnt that Usha was leaving for Chennai to join the IIT he went to her home and found her busy packing. She said that she was going to join the IIT in Madras to study computer engineering and she was on her way to making her dreams come true. Raju felt very happy but also terribly

163

disappointed in some ways. He could not conceal his feelings for long.

"That means I won't be able to see you for quite some time."

"But I'll be in Madras or Chennai as they call it now. It's not very far and the city holds many important matches. You can always come to visit me when you come to play in Madras or whenever you get a break between your games. I'll be only too happy for you to come and see me."

"Why don't you study in the local engineering college? After all, it is also quite reputable."

"Don't be silly. Do you want me to leave the seat in IIT? No way. You must devise your own ways to meet me whenever possible. Don't even think of me not going to IIT."

He knew that she had a point and a strong point at that. How could he ask her to forego her future? What was his standing with her to suggest anything? What had he to promise her? He was not sure of himself as yet. He could not even try to persuade her to stay back and give the pleasure of her company to him. He quietly left, feeling like a batsman bowled by the very first ball. Within the next few days Usha left for Madras leaving a gaping hole in his life. Raju felt that something had been wrenched from his heart, his body and psyche and for the first time he spent a sleepless night.

The second match of the season was held in a different stadium and a few selectors attended the match to see his bowling as the press had raved about him. Raju desperately wanted to impress them but he knew that Usha was at the IIT in Chennai and far from the stadium. His morale sagged even before the commencement of the match. He tried hard, perhaps too hard, and was not his normal self. One of the golden rules of cricket is that each player must play within himself. If he tries to be anyone other than himself or tries to do more than what he is capable of he comes a cropper.

Raju's performance in the match proved true to the rule and he disappointed everyone, including the selectors, who could not be faulted for concluding that his performance in the earlier match was nothing more than a flash in the pan. Raju felt that he had let down the Colonel and Usha. He thought that failing to live up to the expectations of his dream girl was a greater disappointment than letting down the Colonel. He also realised that for the first time in his life he cared for the feelings of a person other than Seth. He had realised he felt some strange and tender emotions growing within him but as he did not watch movies and could not discuss such things with the Colonel, he was unable to identify that tender feeling as love. He did not know what love was as he had never experienced the love of his true parents, brothers or sisters. He had no one except the Colonel who was father, coach, mentor and guide all rolled into one.

THE BALL

The ball is the most important item in the game of cricket. When it is new and shining like a red cherry, it looks like a young girl in her prime, full of bloom and promise. It delights a fast bowler, who uses it as a potent weapon to demolish his opponents; modern fast bowlers are capable of producing fantastic pace. When hurled at great speeds in the range of one hundred and fifty kilometres and above per hour, it produces wonders, like the service of a tennis player who can reach somewhere in the region of two hundred kilometres or more per hour. It allows for very little reaction time as it traverses through a distance of not more than twenty metres before reaching him. The speed of the fast bowlers has been increasing progressively and today a velocity of one hundred miles per hour, or one hundred and sixty kilometres per hour, is par for the course.

As if that is not bad enough, the condition of the pitch, the presence of any grass on it, the wind and overcast conditions all assist the lateral movement of the delivery. A new ball can swing and swerve causing innumerable problems to the batsmen and inhibits them from playing their shots. The speed, coupled with this lateral movement, makes the job of the batsman very difficult, as he has to make his decision and take action in a fraction of a second. A cold, windy day and a grassy pitch produce the maximum movement of the ball and discomfiture to the batsmen. In such conditions the fast bowlers charge in like roaring bulls and trample all over them. The same bowlers however get a sound thrashing if the conditions are not favourable or they err in line or length. The opening batsmen, who are especially selected for the purpose of seeing the shine off the new ball, watch it like an eagle and wear the bowlers out either by leaving deliveries or playing safe defensive shots. As the ball gets older, it loses its hardness and shine and emboldens the batsmen to play their strokes. The best batsmen, who are prolific stroke makers, come in between positions three to seven and play their shots with sound technique and judgement.

The same acquiescent ball will again become a potent weapon when it becomes old if handled by quality spinners. These bowlers are a different breed altogether to the pace men. They bowl slowly, in fact deceptively slowly, but 'turn' the ball leaving the batsmen guessing its likely path. They are able to turn it either way, often confusing the batsmen and sending them back to the pavilion. The spinners do not like the shine on the ball as it ruptures their spinning fingers hence they wait until it has had the newness beaten out of it.

The Indian spinners, who used to form the backbone of the bowling attack, often used to take a new ball and grind it on the ground to take the shine off it. Later, the fast bowlers learnt the art of the reverse swing, which was invented by the Pakistani players. They used to take the old ball and keep polishing just one side of it. Thanks to this, the ball used to swing in the direction of the shine. They would then conceal the ball in their grip so leaving the batsmen guessing which way it would swing. Although dubbed as a trick initially, it has now become a standard weapon in the armoury of all fast bowlers. Similarly, the spinners also started bowling with the new ball to extract bounce to surprise the batsmen. In a few matches, spinners have actually opened the bowling attack with the new ball.

The balls used in different countries, although made according to the standards specified by the ICC, behave differently and can trouble the batsmen from visiting teams. The ball is also hammered and battered by good batsmen and, during a game, is like the Prince of Denmark in Hamlet; the complexion of the game changes as it loses its colour.

One day the Colonel had a call from a certain Commander Bhide, who was one of his batch mates in the NDA. He had also played in the cricket match with the West Indies team and had scored a breezy fifty with plenty of lusty hitting. He was highly reputed for his daring and devil-may-care attitude. Bhide had finally opted for the navy and had continued to play for both the navy and services teams but eventually he had joined the flying branch of the navy and could not continue with his cricket. The Colonel had slowly lost touch with him so when he got the call he invited his old friend for lunch.

They made themselves comfortable with a tall glass of beer in the ease of the Colonel's living room and started recollecting their time at the NDA and their cricket playing days. They visited memory lane and shared many pleasant recollections. The bonhomie that exists between the batch mates of NDA is everlasting and beyond words. Even when they meet after decades, they forget everything and go through their days in that hallowed institution. They relived their younger lives and reflected on all the joys and hardship they experienced while recollecting their old jokes and pranks that they played either individually or collectively.

While in service, batch mates work closely together and the fact that they were fellow students works like a catalyst, improving coordination between the different services. The bond of friendship that is established and nurtured for three years stays permanently and is never broken.

"I heard that you were a flying ace in the navy, so why did you leave?" Seth asked curiously.

"You heard right. I was one of the ace flyers and everything was going my way but then I crashed and my seniors started doubting my prowess. I also had a difference of opinion with my boss who later turned out to be vindictive. He told me that it was the end of the road for me," replied Bhide.

"Difference of opinion, did you say? Knowing you as I do,

you must have told him to go to hell or something like that. Am I right?"

"You're always right!"

Amidst much backslapping and leg pulling, the two spent a very enjoyable afternoon and savoured the lunch carefully prepared by the Colonel's manservant. Bhide also talked about the state of cricket in the country in general and the progress of Raju in particular. What the Colonel did not know was that at the same time in another town in an adjacent state Raju was playing a Ranji Trophy match and was not playing well.

The match was being played in a stadium located far out from the city and drew few or no spectators. Most Indians are crazy about the game; even grandmothers, who do not know the front end of the bat to the rear, talk of cricket and suggest ways and means of beating the opponents. The cricket-loving public of India fill to capacity the stadium whenever Team India plays any foreign team irrespective of the likely outcome. They all cheer their team by making a huge din, beating drums, setting off fireworks and playing impromptu music which all add to the circus. When they find the opponents gaining the upper hand, sometimes they show their ire by throwing plastic bottles and other objects onto the ground. These are not harmful or lethal in any way but definitely annoying to the players. This rowdy behaviour on the part of the crowds is par for the course at any big match and many a time the game has been stopped to control the crowd.

Surprisingly this enthusiasm is conspicuous by its absence when teams are playing domestic cricket, otherwise known as first-class cricket, which is most definitely worth watching. While the players playing for Team India are treated like royalty and paid handsomely, their lesser counterparts playing in domestic cricket get only the crumbs and are kept waiting on tenterhooks for the big day when their name is included in Team India.

When his match started Raju knew that Usha was not coming as she had already left for Chennai to join the IIT. The Colonel had also decided to stay away in order to spend time with his old friend, Bhide. Knowing that the two most important souls in his life were not with him on that day, Raju walked to the middle with his teammates not with a spring in his step but wistfully. His mind was more on Usha and less on the game.

Although he was walking on to take part in an important match, he had been playing a game with a different set of opponents; he was battling his own demons. He realised that, somehow, he had developed a liking for Usha and that his body and soul had started yearning for her company. He also realised that she was the only daughter of a rich and eminent advocate in the city and she was a brilliant student. She had goals of her own, goals which were far different from his. She wanted to go to the USA for further studies and make a name for herself in software. She had a father who had the wherewithal to make her dreams come true.

On the other hand, he was an orphan and living at the mercy of the Colonel and God knows how long Seth would support him. He was striving and struggling hard to make it big in cricket but somehow success seemed to be a distant dream. Unless he succeeded and got into the 'big league', he would not be a worthy match for Usha. He had nothing that he could call his own and depended entirely on the Colonel. He also knew that his uncertain parentage was a permanent stigma that he would have for the rest of his life. He knew that it was not his fault that his parents had abandoned him at birth, but how many people would close their eyes to that? he asked himself. He believed he stood at one end of a spectrum with nothing and Usha was at the other end with everything going her way.

What Raju was unaware of was that a handful of selectors had decided to come down to watch him in action. When the match started, Raju bowled the first spell with a deflated spirit ridden by self-doubts. His bowling lacked fire and pace and the batsmen helped themselves to plenty of runs.

His captain came over to him and asked him, "What's wrong? Are you not fit? Why are you splashing the ball around like that? You're giving the batsmen a free rein! I was counting on you. By the way, you should know that there're some selectors out there watching. You could make or mar your career today."

This pep talk produced some effect on him but not enough to propel him to glory. The captain, fed up with him, sent him to field in the third man position which involved quite a bit of running and was normally considered a punishment position for an erring fielder.

The position was close to the spectators and when he ran to field a ball he noticed through the corner of his eye a lone hand waving at him. It sure was a dainty hand, he thought, and had a familiar gold bracelet dangling from it. When Raju looked up, he found Usha sitting alone in one corner of the stadium waving at him with all her energy. His spirits soared and he pulled himself up from the morass of self-pity in which he had been wallowing. He approached his captain and told him that he had got over his downcast mood of the morning and asked for a chance to bowl. He also promised to deliver. The captain, who in his time missed many chances of selection for the big league, readily obliged. After all, he had nothing to lose. The opponents were getting an upper hand and he was ready to clutch at any straw to get his team back on top. He tossed the ball across to the lad.

After seeing Usha in the stadium, Raju was a transformed man. Gone was the wistfulness in him as his heart thumped with joy. He went to the bowling crease in quick jumps, hopping like a kangaroo. He pulled his socks up and decided to give the match his best shot as he thought that, with Usha by his side, he would be able to cross many frontiers, overcome any hurdle and fight the devil himself. Today is my day, he said over and over in his mind. He measured his run up accurately and went through the preliminaries carefully, like an airline pilot carrying out his checks before take-off.

When he started his bowling run up he looked at the batsman not as an adversary but as a demon, who should be demolished at the earliest possibility. The batsman seemed to him to be a monster with horns on his head, teeth protruding far out and wielding a huge mace in place of a bat. Raju thought that he had the weapons to demolish and destroy the devil and decided to do so without any further delay. He bowled like a man possessed and the first ball flew past the batsman at a breakneck speed missing his bat by a few microns. The entire close in fielders and the wicketkeeper raised their hands and almost jumped with joy. The batsman heaved a sigh of relief, as the bat had not made any contact but could not believe what he was seeing. He had thrashed the same bowler earlier to all corners of the field and scored heavily off him, but now all of a sudden he found that he was facing a very different bowler, menacing and full of verve.

The second ball was more vicious and swung into the batsman off the pitch. It forced him to put his bat down on the ball hurriedly to keep it down and prevent it from flying to any of the close in fielders. He was not so lucky with the third ball, which came even faster than the first two. He did not have a clue how to deal with it so he just put his bat out in front of him, more by instinct than anything else, a reflex action which was certainly not part of his technique. The ball thundered past him but brushed his glove and the wicket keeper gleefully took the catch. All the fielders shouted "Howzat?" in unison. The ball, while brushing past the glove had made the faintest of noises, which would have been lost in the din of any important match. Thankfully, the absence of any spectators made a huge difference and the umpire raised his finger without any hesitation. The batsman, a player of some repute and also waiting in the wings to join the coveted ranks of his seniors, felt disappointed. He made a pretence that the umpire's decision was not fair but that he was complying with it just to ensure that the code of conduct the players have was not infringed.

Raju bowled the next few overs like a man on fire and produced fantastic deliveries, which were unplayable. Even the world's best batsmen would have found it difficult to negotiate such bowling. A couple of close calls and a missed catch robbed him of a hat-trick but he got quick wickets and the opponents fell like ninepins. He put the fear of God into the batsmen and they all caved in. Soon the opponents were all out and Raju emerged triumphant with a haul of six wickets in his bag. Everyone praised him and his selection to the big league seemed certain.

During the break, he went to meet Usha. She told him that she had changed her schedule and decided to come and support him in the all-important match. Raju's eyes lit up and he experienced several feelings, some known and some unknown. He felt very grateful that she had decided to support him and thanked her for changing her schedule. He then began to ponder on the hope that there might be more than just support in her reasons for coming to the stadium, which was way out of her route. A spark of hope kindled and he felt that perhaps all was not lost believing he had a chance, albeit a slim one, of winning her approval. He thanked her profusely and took her to the main stand where the VIPs are normally seated but Usha wanted to be excused and to continue her journey to meet her deadline for reporting to the IIT. She wished him all the best and left when his team started batting. Although she had left before the end of the match she had filled his heart with cheer and tons of hope, hope that his life was not just a grind but definitely with a gold pot in sight. The grass in the stadium looked greener and his whole life looked brighter. He could see rainbows and angels singing and dancing and name and fame encircling him.

During the second innings, Raju performed even better. The demoralised batsmen now saw devils where none existed and, even when Raju bowled ordinary balls, they meekly surrendered and became his victims. Raju finished the match in glory and his bowling figures read like a dream for any bowler, a rich haul of eight wickets and he had caught the attention that he deserved from the selectors.

Raju's performance on that day should have earned him a place in Team India but the selectors follow a strange system called the 'quota system'. The selectors that visited the stadium that day were from other regions of the country and they had already filled their quota but they could not deny Raju something that he deserved. They made a neat compromise and decided to include him in the India A team, which was the second string team of the country. The selectors asked him to go to the MRF pace academy at Chennai and hone his skills further during the next two weeks. They told him that they would send him to the Australian Cricket Academy later for a short stint of three to six months. Raju was elated; he had moved up one rung of the ladder and was getting nearer to his goal.

A BREAK

Everyone looks for and prays for a break in life; cricket players are no different. They play with all the passion and skill at their command and finally pray for a break to get into the big league where the megabucks are to be had. However, when they finally get their break through and start the next phase in their playing career, they do not like a break from the game for this may cause their doom and undo the all-important break they got in life.

The break in cricket may be an off break when the ball turns into the batsman from the off side and a leg break when it turns the other way. The way a ball turns depends upon the tweak the bowler gives it either with his fingers or wrist. Sometimes the pitch also breaks and assists the bowlers. When the ball turns, more often than not it becomes difficult for the batsman to predict its likely path and casts many a doubt in his mind as to whether it has turned at all and if so how much and which way it has turned. The bowling action and the movement of the bowler's wrist often provide the all-important clue to the batsman as to how the ball will turn and how much it will turn. He can then play his shot either defensively or send it crashing to the fence.

There is, however, more to a simple break. While the earlier players used to turn the ball quite a bit with the turn of their wrists or deft use of their fingers, the modern spinners have learnt the art of bowling the wrong ones. They bowl with the action of a leg break but produce an off break, which is called a googly and baffles the batsman. This was standard fare for quite some time and the batsmen learnt to read such deliveries and take evasive action with quick reflexes. Then the off-break bowlers developed a similar ball which they have started calling of late a '*doosra*' and foxes the batsmen. The spinners of both kinds have expanded their repertoire to include an arm ball also called an armer which definitely promises to turn but proceeds straight leaving the batsman stranded in the wrong spot.

The amount of turn and bounce the spinner gets depends on various factors such as high arm bowling action, the pitch, the cracks in the pitch and rough patches developed by the footmarks of the bowlers. The imponderables in the case of a spinner's delivery are innumerable and make the job of the batsmen difficult to solve the equation and come up trumps. Often they fall to the wiles of the spinners. No wonder the batsmen do not want a break and when the ball breaks they would like it to break as predicted. They fervently hope that the pitch will not provide any break to the spinners at all and, when it does, they pray to God and ask Him to give them a break. The only batsmen who survive when the bowler gets a good break are those who are agile with quick reflexes and good footwork. They move their feet quickly, meet the ball and hit it before it gets a chance to break and wreak havoc.

Ramu got his break early in life. He scored prolifically in all the matches that he played in at the beginning of his career and soon caught the selectors' eye. He was called up for duty with Team India at a young age and included in the team embarking on an overseas tour to England. He practised religiously in his early life in the backyard of the Colonel's house and primarily against Raju. He consequently mastered the technique of handling the fast bowlers and posted huge scores against them. England had always been a good breeding ground for fast bowlers and produced some legendary all-time greats. Ramu, batting at number three, found no difficulty handling the English fast bowlers, amassed huge scores and earned a good name. He scored a century at Lords, the mecca of cricket.

Although many excellent cricket stadiums have developed in several countries, Lords still remains a hallowed ground. A century at Lords is the dream of every batsman and a select few have realised this dream and earned their place in the annals of cricket. Ramu was indeed fortunate to achieve such a dream at a young age and so early in his career.

When the team returned to India after a successful tour of England the entire press were agog and hailed Ramu as the latest star on the cricket firmament. The sports writers lavished praise on him and used the most flowery language to describe his wristy off drives and well-timed cover drives. The cricket scribes can go overboard when they either praise or criticise a player. They get into verbal callisthenics, exercise their adjectives and turns of phrase and put them through different gyrations and even invent new expressions. They compared him with Gundappa Viswanath, a batsman of the seventies reputed for his fine technique, and predicted a long innings and very good future for Ramu.

The young batsman, on returning home as a hero, exulted in all the adulation of the home crowd. When he landed at his hometown, he received a hero's welcome and was cheered all the way from the airport to his house. The local press waxed lyrically about the local boy doing the town proud and courted him. Ramu, at the first opportunity, went to the Seth's house to thank him for all the help the latter had provided and said in no uncertain terms that he would have been a nobody but for the untiring efforts of the Colonel. Seth felt uneasy acknowledging his contribution for he knew that he had concentrated all his energies towards the training and development of Raju and that Ramu was only a successful by-product of that process. Nevertheless, he graciously hosted a party in honour of Ramu and invited all the prominent citizens interested in cricket in the city. The party was a grand success and everyone praised the Colonel for successfully training the young batsman. Some even suggested recommending Seth for the *Dronacharya* award, which was given annually for the best coach. The Colonel just smiled away his awkwardness. Fortunately, Raju was away playing a match in a different city and saved the Colonel from considerable embarrassment of the situation; his real protégé still had not succeeded.

The meeting between Raju and Ramu a few days later provided an interesting interplay of human relationships. Raju initially congratulated his friend for the success that he had achieved in such a short time; he complimented him no end. At the same time the green-eyed monster kept rearing its ugly head and he kept asking himself, "Why not me?"

India has always produced many good batsmen but very few fast bowlers. When Kapil Dev burst onto the Indian cricket scene, he brought with him a sea of change in the fortunes of Team India. Raju thought that he had every chance to make it, but somehow never got a good break. Either the fielders dropped catches and ruined his bowling figures or the flat pitches provided him with no help and robbed him of any success. He tried equally as hard as Ramu but Lady Luck smiled on the latter, leaving Raju still hoping for a break one day. He thought that life had been cruel to him from the beginning when his own parents had abandoned him and he believed he could not blame any one for his ill luck other than himself. Although he talked amiably with his friend and put on a jovial façade, a strong undercurrent of jealousy was simmering and threatening to overpower him. He had to make a considerable effort to keep it under check and not let it engulf him.

Ramu on the other hand talked freely, recalling several incidents when they had practised together. He told him of the ways of the fast bowlers of England and gave several hints to his friend as to how to hone his technique further. He felt that Raju should have met with more success by now as he had a godfather in the Colonel, who nurtured and trained him in all the nuances of fast bowling. His father, the Professor, knew little or nothing about cricket let alone batting and he had never got that much help from the Colonel either as Seth's knowledge of batting was sketchy. Whatever he had learnt, he believed, was entirely due to his own efforts. He had won and found a place in Team India, although the odds had been heavily stacked in favour of Raju. He thanked heaven for his accomplishments but wished, sincerely, for the success of his friend too. He made it a point not to brag about his life and ignite flames of jealousy in his friend and tried hard to maintain the status quo in their relationship. He kept Raju in good humour by giving him presents, which he picked up while shopping on his overseas tours.

In the next few months, Raju left for the MRF Pace Academy and then a stint of training at the Australian Cricket Academy. Ramu went on tour at the same time to Sri Lanka and while there he met with mixed success. The fast bowlers of Sri Lanka were not as fast as those that he had encountered in England where he had scored heavily against them.

Modern cricket has become more psychological and, with the advent of televisions and computers, each and every game is recorded and analysed to determine the strengths and weaknesses of all players. Before the commencement of a match, every team carries out a considerable amount of homework and chalks out a strategy against the batsmen to hopefully get them out cheaply. This includes selection of the bowler, the line and length to be used against him and the arrangement of the fielders to restrict his chances of scoring and thus they plot his downfall.

The Sri Lankans found a chink in Ramu's armour and brought in their spinners whenever he batted. The spinners in Sri Lanka, and there seemed to be a horde of them, were a different and difficult lot. They had right arm and left arm spinners who were able to bowl leg and off breaks. It appeared that all the players in the team could give the ball a tweak with their wrists or fingers and turn it at will. Although the pitch and other conditions were similar to those he was used to in India, Ramu found it difficult to negotiate these spinners on their home ground. Soon he became a 'spinners' bunny' and was got out cheaply on several occasions. His career in cricket, which a few months back seemed to be on a steep ascent, looked like stalling, if not collapsing. He thought that he had cemented his place in Team India but suddenly the cement appeared to have developed cracks and was crumbling. Fortune, which had smiled on him so far, seemed to have changed its mind. He lost his confidence and was always forced onto the back foot when he saw a spinner.

Writers get cramp and blocks, tennis players get an elbow and athletes have an Achilles' heel; similarly cricket players lose form and fall into lean patches. The big scores elude them. Simple balls, which produced no problems earlier, trouble them and shots, which they used to execute earlier with a flourish, disappear from their repertoire entirely. The batsmen have to fight with themselves, exorcise the demons within them, regain their confidence and get back into form. Many a batsman has met their Waterloo and been unable to get out of the lean patches and subsequently have vanished into oblivion.

To counter the spinners, Ramu started opening the innings and scored freely off the new ball bowlers. The wily Sri Lankans though sensed his predicament and unease so brought in the spin merchants at the first opportunity, even before the ball had lost its shine and still got him out cheaply. The press latched on to his deficiency in batsman skills and his weakness against spinners, then went to town with the idea that he should go back to the cricket academy; they said he should start learning to play the spinners before returning to the international scene. Cricket is a funny game and reduces heroes to zero in no time. When the tour, which was only a short one, ended Ramu heaved a sigh of relief but realised that things had taken an ugly turn. On returning, he was no longer a hero. On the contrary, he was a fallen idol and had to do something to resuscitate his previously budding career.

Ramu owed his success and failure to his father. Professor

Deb was a specialist in child psychology and had published many papers to his credit but he did not put into practice what he preached and taught at the university. Firstly, he became a professor not by choice but out of desperation. During his youth, he had seen the enormous clout of the bureaucrats and wanted to be one himself but had failed in the civil exams. He therefore wanted his son to become one and if that was not possible at least an academic like himself. With this aim, he had exerted enormous pressure on the young lad from the beginning. Although his wife, who was a psychologist too, had kept checking him, the Professor had put so much of a burden on the young lad that the latter finally rebelled.

Although above average in studies, Ramu wanted to prove to his father that there was life beyond textbooks and he had no inclination to cram his mind full of facts and figures. He wanted desperately to succeed in a line entirely different to that which his father had chosen for him. He had been ecstatic at being allowed to join in with the Colonel and when he was called up for Team India it was his greatest triumph in many ways. The most important though was that he had won the mind game with his dad. He had established once and for all that he had skills of his own and could excel in life in a different field. Once he had achieved this success and won the adulation of the huge crowds, he had forgotten about his personal battle with his father and in so doing the process of his motivation had suffered. Fortunately, he realised that he had crossed the threshold and stepped into the arena of international cricket and wanted to make the most of it no matter what his father thought of him. He believed that he had crossed the Rubicon and there was only one way for him: success in cricket.

Ramu went back to the drawing board and started learning the technique of handling the spinners from one of the legendary batsmen of the country who readily agreed to help him. He was back to his daily grind calling many spinners to bowl against him in the nets and practising under the watchful eye of his new mentor.

Raju meanwhile returned after a successful stint with the Australian Academy. When he met Ramu, he found a different person this time. Gone was the sparkle in his eye, the spring in his step and confidence in his speech. He looked like a king who had lost his crown. Raju, who admittedly had never seen a king or a crown, thought that his friend looked like a ruler who had been dethroned but before he could voice his concern, his friend opened the conversation.

"You look so different now," said Ramu.

"How do I look now?" asked Raju.

"You look like a cut and polished diamond."

"Don't be silly. I'm still the same self, pining for success."

"No! On the contrary, you look like a diamond with all rough edges removed and polished to a sparkle. Success must be just around the corner. Your stint in Australia seems to have done wonders for you."

"You're exaggerating!"

"Not at all. I have felt that special heady feeling when I joined the big league and played with Team India. I know how it feels. I think you're on the verge of making it."

"Thank you for your compliments. I'm looking forward to the day when we both play for Team India. However, what about you? You don't look your normal self. What's bugging you?"

Ramu sighed then told Raju how his life had changed. He explained that, as a batsman, he was always under pressure. That he was out there alone against eleven players and sometimes it seemed the umpire too. As an Indian batsman, he felt he was under extra pressure due to the expectations of the vast number of cricket crazy people. The expectation to perform well was always there and the thin line between success and failure was ever present. So much of what he said is true of how many batsmen feel; a momentary lack of concentration, a single lapse of indecision or a slight hesitation to play a shot and a host of factors can spell their doom. Sometimes shots will scamper past the fielders by a few millimetres and rush to the fence. Other times the opposition miss simple catches and let the batsman score heavily but then, suddenly, some fielder will hold an almost impossible catch and send a well-set batsman back to the pavilion

"Luck or providence, call it what you may, surely plays an important part. Have you noticed that even a legendary batsman like Sachin Tendulkar always looks up to the heavens to thank the Lord Almighty whenever he scores a century or even a fifty?" Ramu paused to collect his thoughts before he continued, "The Sri Lankan fielders caught some of my best shots and got me out. Their spinners bowled well and foxed me. I didn't do well in the last tour so now my future seems uncertain. The selectors are a cruel lot; they don't give second chances. There're many like me waiting in the wings and the selectors will soon find a good reason to sideline me." He looked Raju straight in the face. "I don't have godfathers or political bosses to back me. I'm too young to get a job as a commentator or coach. I may simply disappear into oblivion. Worst of all I'd lose my personal battle with my dad."

Raju was saddened by Ramu's tale so tried to cheer him up. "No, that's nonsense. You've just had a lean phase, a temporary loss of form. I'm sure you will find your silken touch again and both cover drives and square drives will flow from your bat once more."

"I am trying very hard but I'm no longer sure. The Sri Lankans have ruined my confidence."

"Don't let that short tour disturb you. You're a fine batsman. What you need to do is to show your class once again in some domestic matches."

"That's what I intend to do. I've decided to play domestic cricket this season before the selection of the team for the home series against South Africa."

"Have you talked to the Colonel?"

Ramu shook his head. "I'm scared of meeting him. You

know only too well he doesn't take kindly to failure."

"You've got it wrong. He'll encourage you. He knows what the feeling of failure can be like, he's tasted it many a time in his life."

"Okay, let's go and see the Colonel."

Ramu's hopes were rekindled thanks to his friend Raju and the Colonel proved to be very supportive indeed. He told both of them never to lose hope and to always keep trying. "There is no alternative to hard work," he said with finality.

FIRST SLIP

First slip, close to the wicket keeper, is a very important position on the field and only those with the safest hands and quickest reflexes are positioned there. When the fast bowlers beat the batsman and get him to edge the ball the fielder placed here should be able to react very quickly and latch onto the ball. His reaction time will be in microseconds. However, when the slow bowlers deceive the batsman the ball carries at a pretty low height to the slips and the fielder has to be very agile, for even the bowler cannot predict either the height or direction in which the ball may fly. First slip should be able to jump, dive, stretch, bend and perform all sorts of gymnastics necessary to scoop or grab the ball inches from the ground. If he has 'butterfingers' and spills the catch, he will let down the bowler and his team. He needs to be aware that he has no one to back him up and if he misses the ball it will surely find its way to the ropes. There is many a batsman who has been given a reprieve by the first slip that went on to post huge scores.

Ramu always fielded at first slip. Thanks to innumerable practice sessions with the Colonel, he had developed quick reflexes not only to deal with the fast bowlers but also with fast deliveries flying past the bat and into the slips. In his short career of two tours, he established a record of sorts for holding many catches in his chosen position. Besides his valuable contribution with the bat, his catching was a great asset to the team. It is believed that 'catches win matches'. His quick reflexes in latching onto catches without fail stood him in good stead.

When the South African team visited India in the next season he was included in the team despite his not too good performance with the bat in Sri Lanka. The selectors gave him a chance, as the visiting team had no quality spinners. In the same process, they included Raju to play for India 'A' in one of the preliminary matches before the first Test.

Raju was delighted that the preliminary match was scheduled at Chennai. He thought of asking Usha to attend the match but, at the last minute, due to some squabbles between the BCCI and the State Cricket Association, the match was shifted to Mohali in the Punjab far away from Chennai. Raju could not even think of suggesting to Usha to attend. He proceeded to Mohali along with the other hopefuls.

The BCCI, the richest sports body in the country and perhaps in the world of cricket, was always known for its strange ways. It should not have announced the final team to play in the Tests against the visitors so early, as the announcement dowsed the hopes of the players in the India 'A' team. Raju and his teammates had the potential to cross the last hurdle and had pinned their hopes of getting into the senior team by giving a good account of themselves in the match. Hope lies eternal in the breasts of all youngsters and especially in young cricket players. Hiding their disappointment they all decided to give the match their best shot and carve out what glory they could.

The pitch at Mohali was very good; it was hard-baked and looked as if it could produce some bounce, unlike the flat pitches in the other parts of the country. The pitches in India have always been a huge problem for the fast bowlers and many discerning cricket players, and the public, have persistently demanded pitches that would be more favourable to the pace men. Their pleas did not go unheeded and the officials of the BCCI, who were good managers and marketing men but with a poor knowledge of the game, appointed several committees and employed experts. This in truth was the standard practice adopted by the government and other organisations in India for solving any problem and yet, surprisingly, the results have been dismal.

Fortunately for Raju the Mohali pitch looked fine in that it was in good shape with traces of grass still left on it and the winter in Punjab was still producing a nip in the air. The conditions suited him to a 'T' and Raju thought that it was going to be his day and it almost was. Since Usha and the Colonel were not present, his performance was again lacklustre. He had the batsmen in trouble but the match proceeded along the same script of the earlier games and he returned home very disappointed. The only consolation was that the press and the discerning public talked about what would have been the outcome if the fielders did not drop as many important catches in the slips.

When Raju finally returned home, he quietly slipped into his room. The Colonel, sitting in the living room with his crossword, did not say a word; indeed he did not say anything until lunchtime. Only when they had finished lunch and the man Friday had cleared the table did the Colonel say in a gentle voice, "I saw it on the TV. It wasn't your fault. It just wasn't your day, a case of mere bad luck; I don't blame you at all. I think you bowled magnificently. The selectors should have taken note of that but they're a strange lot. Once, Mohinder Amarnath, a great batsman and all rounder of his time, called the selectors a bunch of jokers. Perhaps there's some truth in what he said."

Raju felt relieved and much happier. What mattered most to him was not selection for Team India but the Colonel's approval. If he had met the Colonel's expectations, there was nothing more that he could ask for.

The touring South Africans held the attention of the cricket loving public in India with their competitive spirit and splendid display. The domestic cricket took a back seat; all eyes were on the Indian team and their performance against the visitors. Ramu played magnificently against the tourers' quickies and showed his true mettle. He scored heavily in all the matches and cemented his place in the team again but his success in truth was mainly due to lack of a quality spinner in the visiting team. He revelled in batting against the fast bowlers, who did not get much help from the flat Indian pitches that provided many scoring opportunities to enterprising batsmen.

Meanwhile the BCCI signed a contract with the players and Ramu was included in the senior team and given a fat wad of readies as an advance. He also appeared in many commercials and made more hard cash, which allowed him to get a posh car and a new home of his own. He was no longer dependent on his father and he asserted his authority both at home and on the field. He could therefore play without any circumspection and achieved good results and even his training to play against the spinners stood him in good stead eventually.

When the season ended, Ramu emerged as a winner and Raju remained as the also-ran, still waiting for his day in the sun. The Colonel was still determined to see his protégé succeed so he went to the Professor's house. Fortunately for him, the Professor was not at home but Latha invited him in.

"You look distraught. What's the trouble?" she asked.

"Usha worked out to be a good solution; perhaps too good. Whenever Usha's present Raju performs well, but we seemed to have picked the wrong horse. Usha has a mind of her own, her own set of goals and ambitions and they don't seem to fit into our scheme of things."

"I agree but we didn't pick Usha. Raju picked her himself. You found her photo in his room and we worked on that angle. It's well nigh impossible now to get Usha within his reach. We must find another source of motivation for him."

"I'm beginning to lose faith in this psychological game. Do you really think that some other motivating factor will propel him to success?"

"That's my theory and we tried once with results. We can try the same theory just using another person, but you're at liberty

190

to abandon my idea if you have something better."

"Are you sure that this game of cricket is a mind game? I think either Raju has the skill or doesn't. How can any external force propel him to better performance?"

"Cricket is certainly a mind game and you're playing for high stakes. He should have a strong will to succeed and come up trumps every time but he needs some motivation for that. You've been a good benefactor to him. You've provided him with many things in life and yet at the same time you're his problem. By providing him with all his basic physiological needs you have removed from him the hunger to succeed. If he didn't have all that you provide for him perhaps he might have succeeded by now."

"Your ideas sound too far-fetched for me. Anyway, I can't abandon him and throw him out of the house. He's part of the family now and over the years I've become fond of him. As you know, I lost my wife and my two daughters are abroad. I'm lonely and Raju is filling a void in my life."

"In that case you have to suffer his failures or think of ways and means of motivating him further. You have to make your choice."

"Okay, I'm ready to try out any plan you suggest."

"Let me give it some thought. I'm sure I'll come up with something."

A YORKER

A Yorker is a full-length ball bowled by the pace men to unnerve the batsman. It is aimed directly at the stumps and lands almost at the base of them or on the toes of the batsman, who has to bring his bat down quickly to stop the ball from striking the woodwork. If he is a trifle late, the ball will find its way through his guard. Some of the fast bowlers bowl a swinging Yorker, which is even more dangerous as it swings in the air, foxes the batsman and finally finds its way onto the stumps. With the discovery of the reverse swing, the ball can in fact swing in any direction and surprise the batsman. Many have fallen prey to the Yorker, particularly in the One Day Internationals, ODIs. This delivery is often used in the dying overs of those matches. Only in a few cases can the batsman sense the approaching Yorker and take timely, avoiding action. If he reads it early, he can step forward and send it crashing to the boundary line for a four or six. The bowler then takes a gamble in bowling the Yorker although the law of averages does favour him to either take a wicket or prevent the batsman from scoring.

The Colonel faced a Yorker in the form of a surprise visitor. He was sitting in his living room with his crossword and Raju was watching a cricket match on TV, which had some renowned fast bowlers in action. The Colonel's man Friday announced the arrival of an old man and Seth asked him to send him in. The visitor happened to be none other than the teacher from the village, Raju's first guardian.

The Colonel, as was his wont, was polite and courteous and

made the old man comfortable but the elderly teacher seemed to be carrying a heavy burden on his shoulders. His speech was beleaguered and he looked like a drowning man clutching at the last straw. He did not waste much time and came to the point straightaway. He said that his daughter was ailing badly and needed help immediately. He explained that she had been suffering from some ailment, which the doctors in the village and nearby towns could not diagnose properly. He said that they suspected a serious heart condition and had asked him to consult with some senior specialists in the city. Since that entailed a heavy expenditure, which was way beyond his means, he was helpless.

Raju, although engrossed in the cricket match, got the gist of the old man's lament and his heart went out to his sister. Although he had shifted base to the city long ago he had maintained contact with his foster sister mainly due to his affection for her. He had spent his early childhood in the village and had developed a kind of bond, a distinct attachment to her; she alone had always supported him no matter what he did. He recollected many happy days that he had spent with the little girl, indeed during every visit to the village he had watched with bewilderment the growth of the small girl into a sprightly lass.

Although poor, for the teacher had not made much progress in life, she always delighted him with her company. She could sing and dance with great abandon and displayed a rare spirit for a girl of her age. She always enquired about his progress in life and his success in cricket although she did not know anything about the sport. Raju, many a time, promised to teach her the game and if possible turn her into a female cricketer. She enjoyed every word that he spoke and treasured the small presents that he gave her. Now the news about her ill health disturbed him. He felt a heart-wrenching pain and desperately wanted to do something for her immediately. At the same time he realised his own helplessness as he could do nothing much except to seek the Colonel's help.

The Colonel was quicker to react; he had no hang-ups in life now and could think quickly of the steps to be taken. When he had taken Raju under his wing, he had also taken on some responsibility towards the rest of the family. If he had not taken away the boy from the teacher, Raju would have been of some help to them, however small it might have been. Seth quickly got onto the telephone and arranged an appointment with a leading physician in the city for the next day.

"What are you waiting for, Raju?" he asked.

"I'll get ready and go to the village and bring her back immediately."

"That's more like it. Go ahead and take the car. Make it fast," Seth ordered sounding just like a commanding officer ordering one of his men.

Once he was ready, Raju left with the teacher for the village in the Colonel's car to fetch his sister. The teacher was amazed to find Raju driving the car. In fact everything amazed him. The quick and positive response of the Colonel, his willingness to help, lending his car to them, and Raju driving it with ease astonished him.

"You're a lucky fellow, Raju. If you'd stayed with me, I couldn't possibly have given you all these comforts. Now you're driving a car, speaking English most of the time and living in a good house."

"Yes, I'm lucky in many ways but unlucky in some."

"Always count your blessings. Don't ever think of things that you didn't get. First be happy with what you have."

"If one is too contented you lose sight of your ambition," countered Raju.

"What's your ambition now?"

"To make the Colonel happy."

"What'll make him happy?"

"If I play for India."

"I don't understand."

"The Colonel was a good cricket player and badly wanted to represent his country but could never achieve his dream. His dream will be fulfilled if I play for India."

"You should try your best to fulfil his dream."

"I'm not sparing any effort but I'm not lucky."

"Don't give up hope. Keep trying."

"When did my sister fall sick?" asked Raju.

"She's been sickly on and off since her childhood. I thought that things would work out as she grew up so I didn't worry too much. Anyway, even if I'd worried I could've done very little about it."

"You could've told me at least."

"What could you have done? As it is you are dependent upon the Colonel."

"I'd have mentioned it to him. He's a good, kind man. He would've helped. Have you seen how readily he asked me to go and fetch her to the city?"

"I didn't expect him to be so kind. I was just happy that he took you off my hands."

When they arrived at the village, Raju greeted his sister. Outwardly she looked the same, full of bounce and laughing all the time. She talked and laughed with him as though she had nothing to worry about in her life. Ignorance is bliss, thought Raju. She was like a blithe spirit, totally oblivious of the possible heart condition and its ramifications.

"What did you bring for me this time?" she asked.

"I've got a better present this time. I am taking you to the city with me."

"How nice! I'll get ready straight away." She ran inside the small house and quickly returned with a small bag; in it she had all that she possessed.

Despite soon being on their way, the teacher kept brushing away tears that fell on his cheeks with his shirtsleeve.

The Colonel, along with the teacher, Raju and his sister in tow, did the rounds of the doctor, the laboratories and finally the specialist. Thanks to the Colonel's standing in society, the specialist went out of his way to give them a quick appointment, examined the girl carefully and studied all the reports.

"I've some good and some bad news," the doctor told them.

"First let's hear the good news," Seth said.

"The trouble with her heart is something which is rare and only a few doctors can handle such a case. Fortunately I have a good friend in Mumbai who can treat her." Here the doctor stopped and took a deep breath. "The bad news is that he's a very busy man as he has patients from all over the country and it's very difficult to get an appointment with him. I can probably manage to get one for you but I'm afraid the treatment and other things like hospital charges are going to be very expensive."

"How expensive?" asked Seth.

"Roughly four lakhs of rupees for the operation, add the hospitalisation charges and other expenses at Mumbai, I'd guess it'll be around six lakhs of rupees."

"Let me think about it and I'll see you in a couple of days."

"You'd better hurry up. As it is, the case has been neglected and you don't have much time. She needs heart surgery as soon as possible."

When they returned to the Colonel's house they sent the girl away to another room to take a rest, and then they held a mini-conference. The teacher looked inconsolable and kept crying while Raju stood in one corner speechless. The whole thing depended upon the Colonel and his munificence, he thought. Seth also looked worried, which was most unlike him. Normally very few things ruffled him and he had handled many a crisis in his life with ease.

"We've got a big problem on our hands. Raising that much money at short notice isn't an easy task."

"For me it's impossible," the teacher said amidst yet more tears.

"There must be some way out of it. I can foot part of the bill but not all. I'll try and contact some philanthropic organisations for help but that will take some time. The doctor says that we don't have time on our side. We have to act fast."

"I can't do anything. The life of my daughter is in your hands."

"What do you say, Raju?" Seth asked the lad.

"What can I say? I've nothing of my own. I don't even have the time. I have to go to Baroda to play a match in the Ranji Trophy quarter-finals in the next few days. I don't know whether to play the match or be at my sister's side in the hospital. I'll contact the secretary of our state cricket association and find out if he can help with some money."

"What good will that do?" the Colonel asked but Raju had no answer. "You'd better go ahead with your schedule. You leave the matter to me. I'll do my best and you do your best."

"How can I do my best?" Raju was getting quite upset. "I'll be thinking of my sister all the time and won't give my undivided attention to the game."

"On the contrary you should do your utmost. The only way I can raise that kind of money is by taking a loan from a bank or by mortgaging this house or some other property of mine but the loan will still have to be repaid. Remember that I'm now retired and I've no income other than my pension so you'll have to help me to repay it. You can only do that if you earn more money. That's possible if you succeed."

Raju left for Baroda and, when the match proper started, he tried his best to forget about his sister and concentrate hard on his task. His captain tossed the new ball to him and asked him to open the bowling. Before the start of the game he told Raju about the opening batsmen and their fancy to hook the bouncers and short-pitched balls to score heavily. He asked him to exploit this and get rid of the openers as soon as possible. He also promised to provide a safe pair of hands deep at the square leg and fine leg. The captain had worked out the tactics for other batsmen too but, when Raju started bowling, his mind went totally blank as though some form of amnesia had set in. He lost himself, his knowledge of bowling, in fact everything. His focus shifted to the condition of his sister and the impending surgery on her heart. Instead of bowling short-pitched balls as directed, he bowled Yorkers. The batsmen, although initially surprised, took effective action and belted him all over the ground.

The captain came over to him and asked, " What have you done? Did you forget our game plan? Why are you bowling Yorkers at this stage of the game?" He gave his bowler a mouthful using several expletives.

Raju, shaken up by the verbal assault of his captain, shifted his focus back to the game and bowled as per the game plan. Soon he got the much-needed success and took three wickets in quick succession. When play resumed after lunch, the captain directed Raju to continue the good work. He complied and got another two wickets taking his tally of five in a matter of three hours. Getting five wickets in a match is the equivalent of scoring a century for a batsman and a dream of every bowler, fast or slow.

However, when Raju was about to revel in his success and try to achieve yet better results, disaster struck. The dark-grey nimbus clouds gathering over Baroda turned almost black and the wind picked up. When Raju looked up, he found to his dismay the heavens were about to open. It started raining, then pouring as though the heavens had developed a mighty leak. The players ran to the dressing room and the ground staff was hard put to bring the covers on in time to minimise the damage to the pitch. Play was called off and the umpires waited for the weather to clear before making a further announcement. Unfortunately for Raju the weather gods were not kind to him and his team as the rain continued relentlessly for the next three days leaving the umpires with no option other than to abandon the match.

Raju's hopes of achieving success and catching the eye of the selectors were grounded and stubbed by the jackboots of the weather gods. He tried to contact the Colonel and find out the latest position about his sister but somehow he could never get in touch with him. When the four-day match ended in a draw, without any further ado Raju returned home immediately and was surprised to find the house locked. His neighbours gave him the key but could not furnish any information about the whereabouts of the Colonel and the others. He made a dash to find out from the Professor or his good lady any information about the Colonel.

"How did your match go, son?" asked the Professor. He seemed to be more concerned about the match and less about the condition of the girl.

"It was washed out but I'm worried about my sister. Where's the Colonel?"

"He's taken the teacher and the girl to Mumbai. He said he would let me know once the girl was admitted to hospital and he had found a suitable place to stay. I've yet to hear from him."

"Where should I contact him?"

"I'm afraid I don't have any idea where they all are now. All I know is that the Colonel said that he left some money for you in his study and asked you to meet all your commitments without worrying about your sister. He asked you to rely on him as far as she is concerned."

"Why? I rely on him for everything but that doesn't stop me from worrying about the girl."

"If you worry about your sister you'll not be able to concentrate on the game and give of your best. You'd better go to Kolkata as scheduled, play your match and leave the rest to the Colonel. He's a capable and determined man. He won't let anybody down."

"Okay I'll follow the Colonel's orders through."

After a few days of misery of not knowing the whereabouts of the Colonel and the health of his little sister, Raju joined his team at Kolkata to play against Bengal. As usual, the coach and the captain called a pre-match meeting to discuss the strategy to be adopted for the match. The vulnerability of Surav Ganguly and players from Bengal for the short-pitched balls was brought into focus. Although, some of the players mentioned that after Saurav Ganguly's misfortunes, the Bengal players had learnt the art of hooking the ball and were scoring heavily against such deliveries, the coach and the captain prevailed. It was decided to use the short-pitched ball aimed at the ribcage as the main weapon to bring about the downfall of their opponents.

When the match started, the captain arranged the field according to the plan agreed upon and tossed the new ball to Raju who had his own doubts about the wisdom of such an attack. He followed his orders and started bowling short right from the word go. The Bengal players were initially unnerved and took some evasive action but finally one of the opening batsmen took courage and decided to attack. He took his stance a foot before the crease and hit the ball before it could rise to an inconvenient height.

Soon he started plundering runs and Raju, despite his fiery pace, looked a mediocre bowler. He went up to his captain and asked him to change the tactics and rearrange the field. The captain wanted to persist with his plan and asked Raju and other medium pacers to stick to it. The bowlers got the worst end of the stick and their bowling figures looked awful. Raju on his own defied the orders of his captain and bowled his normal line and length. This change immediately brought results and five of the opponents were back in the pavilion within a short span of a few overs. The captain and coach saw the wisdom of Raju but, by then, the damage had been done and the ball had lost its shine and the fast bowlers their sting. The captain brought on the spinners whom the opponents handled with relative ease and managed to amass a huge score at the end of the day. Back in the dressing room, Raju said that the captain and coach should have changed the game plan immediately after the first few overs.

As cricket players grow in stature, their ego also grows proportionately and by the time they play for Team India, they often have inflated egos and do not like to be told that they are wrong. This malaise rests even with players who make a few appearances for their country. Very few people like to be told, " I told you so!" and cricket players are definitely not in the select category. The captain, who had played for India a few times, definitely did not like it and in the second innings did not toss the new ball to Raju.

The whole team shook their heads at the action of their skipper in not giving the first use of the new ball to the fastest bowler of the team. They felt let down by their skipper and consequently did not put up a creditable performance. They dropped catches, misfielded and conceded more runs than what were actually due. When the team batted, the batsmen also showed a total lack of enterprise and let the game easily slip out of their hands. The end result was that Raju's team lost and lost badly. Although Raju himself bowled well, his bowling was not appreciated. On the contrary, all the media criticised him for bowling consistently short in consecutive matches and doubted his abilities. His hopes of making it to the next level, which was the Duleep Trophy and scheduled to begin immediately after, were completely dashed. Raju returned home once again disappointed and found the house was still locked. Much later, he went to the Professor's house where, to his amazement, he found the Colonel talking animatedly to the Professor's wife.

SQUARE CUT

A square cut is one of the most delightful strokes to watch. When executed by a batsman possessing a good technique, it is a visual delight, for the ball travels like a flash to the boundary line square of the wicket. All top batsmen master this stroke at the beginning of their careers and then fine-tune it as they progress in their cricketing life. Rolling their wrists and hitting the ball with the meat of the bat, the batsmen execute it with sheer classiness. Some batsmen, like Gundappa Viswanath, earned a great reputation for the elegance and finesse with which they played this stroke. It is employed when the ball is pitched outside the off stump and provides a little width to the batsman. The execution of this wonderful shot depends more on technique and much less on strength; indeed those with a reputation of executing this stroke with ease were generally of small build and not endowed with much brawn.

The shot, although a treat to watch, is not without its inherent perils. If the ball is moving laterally or spinning and is not exactly in the position the batsman expects it to be it can take some inner or outer edge of the bat. Often it finds its way into the wicket keeper's gloves and so brings about the doom of the batsman. The fielding team always station their best fielder at the 'point' at which a square cut passes through on its way to the ropes. Renowned fielders like Jonty Rhodes and Nawab of Pataudi made sure that the batsman, despite his elegant stroke, never got any runs with this shot. In the one-day version of the game it has become a standard practice to keep a fielder as a sweeper whose main task is to patrol the area around the boundary line square of the wicket to prevent any ball reaching it.

The square cut however is fraught with danger when executed against a spinner. Whether it is an off or leg break the ball may take more or less turn than gauged by the batsman and is likely to be at a position other than the expected. The batsman in all probability will miss the ball or make a faint contact with it. In such cases, it will land safely in the hands of one of the close in fielders and put paid to his innings.

When Raju visited the Professor's house, he was like a batsman who had played the square cut and had come a cropper. He was now worried on many counts. First, his performance in the Kolkata match was none too good. He had not had any news about the health of his sister and he did not know the whereabouts of the Colonel. He thought that his life was going very wrong and taking him in directions he did not want to go. When he finally found the Colonel at the Professor's house, initially he heaved a sigh of relief. At least one mystery was solved, he thought. On discovering the Colonel laughing, he took it that his sister must have been all right so that solved the second worry. Yet he could not understand as to why the Colonel was in such a good mood.

"So, you're back from Kolkata after a lacklustre performance again?" Seth half asked, half commented.

"It was the fault of our coach and the captain. Their game plan was wrong. Things didn't work out according to the plan but they didn't bother to change it and we lost the initiative," Raju replied.

"What about your own judgement?"

"I tried to tell the captain, but he wouldn't listen. The coach was just as stubborn and not amenable to any discussion."

"A bad workman finds faults with his tools."

Raju looked somewhat hurt before saying, "When I tried to bowl a normal length and started troubling the batsman the captain took me off. He cared more for his ego and less for the interests of the team. If the captain himself forgets that team work alone matters, how the can team win?"

"You may be right but the people watching the game will put the blame squarely on the bowlers. They'll just say that they provided a free lunch for the batsmen and threw the game away. The bowlers will get the worst end of the stick."

"What could I have done?" Raju was at a loss.

"That's precisely the question bothering me."

"How about my sister? Where is she?"

"Your sister must take a back seat. Right now we've a bigger problem."

"What's happened now?" Raju asked incredulously.

"I'll show you at my house."

He took Raju in his car having bidden a hasty farewell to the Professor and drove straight home. When they entered the house Raju found a middle-aged woman sitting comfortably in one of the sofas. As soon as she saw Raju, she sprang up like a coiled spring and rushed to him. She hugged him and planted a kiss on his forehead taking Raju completely by surprise. She ran her hands over his face, shoulders and finally down his arms before saying, "He's grown up to be a fine young lad. Thank you so much, Colonel Sir."

"What's all this? Who's this lady?" asked a surprised Raju.

"She's your mother, or so she claims," said the Colonel dispassionately.

"My mother! How do I know that she's my mother?" Raju had been thrown into turmoil.

"No way except for her word."

"Of course I'm your mother because it was I who abandoned you outside the village about twenty years ago. I have been keeping track of you and waited all these years to reclaim you." The woman beamed at him.

"If you're my mother why did you abandon me and why are you reclaiming me now?"

"It's a long story and takes time to tell but in short I was

205

forced to disown you and get rid of you to save myself from disgrace. You were born out of wedlock... before I got married. Your father, who promised to marry me, took advantage of me and abandoned me when I was pregnant so I'd no option other than to abandon you. I couldn't afford to keep you, and my reputation, well it was important to try and keep it in tact. I was economically dependent upon many people and I'd little option other than to obey their wishes."

"Why do you want me back?"

"Now I'm economically independent so I can support my son. I have wanted you back so badly. I loved you so much despite your absence and I decided to have no other children all these years, which was much against the wishes of my legal husband."

"What about my father?" Raju asked rather quietly.

"I lost track of him after he abandoned me. He didn't care much for either of us for many years. Only when death beckoned him did he remember us and wanted to make amends for his mistake."

"You still didn't answer my question. Why do you want me back?"

"It's a silly question to ask. Why does a mother want her son back? I always have and always will love you, love. What more can I say except that I'm so sorry that I abandoned you as I did. It has caused me much pain both in my heart and soul. I want to redeem myself now."

Raju felt completely at a loss. He felt this was a strange twist in his life and didn't know how to react. He saw a woman standing in front of him who claimed to be his mother. He had read various tales of filial affection of sons towards their parents and particularly towards their mothers but he felt nothing, no feeling of either good or ill will towards this strange woman. He seriously wondered whether there was something wrong with him or his mental makeup.

He was also unsure whether to believe the woman or dismiss

the whole idea as a prank. Why would anyone come forward and claim to be his mother if she were not so? Why would she disclose her mistake at this late stage and be willing to take on the responsibility of a grown-up young man now? What would she gain from it? 'She must be my mother,' he thought. Why then did she take so long to come forward? He could find no answer to that question. It also occurred to him that he stood a good chance of attaining name and fame if luck favoured him.

If he got the chance to don a Team India cap, he would stand to make a lot of money, in fact a fortune. Perhaps the woman had sensed his potential wealth and had come to claim him now in order to reap a good harvest in the next few years. After all, he mused, plenty of people will do a lot of strange things for a few dollars more. While his head was reeling, full of unanswered questions, he looked at the Colonel and found him sitting absolutely unruffled and smoking his pipe at leisure. How could he be so nonchalant? Raju wondered.

"What do you say, sir?" he asked tentatively.

"What is there for me to say? She says that she's your mother. She told me of some identifying marks on your body, which are correct, and she even recollects the exact date you were born. She has also told me, correctly, all the details as to when she gave birth to you and when she abandoned you. I checked up and found that what she says cannot be faulted.

"It seems your biological father, who ditched your mother, had a change of heart before his death and wanted to expiate his sin. He left a good amount of money to your mother and asked her to reclaim you and look after you. She says that she even renounced her husband of twenty years to take possession of you. It all sounds like a cinematic tale, I know, but she tells it with so much passion that I can't find any reason to doubt her. When she has sacrificed so much just to reclaim her only child, how on earth can I say no to her? How can I keep you with me and deny her the motherly affection she feels? Now it's between the two of you, mother and son. I only looked after you in the interim and I've not done too badly."

"What does she want now?"

"She wants to take you with her."

"But I do not want to go!"

"Why do you say that?"

Raju looked at the Colonel as he tried to explain. "You've been like a father to me for the last so many years. Although the village teacher had taken care of me in the initial stages, he could hardly provide anything. I've spent all my formative years with you. Thanks to you, I've had a good schooling, fantastic training in cricket and a fine lifestyle. I've had everything that a young lad of my age could wish for. My feelings, respect and adoration for you are beyond words. You've been more than a father to me. You've provided me with everything and dragged me up from a being a simple village lad to a fine city boy playing first-class cricket and knocking at the doors of Team India. I know the pains you've taken and the kind of affection you have shown to me. I'm grateful to your entire family; indeed, I feel I'm part of your family. You always made sure that I felt it was so; even your daughters have taken kindly to me. You took me on a trip to the USA, which was way beyond my expectations. You've shaped my dreams and I'm sure that I will realise my dream fully in the near future."

Raju stopped at this point, somewhat overcome with emotion. He turned and looked at the stranger who claimed to be his mother. "Suddenly some woman comes and wants to take me away from all of this...this paradise. I don't know what is in store for me and what this lady can provide for me. She may be my biological mother but she can't replace you in my heart, mind and soul. I will be totally at a loss anywhere except in your house and your company, which I cherish more than anything. Without you, I'm nothing, whereas with your help, guidance and kindly manner, I may be something in the future. What should I do? Have I got an option?"

"I'm afraid I can't help with this. What right do I have to deny this lady, who claims you as her son? How can I dissuade her from taking you with her? You tell me!"

Raju looked at the lady and said, "What were you doing all these years? Why are you tearing me away from this paradise? How will you help me achieve my dreams? I don't know anything about you! I'm trying very hard but I'm finding it difficult to accept you are my mother. I'm not able to muster any love for you. On the contrary, I'm feeling hurt that you are wrenching me away from my normal life and going to put me through new problems, both physical and mental. Do you want something from the Colonel? He is a kind man and will no doubt oblige you. Why don't you leave me alone?"

The woman looked shocked. "Is that the way to speak to a mother? You don't know how a mother misses her son. I've been through hell these past years and now I want to make amends for my mistake and look after you with all that I have. I've given up many things just to reclaim you. I may not be rich like the Colonel but I'll provide whatever you want within my means. I'll do whatever any mother would do for the well-being of her son, I can assure you of that."

"What about my sister? You haven't told me about her at all. How is she getting on?" he asked the Colonel.

"Why are you worrying about your sister now? You've found your mother at last. I'll take good care of your sister. You go and spend time with your mother and enjoy the motherly affection this lady will give you. You don't know how kind mothers can be; it'll be a new and wonderful experience. Perhaps her motherly affection will egg you on to achieve all the success that you are still dreaming of. "

When Raju found that his efforts to persuade Seth to keep him had failed and he was unable to dissuade his mother from taking him away, he resigned himself to the idea of leaving the Colonel. He packed his bags and followed the woman with great reluctance. The lady got an auto rickshaw and took him to her home, which was a small, nondescript two-room house with a kitchen and bathroom adjoining. Raju found that his lifestyle had changed dramatically and he would have to live in the squalid surroundings. Sadly, he resigned himself to his fate.

During the next few days, his mother tried her best to make him comfortable and provide him with the basic necessities in life. She spent most of her time with him asking him never-ending questions about his childhood, schooling and his life with the Colonel. Raju was amazed to see that the lady wanted to know every small aspect of his entire life. As he relived it and narrated his story leaving out no details, she kept sobbing and wiping her tears with the end of her sari. He found it difficult to bear seeing the woman cry like a child, yet could not leave her. He had never seen grown-ups crying. The Colonel never had a reason to cry nor was he a crying type. No one cried in the Colonel's house and Seth had always chided people saying crying was a display of helplessness which he despised. He always wanted everyone connected with him to keep trying and never say die. Never give up, never give up the ship and never throw in the towel were the standard expressions he often used with his friends and visitors. Brought up in such an ambience Raju found his mother's crying very strange and he despised her.

Why did she commit so many mistakes to begin with? he asked himself. Why cry now after so many years? If she really cared for my welfare she should have left me in the comfortable surroundings of the Colonel's house and let me progress in life. Why take me from all that happiness? He kept asking himself many questions but could not muster up the courage to ask his mother. He suffered in long silences as his mother cried frequently and, although the doubts persisted, slowly a small seed of love for her started germinating in his heart. While his mind rejected any such idea, his heart finally went out to his mother and he started imagining the agony that she must have gone through all these years. Until then, he had harboured a grudge against his parents for abandoning him but now he started to feel happy that he was, after all, not an orphan and was in the care of his mother. At least no one would dare to speak of his doubtful parentage anymore, he thought. He slowly grew closer to her and told her of his dreams and how he was facing failure despite his best efforts.

"You are my son. The two of us have had a turbulent life over the years. Now that I have succeeded in getting you back, I'm sure that success will not elude you for long. I'm sure that your dreams will come true. Remember that your dreams are my dreams. If you become famous I'll be the first person to celebrate."

"That's what all mothers probably tell their sons, but it's not that simple."

"Don't you worry, you do your best and you'll get what you want as I did."

Raju adjusted to his new surroundings and his new lifestyle. He slept on a cot without a mattress and covered himself with a sheet when the nights turned nippy. He had no bathroom with running hot and cold water nor the large dining table to sit at comfortably to eat while being served by the Colonel's servant. He sat cross-legged on a mat and ate from a stainless steel plate but he soon got used to it as his mother would sit next to him and feed him with great love and affection. It was yet another new experience and slowly he started getting used to the new and very different lifestyle. He had lost the Colonel and his kindness but he had gained his mother who was full of love and affection for him.

The cricket season was drawing to a close and Raju had to wait for the next year to start afresh. Meanwhile Team India, on tour to Australia, had some injury problems and the manager of the team asked for replacements for a couple of fast bowlers. Raju hoped that selectors would think of him and eagerly waited for the names to be announced. Alas, his hopes were dashed again when two others were selected and flown out immediately. He resigned himself to waiting for the next year and to produce better results to catch the eye of the selectors.

While waiting for the next season to begin, Raju decided to find out about his ailing sister. He made his way to the village and to the teacher's house. Thanks to the munificence of the Colonel, the teacher now lived in a better house with some amenities. He spotted his sister sitting outside sunning herself. As soon as she saw him, she rushed inside, got into bed and covered herself up. Raju instantly realised that she was pretending to be sick. He gave her a whack and asked her, "How are you, how's your health?"

His sister looked embarrassed, "I was never sick at all. I just acted sick because my father asked me to do so."

The teacher was left with no option other than to tell the truth. The Colonel had devised a scheme in which the girl was to feign sickness, a terrible sickness at that and both of them were to follow his scheme.

"You mean to say that you all fooled me?" Raju was taken aback by the deception.

"I'm afraid so. We wanted you to feel the pain and perhaps be motivated into achieving something. It was the Colonel's idea entirely. We only played our roles as dictated by him."

Raju did not know what to say. First he felt infuriated that the Colonel had put him through the wringer but soon he realised that the latter's intentions were honourable and could not be faulted. He could not make up his mind whether to thank the Colonel for the trouble that he had taken or to curse him for the agony that he caused.

STRAIGHT DRIVE

A straight drive as its name implies is played with a straight bat and is attempted only by batsmen with sound technique. It looks more like a defensive push against a ball pitched on the off or middle stumps. The batsman presents a straight bat and strokes the ball with the meat of it. Normally the straight drive is executed against a ball bowled with considerable pace as the batsman uses the momentum of the ball to propel it back, straight all along the ground, past the bowler and to the fence. When the bowler finishes his follow-through and finds the ball racing past him, he looks at the batsman not only with anger and contempt but also with concealed admiration.

On striking the bat during the straight drive, the ball makes a distinct sound, which is sweet music to both the batsman and the spectators. Since only a few batsmen can execute this shot, the area behind the bowler's arm is normally left unmanned. The batsman who executes the shot correctly knows that the moment the ball leaves the bat it will reach the ropes and will not even attempt to run between the wickets. When batsmen like Sachin Tendulkar and Brian Lara perform this shot it is a sight for the gods and the true connoisseurs of cricket.

Ramu learnt to play the straight drive by watching the great players on TV repeatedly. With constant practice, he mastered the shot and won the admiration of his peers whenever he played it. His rapid progress in the game had been mainly due to his delectable square cuts and excellent straight drives. Other shots, like the cover drive and on drive, form part of the repertoire of every batsman and need no special mention.

During his tour 'down under' to Australia and New Zealand, he played the straight drive many a time and won great recognition. He scored prolifically and soon became a darling of many fans, including a number of attractive and fashionable girls who sent him letters expressing their intent to marry him. They sent their photographs and brief accounts of their wealth and status. On his return to India after the successful tour, he became a well-known personality and started rubbing shoulders with celebrities including some gorgeous girls from Bollywood. He found it difficult to keep away from the numerous admirers, who grabbed every opportunity to be seen with him. His image was used in many commercials endorsing several consumer products and he had to find a PR man to manage his monetary affairs and commercial contracts. He was on a roll and the money was pouring in.

Raju, in sharp contrast, had made little progress from square one and had found the going tough. Cricket is not a game for ordinary folk, as the players need to spend money in order to develop. To get meaningful and valuable practice they have be part of a club with adequate resources like a practice pitch, nets and the necessary cricketing gear. To be a member of such a club, one needs either connections or money. It is only on rare occasions that one gains admission to such clubs by the sheer dint of one's talent.

Raju had had no such problems up until this point as the Colonel had provided a pitch and the gear for his exclusive use. After leaving the Colonel's house however, he was at a loss to find somewhere to practise his bowling. Fortunately for him, he found a place that had some facilities although they were not as good as he was used to at the Colonel's house. He decided to make do with what was at hand and continued his practice.

The Colonel, however, showed no more interest in his practice or progress. Raju suffered great pain at his loss and thought that the only way to get back into the Seth's good books was to produce top-class results. He felt success would be some repayment for all that the Colonel had done for him so he worked with renewed vigour. His mother somehow managed to provide the necessary money whenever he needed to replenish his cricketing gear and quickly the next season started. As usual, he was picked for the state team.

The selectors by this point were unanimous that Raju was the fastest of the bowlers in the state and he had achieved moderate success in some matches. Although there were many contenders, some with connections and some who had strings to pull, the selectors could find no reason to ignore him or sideline him. He was their spearhead in the bowling department and there was no denying it.

His mother expressed her intention of accompanying him to all the matches he would be playing away from home. It was a strange request, as none of his teammates took their mother along with them. Most of the players playing for their respective state teams in the Ranji Trophy tournament and other such matches were poorly off in comparison to their counterparts in Team India.

The wide chasm of financial resources made available to the players in first-class cricket and their seniors has always intrigued and irritated the players. Nevertheless, they have never raised their voices lest they offend the Lord High Commissioners of Cricket who decide the fortunes and fate of the aspiring young players. They suffer many privations such as travelling in crowded trains without a reservation and putting up with substandard accommodation. Even the players who were star attractions and brought in plenty of money to the Board of Control of Cricket always had a raw deal until the players' contract system started.

They were made to make do with less money and put up with many privations whereas the officials of the Board who did not know the front end of the bat from the rear used to jump on board the gravy train. These officials always travelled in style and stayed in the best of the hotels and had many free lunches, despite being well able to afford the same from their own resources. The members of the various state associations and the controlling board were drawn from the influential section of the cream of society and their attitude towards cricket was mainly to skim the cream and share it amongst themselves. Some made the BCCI their exclusive club and kept all intruders at bay. They controlled the affairs of the board, behaved like uncrowned monarchs and brooked no dissent. Any cricketer who crossed their path or raised his voice against them tasted their ire and felt the heat.

Raju started feeling the pinch. His mother, despite her best efforts, could not match the Colonel in looking after his needs. Yet she wanted to accompany him to the matches. How could he convince the management of his team that they should allow his mother to accompany him? He broached the subject with the team manager who was known for his stinginess with great trepidation. However, the manager much to his surprise readily agreed but made it clear that it was a one-off case and the same privilege would not be extended to other players.

When Raju played his first match at a far-flung stadium, his mother was in the stand next to the dressing room. As the team took to the field, everyone expected Raju to bend, touch his mother's feet and take her blessings as per the normal Indian custom. Raju would not make this particular gesture; he had been ignorant for so long of how sons behaved with their mothers and did not feel like starting at this point in his life. He thought that such an action would be a show of obsequiousness and did not want to make a scene but his mother called him, planted a kiss on his forehead and wished him all the best in the match.

"You are a lucky guy, Raju. For so long you had the Colonel and now you have a very supportive mother who insists on sitting in the players' stand and watching you play. Surely your mother will bring you luck," said one of his teammates.

"Lady Luck is very fickle. My chances are as good or as bad as yours," replied Raju.

The match started and this time the team had a new coach who believed in flexibility and playing according to the situation. He did not believe in game plans and set patterns and thought that innovation at every moment was the key to success. He also believed that surprise could be a very good tactic. He gave full freedom to the captain of the team and asked him to change his tactics as the situation demanded. He refused to be a 'remote control' and allowed a free rein to the leadership qualities of the appointed player. He also emphasised that the captain was as good as the team and could not win a game merely on his superior tactics or aggression. He asked all the players to lend their captain support and even provide advice whenever necessary to achieve the final goal of winning the match. He finished by saying, "The world loves a winner and, if the team wins consistently, some of you must have a chance for inclusion in Team India."

The captain, given the freedom of choice, surprised all the team members as he tossed the new ball not to Raju but to another medium pacer who was not as fast as Raju and definitely not in the same league. The surprised team members immediately protested and advised the captain who refused to change his mind. He said that he wanted to try something new and use Raju later at an appropriate moment. What he did not tell his team was that he wanted to give chance to another member of his own community.

Caste, creed, community and region are the bane of Indian cricket and these feelings rear their ugly heads frequently. The captain considered Raju a bastard of indeterminate religion and caste despite the patronage of the Colonel and the presence of his mother in the players' stand. He thought that Raju was growing too big for his boots and wanted to cut him down to size. He was also jealous; he had played first-class cricket for more than ten years and had never got a nod from the national selectors. 'Why should this youngster get it?' he thought. He had harboured contempt for Raju but had never got a chance to exercise it before. He was only interested in providing an opportunity to another bowler of his choice and did not give a damn about the interests of the team.

The bowler he had selected wasted the new ball and gave away runs freely. When the opponents took him to the cleaners, the team members almost rebelled and demanded that Raju be given the bowling. When the captain finally yielded to their demand the damage had already been done. The ball had lost its shine and Raju the sting in his bowling. He still bowled his heart out and stemmed the flow of runs but could not achieve a breakthrough. In fact, none of the bowlers could achieve anything and all were hit for many runs as they lost their fighting spirit and their morale sagged.

At the end of the day, the opponents finished with a score of two hundred and seventy-five runs for no loss. This intimidating score put the visiting team on its back foot and in an irretrievable situation. Team spirit is like a plant in the nursery. Given the right nourishment, it grows rapidly and blossoms quickly. If it is nipped in the bud, it becomes almost impossible to recover and nurture back into life. It requires a lot of resilience on the part of the plant to overcome the adverse ambience and to manage to grow again. Very few sides showed such resilience. In the particular cases of teams which had been done in by their captain and yet managed to win, there are few and far examples in the annals of cricket.

It is no wonder then that Raju's team took a severe beating and his bowling analysis showed him in a poor light. The captain, instead of mourning the loss of the match, revelled in it as he felt he had finally put Raju in his place. He knew that his own game was on the wane and the state selectors had warned him that it was his last chance to either prove himself or be dropped. He had seen the writing on the wall and was not surprised at all when he was omitted from the team for the next matches. That awful match then had turned out to be his swansong, written by himself.

The remaining matches, under a new captain, were played out to a similar script in that the new captain was also contemptuous of Raju. He exercised his prejudices and did not give Raju the necessary opportunities to prove his mettle. The interest of the team was given the heave-ho and personal interests and records took precedence over team success. In such an atmosphere, Raju was left high and dry without showing anything noteworthy against his name. The international matches involving Team India always got great media coverage and all the experts converged to have their say though the same experts gave domestic cricket scant attention. In this jungle world of the media, everybody stated the obvious but in different tones and varying styles. The press indulged itself in concocting huge stories out of trivial incidents but ignoring the talent in the domestic cricket scene.

Fortunately for Raju there were some discerning cricketers of yesteryears who went round scouting for new talent and wrote about them in their columns. Sunil Gavaskar discovered Saurav Ganguly, who later turned out to be the most successful captain of the Indian team, but such instances were few and far between. Yet, thankfully, one critic noticed the dormant talent in Raju and wrote many columns about him. This put pressure on the selectors, but they always stuck by the statistics and Raju's bowling figures showed no great achievement. At the end of the season, once again, Raju found that he made little or no progress.

The Colonel visited him one day and commiserated with him. He said it was not the end of the world and asked him to persevere. "After all, you're still young and you've many years of cricket ahead of you. Don't lose heart."

Raju muttered something but without any real conviction or hope. Later he found the Colonel having a long chat with his mother supposedly out of his earshot. He wondered what they could possibly have discussed for so long. The way they were talking about something so animatedly showed that they did not appear to be strangers but friends of long-standing. This intrigued Raju, who did not know what to make of it.

SELECTION

A batsman has a repertoire of shots at his command. A square cut, a straight drive and a pull to name a few. Which shot he selects will depend on various factors such as the situation of the game, which sometimes prevents him from executing certain strokes, the line and length of the ball, the position of the fielders and his own form and confidence level. Above all else though is his own technique and finesse in executing the appropriate shot.

The player first acquires the technique by constant study and practice of 'textbook shots'. Even experienced batsmen practise these during the gap between overs in the game and check their swing, which is similar to the natural swing of golfers. The finesse however, comes with inborn talent. A roll of the wrists, a good follow through, opening the full face of the bat and exquisite timing are just some of the finer points that result in the finesse of top-class players.

Some cricketers have very good eyesight and extraordinary coordination between the eye and reflexive action. Many of them spend endless hours of practice, learning the shots textbook style but only a blessed few have the talent to execute the shots with a certain flair, sending the ball racing away to the boundary all along the carpet. The batsman knows when he has executed the perfect shot and does not even bother to run, as he feels certain that the ball will kiss the ropes in a flash. A batsman is like a warrior in some mythological story; with a quiver full of arrows of magical powers, he selects the right weapon at the right time.

Similarly, the bowler has many potent weapons in his arsenal and keeps selecting the right weapon for the right batsman and for the right occasion. He hones his skills by constant practice but he also should have a natural rhythm in his bowling action and the physique to support his action that will keep him going for long spells without injuries. It is the finesse that separates the men from the boys, and only a discerning few can spot such finesse in the players.

Raju did not know that one of the selectors of the national team was present in the stadium. The selector, a cricketer who had established several records during his halcyon days, had come unannounced and quietly slipped into the stadium. He asked the few officials to keep his presence a secret and asked for a lonely spot where he would not be disturbed. Cricket players of repute, past and present, have a big following in India and the adulation of the fans often spirals out of control. The selector wanted to avoid the limelight and watch the game to possibly pick some members for Team India. He had heard about Raju in particular and wanted to see his performance firsthand. Equipped with a binoculars and a notebook he hid himself in a corner of the VIP box. The game began and the players played their natural game without their style being cramped by the presence of the selector.

During the lunch break, the President of the local Cricket Association quietly entered the room with a tray of food and sat next to the visitor. He waited for the selector to finish his lunch in peace before he asked a question. The President, an eminent lawyer and a good cricket player in his youth, was a much-respected man and could not be ignored.

"I understand your job is rather tough. How do you do it?" asked the President.

"It's a very difficult process. We've good domestic cricket and the game is played at various levels, the schools, colleges, universities and clubs. We've several tournaments for players of different ages: Under-13, Under-17, Under-21 and the Ranji Trophy matches where state teams take part in a league and knockout format. We also send teams to the Under-15 and Under-19 World Cups and send our India-A team on tours abroad. A good player with consistence performances can progress continuously through these tournaments and earn his place without much trouble. However, consistency is at a premium and many players fall by the wayside after excelling at certain levels. We then select players from the teams playing the Ranji Trophy. We have an onerous and thankless job as the cricket scribes always fault our selection and claim we have devious motives of our own."

"What do you look for in the players?"

The selector explained that he needed to see talent and performance. The two, he thought, should go together but unfortunately it did not always seem to be the case. Some talented players he felt failed to perform and some players who performed very well and stood out in the record books really did not have the talent. The selector paused then continued. "If I pick up a player based on my judgement of his talent and potential the press will haul me over the coals unless the talent is reflected in the performance. I see the bowler, Raju, and I feel he has the potential to make a very good fast bowler but there's still something lacking. He's a little rough at the edges; he needs a more polished performance. It could be done easily enough; exposure to international cricket and coaching by the experts would help but his performance in today's match has been very disappointing for reasons beyond his control."

"Why do you say that?"

The real problem according to the selector was not in Raju's action, pace or physique but in his relationship with his captain and teammates. He felt that somehow Raju did not get on with them and so he had not been given the opportunity to shine. "The captain didn't give the new ball to him and many fielders didn't support him by taking the catches offered so at the end of the day his bowling figures read dismally. If I pick him for the national squad purely on my judgement unsupported by the performance record, I'd be branded an idiot, along with many other things." It was obvious that the selector knew all too well the response he would get if he picked Raju. "Some would call me a communalist, some would say that I'm too parochial and even the other members of the Selection Committee wouldn't support me. After all, selection is nearly always a subjective process, if it were not so then Team India would be selected solely on the basis of the records of performance. We could do that without watching any of the players."

They then turned their attentions to one of the batsmen who had scored one hundred and fifty-eight at a brisk rate. The President asked what the selector thought of him. "He proves my point. He has some technique but it's not particularly sound. He's got guts and he is willing to wield his bat and go through his shots undaunted by the situation but he was lucky in many ways today."

The opening pair had already put on a good partnership and laid the foundations for a high score so the batsman they were discussing had been able to go for runs from the word go. Many of his shots had just nipped past the fielders' hands and with one or two fumbles in the field, he had been dropped twice when he was twenty-six and seventy-four.

"In my opinion," the selector continued, "he was downright lucky today whereas Raju had a bad day at the office. Tomorrow the press will report the match, hail the batsman and Raju will find no place in the write-up at all. That puts me in a spot if I select Raju. If I select the batsman, I'm sure he will at best be a one-match wonder and again the blame for his selection will be placed squarely at my doorstep. Now, I understand you are a learned man. What should I do? Follow my instinct or go with the records and statistics?"

"I appreciate your predicament but I'm glad that you decided to take the trouble of watching the players in action. The previous selectors never attended matches and this was the biggest grouse of all the players."

"They were going by the record books and awarded points for every fifty runs scored or for every wicket taken and kept a tally and then selected those who topped the list. They didn't trust their own judgement as they didn't want to incur the wrath of the public and the press who, if you ask me, don't know the front end of the bat from the rear!"

"Not all scribes are bad, surely?"

"Some of them know about the game but they write to make a point and to whip up public opinion. You know how in India everybody is so opinionated; they play the role of a selector and decide what the composition of the team should be. If the team doesn't include any of their favourite players they call the selectors all the names under the sun. I once heard a lady in her fifties who had never touched a cricket bat speak at length about the partiality of selectors in not selecting a player. In a country like ours with such a huge following for the game it's difficult to satisfy the entire range of cricket lovers. We do our job and leave it at that."

"Some of the players selected for Team India made quick exits from the team. How do the selectors feel in such cases?"

The selector sighed. "Downhearted. In a match between the NDA and the visiting West Indies team there was one young cadet called Sengupta who scored a century and was selected for the Test squad. He scored only four runs and faded into oblivion after one Test whereas some batsmen, who were playing for Oxford and Cambridge, were drafted into the team when it was in dire straits against England. They had had no experience in domestic cricket but acquitted themselves very well and played successfully for many years. There's no foolproof theory for selection. If there is one I'll be the first to learn it."

"Your statements sound like a lament," the President said sadly.

"It's true. The job of a selector is a thankless one. While the success of a player is attributed to the player's talent, his failure is blamed on the selectors. Previously we had only the print media to contend with. Nowadays the all-pervading television is playing havoc."

The selector explained his reservations regarding television. The constant replays that showed clearly the talent or lack of talent in a player and the commentators, who, often ex-cricketers and not without their own faults, were too quick to make derogatory comments about the team and then blame the selectors. The TV channels, he told the other man, had even started 'Master Selector' contests. With the advent of these contests everyone in our country who owned a TV set, and that was about five hundred million, has turned into a selector. The cricket loving public of India had an important say in the selection.

"If you remember, the public protested when an out of form Kapil Dev wasn't included in a Test. They said that 'No Kapil, no Test' and held the team to ransom. Recently when Saurav Ganguly was omitted from the team due to poor form, the public and the politicians, including the Chief Minister, got in on the act. They burnt effigies of Greg Chappell, the coach, and if Surav hadn't been subsequently included, the party in power would've in all probability called a strike and paralysed the city of Kolkata and West Bengal for a day. I sometimes think that with the advent of the modern technology the umpires are becoming redundant and the day's not far off when the selectors will be redundant too."

"Anyway, coming back to today's match, has anyone caught your attention?"

"I heard you're an eminent lawyer and you're asking me a leading question!" the selector said with a grin.

"What about the process of selecting the selectors?"

"That's beyond me; I can't comment. I didn't ask for the job but, when they asked me to be a selector, I couldn't refuse. I love the game and I'd like to do whatever I can to improve it."

"Some of the selectors have had little or limited experience of Test cricket. Some were one-match wonders. How come they get drafted in as selectors?"

"You should ask the BCCI that question. They do have some method in their madness. They appoint one selector from each zone to ensure that the cricketers from all parts of the country get a fair chance. Their intentions are honourable."

"But the results seem to be disastrous and they do say that the way to hell is paved with good intentions."

"I'm only a cricketer and not a learned man. You're using flowery expressions and making it difficult for me to answer."

"I also understand that some horse trading goes on and players from some regions of dubious merit get selected." The President's voice had fallen to a whisper.

"I've also heard that. In our country we are all parochial to some extent. Some selectors insist on getting players from their zone selected at the cost of candidates that are more deserving but what can we do? Previously the cricket had the Bombay lobby and North Indian lobby. To break up the lobbies the BCCI adopted the zonal selector system. But no system can be foolproof as there's a human element involved and selection is a subjective process."

"The public doesn't understand all this. They even doubt the composition and integrity of the members of the BCCI."

This point raised by the President was true. The BCCI should have been solely manned by players of repute with managerial skills. Unfortunately, when the BCCI elections were held, all the politicians and the top bureaucrats threw their hat into the ring. The result was that many members of the BCCI knew very little about cricket and their sole interest had been to win the election and enjoy the many benefits as members of the BCCI. Several of the officials were accused of embezzling funds, which should have gone rightly to the players of past and present. It is only recently that players of the domestic tournament have been paid well and pensions awarded to the players of yesteryear. There was the case of BS Chandrasekhar, a renowned spinner of the seventies, who, when driving a scooter, was hit badly by a truck. Only when the public made a hue and cry about it did the BCCI send him to the USA for corrective surgery and other medical help.

The President was becoming quite incensed with what he was hearing. "Why don't the players protest?"

"In my time the captain took the lead and represented our grievances and asked for more money. He's been unceremoniously thrown out. The competition is so intense that each player is scared of losing his place in the team. If the captain himself could be thrown out, what could happen to lesser mortals? Today we have a Players' Association but it's defunct too."

"There seems to be a lot of rot that has well and truly set in in Indian cricket, don't you think?"

"You've to decide that yourself. We, as players, consider it a great honour to represent our country. When we perform well we taste the adulation and praise of the public, which gives us immense happiness. The adulation that the fans show me still four years after I've retired is something to be seen to be believed. That's enough for me. I made a modest sum of money and one day the BCCI will organise a benefit match and present the purse to me and I can live the rest of my life in comfort. I'm very satisfied with my lot."

"You played a very good game and played a very important role in many tight situations and established several records."

"Thanks for your kind remarks."

"You were also known to be a very superstitious cricketer."

"True. I was always superstitious. I always prayed before the start of the match. When I made my debut in international cricket, I scored a ton. At that time, I carried a blue handkerchief in my pocket. I made sure that I always carried the same handkerchief whenever I played an important match. The handkerchief did its trick most of the time."

"We used to see you on TV. You seemed to have some other superstitions also."

"Almost all the cricket players are superstitious," the selector replied with a broad smile.

He then went on to describe some of the greats and their

beliefs. How Sachin Tendulkar, the greatest batsman in the country, looks heavenwards when he scores a fifty or hundred. That Azharuddin always used to keep a charm hung round his neck and he went on to score three centuries back to back on his debut, a rare feat indeed. He ultimately became one of the best batsmen in the world. Mohinder Amarnath apparently used to keep a red kerchief in his right pocket, while Krishnamachari Srikanth used to walk to one side of the crease before taking his stance for every ball that he faced. Even foreign players like Mahanama from Sri Lanka used to kiss the bat before facing every ball.

The selector finished by saying, "It is not just cricketers. Vijay Amrithraj, the famous tennis player, used to touch the cross that hung around his neck at the end of a chain before receiving serve. Superstition is common amongst all sportsmen, so I was nothing unusual."

"I hope I didn't offend you. Anyway it has been a great pleasure talking to you."

By this point the match had resumed and the lawyer made himself scarce. He thought that this particular selector had his head screwed on. Earlier he had believed that all selectors were nincompoops but now he had changed his opinion of them. In fact, this particular selector had gone up several notches in his estimation.

BOUNCER

A bouncer is one of the most lethal weapons in the fast bowlers' arsenal. It is pitched short so as to rise to an uncomfortable height, endangering the body of the batsmen. Nari Contractor, the captain of the Indian team on tour to West Indies in the sixties, was struck by a bouncer from the fast bowler, Griffith, and was badly injured. The new hard ball hit him square on the head and split his skull open. Contractor had to be carried away from the field straight to hospital for an emergency operation. Thanks to the immediate medical aid, he survived but he never played cricket again. In his post-playing days, he always appeared smartly turned out and handsome but sported a large scar on the side of his head to remind him of the bouncer.

When such injuries began to occur once too often, the batsmen started wearing protective headgear. Specially designed helmets to protect the head became standard kit for all batsmen. The helmets were designed with a mesh in the front to protect the face and shields on the side to protect even the ears.

The batsmen first adopted the technique of avoiding the bouncer by ducking underneath it. As long as they kept their eye on the ball until the last second they had no difficulty in getting out of the way of the bouncer. Some ducked, some bent backwards and some stepped back to keep out of harm's way. However, a bouncer, which bounced only up to the height of the ribcage proved to be even more dangerous. It was too low to duck underneath and it compelled the batsmen to fend it off with the bat. In such cases, the ball, more often than not, used to fly off the bat or the glove in any unexpected direction to be caught by the close in fielders.

Many reputed batsmen like Mohammad Azharuddin, Saurav Ganguly and Virendra Sehwag had problems facing such deliveries and often fell prey to the bouncers. The Australian quickies developed a fine art of sensing the weaknesses of these batsmen and used this lethal delivery to take many wickets.

Yet, some intrepid batsmen revelled at the sight of the bouncer and took the fight to the bowlers. They hooked the ball for a definite four and at times possibly for a six. They succeeded as long as they could hit into the ground, which they did most of the time but on occasion found the fielder at deep fine leg and provided him with catching practice. Mike Atherton, one of the past captains of the England team, was one of the finest hookers of the bouncer. Mohinder Amarnath and VVS Laxman in India also showed guts and the technique to deal with the rising ball effectively. Therefore, the bouncer sometimes boomerangs and instead of forcing a wicket gets hit for a six.

Usha felt like a bouncer jumping with joy. She had finished her Masters in Computer Engineering at Penn University, Philadelphia. She had received attractive job offers before she had completed her degree and could pick and choose. Normally the students from India do not present their dissertation at the end of their course and wait until they land a job, for their F1 visa expires on completion of their studies. They complete their degree formally only after landing the job, as the employer applies for a change in the visa. Usha, the brilliant girl, had no such problems and during a campus interview picked up a plum job with one of the best software companies. The combined reputation of IIT, Penn University and her excellent grades helped her to get a job with a good compensation package and perks. She wasted no time in completing her degree and joining the firm.

In the first few months she enjoyed her newfound freedom. Firstly, she had achieved her dream of doing a Masters in Engineering in the USA. Secondly, she had got a fantastic job that she found both challenging and interesting. She immersed herself in her work, enjoying the ambience of the office and flexible working hours the company provided. Soon her bosses spotted her talent and quick uptake and started rewarding her with bonuses, awards in terms of cash vouchers and other incentives. This quick appreciation gave her great job satisfaction.

Her personal life also changed beyond description. She was far away from India with no restrictions imposed by society, parents or peers. She felt like a blithe spirit, a bird released from a gilded cage after so long. Her soul took flight and winged its way to complete freedom; she could do what she pleased. So the first thing she did was to cut her long hair to a more comfortable shoulder length and in doing so changed her hairstyle completely. Then she discarded her Indian clothes and acquired a new wardrobe full of jeans, trousers and tops to match. Finally, she went to a gym and got herself into shape. All in all, she gave herself a complete makeover.

She then went out and bought a new BMW and enjoyed driving the wonderful car on the beautiful road network of Philadelphia, New Jersey and New York. Quickly she found that as long as one followed the rules, driving on American roads was a pleasure and free from any hassles. With her car, she visited all the important cities and the historic places around while at the same time she made man, good friends, both Indian and American, and visited them whenever she wanted. She shared an apartment with another Indian girl, who she enjoyed the company of, and between them they divided the housekeeping work and kept a very neat and tidy apartment.

With money to burn, she could afford fine dresses, accessories to match and many gizmos for the apartment. She changed her life style completely and soon became part of the 'in crowd' of well-to-do Indians. Since she was an alumnus of IIT and Penn University with good looks and grades to match she commanded respect instantly. Whenever she visited the Indian temple all eyes turned and the other Indians looked at her with a mixture of admiration and envy.

She missed nothing about India except perhaps her indulgent parents, particularly her father, who had always made sure that she got whatever she wanted in life. Her mother had been just as indulgent but in a different way, in that she had never allowed Usha to go anywhere near the kitchen nor do any household work. "It was servant's work," she used to say. Her parents had raised her with a more male set of attitudes towards the world and had given her only one task: of confining herself to her studies in school and college.

They revelled in her success whenever she won accolades from the teachers and prizes at college. They wanted their daughter to prove that girls were in no way less than boys in any respect, particularly in studies and Usha always lived up to their expectations. She had her name inscribed permanently in the roll of fame at both her school and college. Thanks to their encouragement, she cleared all the hurdles in life with ease and achieved her dream. Into the bargain though, she had picked up a handicap and had learnt little or nothing about housekeeping. When she had to share the housekeeping work with her flatmate, she wished that her parents had been less indulgent but, with her quick mind, she soon learnt the art of cooking and how to deal with other chores by studying the cookery books and learning online. She thought that she was on a roll and that everything was going her way except for one small item.

Every night before retiring to bed it was her task to roughly rinse the cutlery and crockery before putting them in the dishwasher, tidy up the kitchen and square up the dining room. She also had to clean the toilets on alternate days but back home, she had always had a horde of servants at her beck and call keeping the house immaculately clean. Even when she wanted a glass of water she used to shout out an order and someone used to fetch it. Usha realised that despite all her qualifications and the best of jobs she would have to wait at least ten years or so before she could employ that type of servant. A small fortune would in fact be needed to have as many servants as her parents had. Back home she was like a princess in a huge mansion but in the USA, although well paid and enjoying life, she was just an ordinary person. So although she was thanking the stars for all that she did have, she felt that she was missing something but could not put her finger on it.

Since being a brilliant computer engineer, she decided to analyse her problem and find out what was bothering her analytically. She took out her think pad, listed all her assets on the left and found the page almost filled. Then she put her troubles on the right. First on the list were her indulgent parents; she was missing them badly. This did not seem to be an insurmountable problem as she kept herself constantly in touch with them by telephone and through e-mails. She used to have long chats with her mother, even learning how to cook some Indian dishes that way. Secondly, she was missing her friends but she had made new, equally good friends who encouraged and supported her in all her endeavours. The third thing she jotted down was the fact she missed her palatial house and the small army of servants, but she thought she had a nice apartment and soon she would be able to buy a house with the kind of salary that she was getting and the prospects of quick raises. She scored off that point too.

She found herself staring at a blank page that was of no help in pinpointing her troubles. Yet she was missing something and she felt there was a void in her life. She wanted to wait and hope that the elusive answer would present itself sooner rather than later. She recalled how she surprisingly found the answers for her computer problems at odd times like while taking a shower or cooking a dish. Strange though it may seem, she thought, but solutions to insurmountable problems

235

often present themselves at odd times.

She called her parents more often and chatted with them for a long time, sometimes for half an hour or more. She told them mainly about her achievements at work and how she was enjoying her life. She found her parents loved every minute of her telephone calls but, during one of their chats, they told her that they were looking for a suitable boy for her.

The words 'suitable boy' struck like lightning and she quickly realised what she was missing in her life. A suitable boy indeed! She had heard of the famous novel and made it a point to read the book immediately. When she had finished it she suddenly realised what she had been missing all along: Raju. She could not believe it when she realised that she was missing him. What was he to her? Nothing! she thought. He was definitely not her class; he had nothing in common with her either in studies or other interests. She had met the fellow only because the Colonel had requested her to help motivate the lad. Strangely though she also remembered that whenever she attended a match Raju performed very well. Either it was pure coincidence or the Colonel was right.

She had only been able to attend a handful of matches before she had joined the IIT and had met him on a few occasions later. She had slowly lost track of him but the few meetings she had had with him during their formative years had left a permanent impression on her psyche. Raju's image as a tall, handsome fellow with gentle manners, which had been stored in the labyrinths of her memory, suddenly shot into focus and demanded her attention.

She recollected how he used to behave towards her as though she was a queen and he was one of her subjects. He was almost obsequious, she thought. She also recollected the look in his eyes, the unbridled admiration he had shown for her. The Colonel even mentioned once that the boy possibly loved her. Now it made sense to her: perhaps his admiration was not for her talents alone but was part of his love for her. She thought it was pleasing to know that someone loved her.

On her part she had never shown any interest in him as a person except as a cricket player waiting on the wings and in need of some extra motivation. She had helped him on a few occasions when she could. Otherwise, she had never entertained any thoughts about him; in fact, she had believed that he had not warranted a second thought. So why was she missing him? She asked herself this several times but could not come up with any satisfactory answers.

She did not know that the body chemistry between two young people of the opposite sex follows its own rules and there was no way to rationalise it. It springs many surprises and the heart pines for someone whom the mind does not recognise. The heart has a mind of its own. With a good lot of spare time on her hands now she suddenly wanted to know what progress Raju had made. She browsed various sites on the Internet for cricket in India and started to keep a track of his career. She found to her utter dismay that he had made little or no progress at all after she had left the country. She called the Colonel's house to speak to Raju and learnt that he had left for his mother's place. The Colonel told her about his mother and the changed scenario.

"Is this real or something engineered by you, Uncle?" she asked suspiciously.

"This is real, my dear girl. I must thank you for playing along with me before and sticking to the script I prepared for you."

"I'm sorry to see that Raju has not made much progress. What new trick are you going to try to spur him to success?"

"I've run out of tricks. Now he's grown up and he knows what's at stake. He should motivate himself and propel himself to success. I gave up a while back."

"I can't believe that you gave up. It's most unlike you."

"True, but I've no other tricks. Now that you are a well-educated girl, I'll take any suggestions you might have. I've tried various methods suggested by the psychologist and achieved nothing worthwhile."

This conversation with the Colonel had caused the cogs in her mind to, first, leap into motion and then spin ever faster. Spurred by some unknown or unacknowledged motive, she swung into action and studied about cricket in general and fast bowlers in particular. She carried out an in-depth study, indeed she almost carried out a full research project in order to get all the facts right. Thanks to her incisive mind, she got even the nuances of cricket right. Philadelphia had a good cricket tradition and the local library and museum provided her with the necessary material. She learnt of the success of bowlers like McGrath, the speed of Bret Lee and Shoab Ahktar and others who had made names for themselves for their pace and accuracy in bowling. She also studied about the new rules of the ICC, biomechanics and the extent to which bowlers are permitted to bend their arm before delivery. She studied dynamics and the art of swinging the ball and reverse swing; in truth, she covered the lot.

Meanwhile she learnt of the progress of IT in India and the fat salaries the IT experts were getting in Bangalore, Cyberabad and other IT centres. She found that she could be as equally successful in her own country, have a better lifestyle and be closer to her parents and friends by working in India. Money did not matter much to her. She was sure to get a good pay packet with ESOP and other perks. Anyway, her father made a fortune and, as the only daughter, she was bound to inherit the lot. She had been brought up like a princess all her life with so many servants at her beck and call and she realised she could live like that again once she returned to India. She thought that, all said and done, she was an alien, a foreigner in the USA, and that it would take at least another ten years before she could be naturalised as an American. Somehow it seemed that it was not all that important nor worth all the trouble. What she heard of the new work environment and the opportunities for bright young people in the IT sector in India reinforced her new ideas. Once she had decided, she acted with the pace of a fast bowler.

LATE CUT

The late cut is a connoisseur's delight in cricket and only batsmen endowed with fine technique execute this masterful stroke. The batsman watches the ball like a hawk and waits until the last fraction of a second to determine the direction in which the ball is travelling before bringing down the bat with a quick movement and rare finesse. The stroke can often surprise the wicket keeper and the close in fielders as it races to the boundary much to the delight of the spectators. All the cricket cognoscenti appreciate the stroke and sports writers will devote pages to it. This cut is not attempted by lesser batsmen and, when executed properly, will evoke appreciation even from the fielding team. Reputed wielders of the bat, like Zahir Abbas, Sachin Tendulkar and Gundappa Viswanath, executed this stroke often with great panache and won much praise from the purists of the game.

The late cut however is also fraught with dangers as it may be the downfall of the batsman if he overestimates himself and executes it too late, as the ball will hit the stumps. Timing plays a very important role in the implementation of this shot and those who perform it stand apart from lesser mortals. The various cricket academies that have developed in different parts of the world teach this shot at the very end of the curriculum. The numerous cricketing manuals and copybooks also list this stroke in the final chapters and caution the batsmen not to attempt it without mastering all the other shots first.

When Usha returned to India, leaving her cushy job in

Philadelphia, she made her parents very happy. They were delighted with her decision and did not bother to ask her reasons for returning home. Her father felt proud that his daughter had decided to render her services to India and not serve some employer abroad. He decided therefore to host a grand party to celebrate her homecoming.

The spacious lawns of the lawyer's house were cut and manicured to perfection. Lights, arranged in helical patterns around the tall trees surrounding the lawns, illuminated the place while potted plants, placed strategically, added colour and grace. A well-stocked bar was in the left hand corner and a table with a huge spread of the choicest dishes stood on the right. The immaculately dressed lawyer and his bejewelled wife, wearing broad smiles, stood at the entrance to the lawns to receive the guests. Liveried servants went round with trays of glasses carrying the best of drinks and almost everybody who was anybody in the city turned up. Everyone loves a party, particularly one that is hosted by an eminent lawyer known for his riches and hospitality, and so the delighted guests eagerly arrived.

Usha, resplendent in a light blue sari with a gold coloured border and sequins artistically attached, was the cynosure of the party. The guests all made it a point to congratulate the lawyer on Usha's success and how such a brilliant daughter was a credit to him. The proud parents naturally basked in the glory of their daughter. Usha circulated, meeting all her friends and narrating some of her interesting experiences while abroad. Of course all the guests listened to her with rapt attention. At one point, Usha surveyed the scene and realised that somehow she felt the party was not complete. She could not find the Colonel. She made some discreet enquiries and learnt that, although invited, the Colonel had expressed his regret at being unable to attend due to an indisposition. It seemed that everyone, or almost everyone, enjoyed the party but not Usha. She missed the Colonel.

Later that night she asked herself why she had missed the

Colonel. After all, he was not a family friend or a relative but a mere acquaintance. She had not known him until he had approached her and asked her to help him out with his problem. Before she could really analyse her thoughts she was whisked away by her parents for a discussion in the living room.

Next day she made it a point to visit the Colonel at his house. Seth, who was nursing a minor ailment, immediately rushed to the living room to welcome his surprise guest. With one look at her, he felt much better and even rejuvenated, for Usha looked totally different from the young girl whom he had asked a favour of. Now she was radiant, brimming with confidence and smiling broadly. The small sparkle in her eyes had grown to a shining light; she exuded confidence and obviously had a good future before her.

"Nice to see you, Usha, and, if I may add, you look beautiful, in fact radiant."

"Thank you, Uncle."

"I heard that you did very well at the IIT and in the USA. What's made you return to India and to this city in particular?"

"Now India is booming, as they said it would, there are plenty of opportunities to be had and a good life to be made here. I'd like to do my own thing in India and not work abroad; I didn't really like the way of life over there. Besides, I wanted to stay close to all those that are near and dear to me."

"Splendid! Congratulations on your excellent decision. All along, people have been talking about the brain drain. Your decision shows that the best brains, like yours, can be an asset to our country."

"Thanks." Usha paused momentarily before asking what was really on her mind. "What progress has Raju, your protégé, made? Where is he? I haven't seen him around." Usha sat quietly listening to the lacklustre progress and the appearance of Raju's mother, which ended up with the lad living with her. "Do you mean to tell me that you've given up on him?"

"I'm afraid so," Seth replied.

"It's most unlike you, I heard so much about your perseverance. How could you give up on him?" Usha sounded a little annoyed.

"I had no alternative."

"I've been thinking about the problem. If you make a product and it doesn't work you should go back to the drawing board and start afresh."

"What do you mean? You can't equate a cricket player with an industrial product! I heard that you're a brilliant computer engineer but you can't design and produce a cricketer of international standards just like that."

"Of course you can, provided you use the right systems, tools, programme and technique." Usha spoke as calmly as she could.

"What do you think I was doing all these years?" This time Seth had a slight edge to his voice.

"If you don't mind I'll do some plain talking if you promise not to take offence."

Seth, although a little annoyed was intrigued, so said, "I give my solemn word. Go ahead."

"To put it in a nutshell you've been a great asset but also a great liability to Raju."

"What makes you say so?" The Colonel found it difficult to contain his irritation at the word liability. "What do you know of cricket? Have you ever played the game?" he added.

Usha just looked at him. Although annoyed he had given his word and he was also affected by her commanding persona. Here he was, a Colonel who had commanded troops, tough troops in an elite battalion, but now he found this wisp of a girl commanding him and demanding his undivided attention. She had acquired a certain aura during the intervening years and so he listened to her spellbound, like the wedding guest to the ancient mariner.

"One need not be a botanist to smell a flower!"

"Go on and unravel your fancy theories then. I'm all ears."

"When did you play competitive cricket last?" Usha asked.

"Back in the fifties and sixties. I played for about fifteen years, fifteen long years."

"That's the trouble. We're in the twenty-first century and already six years have passed. Cricket today is totally different from the game that you played in your time. Your techniques and methodology is archaic and obsolete. Even the spirit is different. In your time people used to say, 'It is immaterial whether you win or lose but when the final scorer scores what mattered was how you played.' Today there is only one thing that's winning. There are no flowers for the loser. The winner takes all.

"The sport has had a quick makeover and is now an entirely different ball game. Today's cricket is for professionals who use cricket-4G, which means Technology of the Fourth Generation. When you played, you were an amateur and used cricket-1G technology. How can you design a successful product with obsolete technology? The only answer is to get back to the drawing board with up to date ideas. Today technology rules the roost. If you don't use it you stand no chance and you're a goner."

"You surprise me with your language, accent, knowledge and ideas, young lady. I'm beginning to admire you. I do have an open mind and I'm ready to try anything. What do you suggest?"

"Start afresh using the state of the art technology, which I will provide. After all, you set me a task once and I want to finish it to my satisfaction. I've never failed so far. I don't like the idea of failing and I don't want to fail you."

"I can't believe that a girl is talking like this about cricket."

"Leave the gender bias in the dressing room and let's get to business, Uncle!"

They got down to business the next day. The ground in the Colonel's house was re-vamped and put back as it was before.

When Raju was summoned, he felt immensely happy that the Colonel had started taking an interest in his game again and rushed to his house with his gear. He felt he had been drowning and the call from the Colonel revived his hopes of survival and success. His spirits soared and he felt he was on cloud nine when he saw Usha, a new Usha, who now looked in his eyes gorgeous and sounded to his ears so smart. She had had some intrinsic beauty earlier but she now was utterly stunning.

He felt speechless when she greeted him with great enthusiasm and enquired about his life in general but, in particular, his progress in cricket. He found neither words nor courage to tell her that when she went abroad to study she had created a vast void in his life, a void that nobody had or could fill. He had felt abandoned by the girl and the Colonel, the two people who had mattered most in his life. Now not only had he got a call from the Colonel, but Usha, the girl of his dreams, was standing in front of him asking after his welfare and progress. What more could he ask for? He was only sorry that he could not report any worthwhile progress to her. In fact, the only things to report were the decline in his station in life and his failure in cricket.

To Raju's surprise though, without any further ado, Usha and the Colonel got down to the business of redesigning and reforming him as a front line fast bowler. Usha displayed her gadgetry: a digital video camera, two other video cameras, a speed gun, a laptop and a DVD player. She placed the video cameras and the speed gun at strategic places around the pitch and adjusted their settings. She held the digital video camera in her hand and stood behind the net in line with the stumps. The stage was set finally with the Colonel standing next to the lone stump at the bowling end. Then she asked Raju to bowl.

The Colonel liked the way she asserted herself and started taking charge of everything, including him. He always liked girls with a bit of zip and had brought up his own daughters to be so. He waited to view her methodology. When Raju had bowled a few overs and had warmed himself up, she tossed him a new ball, declared that all systems were go and told Raju to bowl as if he was opening the attack in an important match. She let all the cameras roll for a short while until Raju had completed a few overs. Then she asked everyone to adjourn to the living room.

Usha showed the action replay on the TV having linked her laptop to it. With the help of the software that she had designed and the inputs from the speed gun, she showed that Raju was bowling at speeds not exceeding one hundred and thirty-five kilometres per hour and that he was delivering the ball with almost a straight arm, bending it by only two degrees. She clicked the mouse and the screen showed the latest rules from ICC, which allowed the bending of the arm up to fifteen degrees without risking the ire of the umpires. She also showed footage of bowlers like Bret Lee and Shoab Akhtar, and the slinging action of some Sri Lankan bowlers.

"These bowlers would easily have been called 'chuckers' according to the old rules. In fact, eminent players like Bishen Singh Bedi are running a campaign to chuck out the chuckers. But the present rules permit these bowlers to deliver the ball at great pace," she explained. She then talked about biomechanics and aerodynamics. She spoke about the importance of the speed and the probability of the swing with more speed. She spoke of the influence of extraneous things on the pace and movement of the ball. She also spoke of reverse swing and how bowlers like Andrew Flintoff were achieving it with ease.

Raju and the Colonel listened to her with rapt attention, forgetting that she was 'only a girl'. They not only absorbed everything that she said but also wondered where on earth she had picked up all this knowledge about cricket and fast bowling.

"What you say makes great sense and is splendid," Seth said, "but where did you get all this information from?

"Philadelphia has a great tradition of cricket. Although the game is not played anymore now, the library has a very good collection. Above all the Internet today is a fount of information and knowledge."

"What do you suggest? How should we go about our task?" Seth asked.

"First, Raju should unlearn all that he has learnt over the years and start afresh with the new rules in mind."

"It's easier said than done!" exclaimed the Colonel; he found it difficult to contain his irritation this time. He could not stomach the fact that the young girl had the temerity to tell Raju to unlearn all that he had taught him. Nevertheless, he tried to keep his cool as Usha outlined the plan.

"Let him start by throwing the ball at full speed and we'll measure it with the speed gun. Then we'll get him to bowl with a faulty action, chucking the ball at full pace so we can measure that speed achieved and see the angle that his arm bends at. Next, we can work on reducing the angle to permissible limits while still achieving the maximum speed. Finally, we'll work on the swing so he can swing the ball both ways. Meanwhile we'll send him to the gym and condition his body to be stronger and more aerodynamic."

"Your plan seems theoretically sound but I don't know whether it will work or not," the Colonel said dubiously.

"I'll give you the ideas while you two do the work and let's progress step by step. You provide the raw material, I'll provide the technology but Raju will have to do the hard work. We'll form a triad and produce the desired result."

The Colonel was clean bowled. He could not stomach all these new ideas coming from a girl, who did not know the front end of the bat from the other and who had never bowled in her life. Then he chided himself for considering her simply as a girl and not as a brilliant engineer who had specifically come to help him. Once he had overcome his gender bias, he followed her instructions to the hilt and put Raju through his paces as prescribed by Usha.

As for Raju, every word that Usha spoke sounded like sweet

music. Whenever he looked at the beautiful girl, he could not believe what was happening. He had been brought from the village and trained by the Colonel all these past years and now Usha, with latest technology, was hell-bent on reforming his game; he was starting afresh. He took her every word as a divine dispensation and followed her instructions carefully and diligently.

CHUCKING

Bowling is basically hurling the ball at the batsman using an overarm action. Unlike baseball, where the pitcher throws the ball directly at the striker, the bowler goes through a run up, picks up speed and bowls by taking his arm overhead and bringing it down in a complete circular movement. He delivers the ball once the arm has reached its highest point and has started to descend. The most important thing in the bowling action is the movement of the arm, which should be one complete action with the arm kept straight throughout. Any ball bowled by checking the arm or by bending the arm and straightening it before the delivery is considered a 'throw' and declared a no ball. Such bowlers are called chuckers.

Earlier these players either had their action corrected in the early stages of their career or were thrown out of the team at the first opportunity. The difference between normal bowling and throwing is clearly evident to the eye and the chuckers had no place in any team. This was mainly due to the unfair advantage that such flexion gave the bowler with the wrong action in terms of speed, bounce and turn over not only other bowlers but also the batsmen. The chucker could put the ball exactly where he wanted to without extra effort. In short, 'it wasn't cricket'.

Somehow, some chuckers found a place into international teams and the near epidemic of chucking started in the fifties. The classic case was that of Charlie Griffith of the West Indies who used to generate tremendous pace and terrorize the batsmen. He broke the skull of Nari Contractor, the then

Indian captain. When many players complained, he retired from international cricket.

The controversy reared its ugly head again more recently with Muralitharan, the Sri Lankan off spinner who, with his suspect action, could make the ball turn almost a yard, much to the discomfort of the batsmen and he took many wickets. Several umpires called 'no ball' due to his faulty action. Initially the Sri Lankan cricket authorities explained it away by saying that the bowler had suffered a bout of polio in his childhood. His suspect action therefore was due to a bent arm, the legacy of the disease, but that it was correct and did not demand any improvement. Thanks to him, Sri Lanka began winning matches and backed him to the hilt. The same bowler was repeatedly no balled for a faulty action in Australia and soon matters came to a head when the captain took his team off the field as a mark of protest. Subsequently the bowler was put through biometric tests and the ICC in its wisdom cleared his action. Interestingly enough, BS Chandrasekhar of India also had an attack of polio in his childhood but he was never called for chucking.

Taking their cue from Muralitharan, speedsters like Bret Lee and Shoab Ahktar bent their arm and straightened it before delivery and generated speeds of up to one hundred miles per hour or one hundred and sixty kilometres per hour. This pace got them many wickets and all batsmen cried foul. Honest and straight-armed bowlers like Srinath from India suffered and ended with poor statistics. The spinners like Rajesh Chouhan and Harbhagan Singh from India and Shoab Mallick from Pakistan were sent to the Australian Academy for biometric tests and to have their bowling action reformed.

The ICC in its wisdom initially formed a rule permitting straightening the arm 10 degrees for fast bowlers, 7.5 for medium pacers and 5 for the spinners. This was like treating the bowlers to something equivalent to the Hindu caste system in India and caused uproar. Finally, to mollify the various teams, the ICC modified the rules and permitted all bowlers, quickies to spinners, irrespective of their speed, bending of the arm up to 15 degrees. The main argument in favour of this rule was that if the angle were more than the specified then the suspect action would be apparent to the naked eye. Most of the umpires and public do not seem to fully understand the rule but the new legislation put an end to the debate; it legitimised bowlers hitherto called chuckers and opened a can of worms. "Bowling it may be according to the rules, but it's not cricket," shouted many players of yesteryear.

Seth hated controversies and tried his best to stay clear of them. Fortunately for him the army and the other two services had remained apolitical and devoid of any major controversy, especially religion, which has always been a strong divisive force in the country. During his younger days, there had often been clashes between the Hindus and Muslims and the army was called upon to supervise protest marches and, if required, to control the mobs indulging in killing, looting and arson. Each battalion honoured the four predominant religions: Hinduism, Islam, Sikhism and Christianity. Before embarking on any campaign the battalion used to offer prayers in the temple, mosque, the church and the gurudwara, the Sikhs' temple. As time passed, Seth found that the frequency of these religiously fuelled clashes reduced considerably but they did persist in some pockets of the country.

Religion played no role in cricket and players of all religions found their place in Team India by sheer dint of their merit. The team had outstanding players from the minorities who were very important members and often served as captains. The Nawab of Pataudi and Azharuddin, two Muslims, captained the Indian team with great distinction for long years. Bishen Singh Bedi, a Sikh, was chosen as captain without any hesitation. Navjot Singh Sidhu, Harbhajan Singh and other Sikhs found their places in the team by merit and their inclusion was never questioned. The Indian team once had a fast bowler called Ashis Winston Jaidi. His name had Hindu, Christian and Muslim components.

The most defining moment though was when India won the Nat West series in England with Mohammed Kaif scoring the winning run. Saurav Ganguly, the captain from Bengal, a state that was once torn apart purely on the basis of religion and which had witnessed the worst unrest at the time of partition, spontaneously hugged Kaif. He was from Uttar Pradesh, which still suffers from religious strife on a regular basis.

While religion polarised the body politic, the game of cricket acted as a unifying factor. All Indians, irrespective of their religious faiths and political affiliations, rooted for Team India and prayed in their own way for its success. While religion was a divisive force, cricket was the strongest unifying factor of modern India. On the political front, the two main parties paid more attention to religion and put the economy on the backburner. Some called themselves secularists and dubbed the other party communalists, who in turn referred to themselves as nationalists. The so-called secularists and the communalists agreed on several common factors regarding the economy and the reforms needed to revive it. A combination of the two parties could have taken the country on the road to prosperity but the secularists, to gain the vote of the Muslim minority, preferred to join hands with the leftists who put up road blocks in front of every economic reform. The path to progress in India, it seems, is paved with religious misgivings.

Seth found himself for the first time embroiled in several controversies of his own. First Usha, a wisp of a girl who had never bowled a single ball, was telling his ward to unlearn everything that he had assiduously taught him over the years. Next she wanted Raju to literally throw the ball while keeping his arm bent but within the limits of the 15 degrees rule.

Seth was certain that he was not a male chauvinist pig; after all, he had brought up his daughters as boys and had always championed the cause of women. He never once resented the fact that Usha was a girl but he still could not stomach the idea of a female talking so authoritatively about cricket. There was women's cricket but it was an entirely different ball game. Chucking and throwing, to Seth, was not cricket; it was an anathema to him. So how could the girl advocate such wrongful practices so blatantly? he thought. True, he sought her help to motivate Raju but he did not anticipate this type of response from her, especially six years later.

Yet he could not dismiss her outright. She shared a common goal in shaping Raju for success and, in that way; she was an ally and not an adversary. She spoke of modern technology and software which he did not understand but software surely does not produce cricketers? Especially fast bowlers, who basically, he believed, needed to bend their backs and bowl their guts out to succeed.

As he was musing on these random thoughts, Usha entered unexpectedly.

"What a surprise!" He asked her to sit down and ordered a coffee for her. His long years in the army permitted no response other than politeness even when Usha took liberties; she came over and sat in the chair next to him, pulling it very close.

"Forget about coffee. First, I wanted to apologise if I offended your sensibilities. Secondly, I want to put across my point of view dispassionately, without emotion and sentiment clouding my judgement."

A bit taken aback, the Colonel said, "I must say that's very decent of you."

"You're still being very formal. Why don't you relax? We both want Raju to succeed. You did your part. Now give me a chance to do it my way." She smiled beguilingly before adding, "Please," in a very entreating way. When she spoke like this no man could have refused her request.

The stiff upper lip that he learnt from his days in the army, which was part of the legacy of the British, gave way to a smile. All reservations and doubts in his mind about Usha and her strange unorthodox ways melted away. He did not understand why the young woman was going to such lengths for the sake of Raju's success but, if that were her intention, it would be foolish on his part to hold her back.

He pulled her close and kissed her on the forehead. A single kiss can say more than a million words. It indicated to Usha that she had crossed all mental and emotional barriers that the Colonel had built around himself. She had found acceptance and agreement. She had been fighting for it for the last few days and now she had got what she wanted.

"Now let's study the ICC rules clearly, interpret them and then let me explain the software that I've produced."

"Go on, I'm all ears!"

Usha gave a detailed explanation of all three aspects, then made out a plan to start with. It took Raju's development from the drawing board through to a fully evolved plan of action.

"From now on you teach Raju about ethics and other sublime aspects and I'll take care of the technical side of his bowling."

"I agree, fine, but why ethics?"

"The game of cricket is getting a bad reputation. Every day it's in the news for all the wrong reasons. One day it's the violation of the code of conduct and imposition of penalty fines on the players. Another day it is doping and banning and controversy between different organisations. Lastly, the matter about betting in cricket, the millions that change hands and the way the bookies are getting the matches fixed. Match fixing is the hottest scandal in cricket today."

"True, in my time cricket was more a gentleman's game. When the umpire declared a batsman out the latter never questioned the decision. Even when he felt aggrieved he kept his dissent to himself. Today the bowlers and fielders appeal excessively, put pressure on the umpire and, when the decision goes against them, use several expletives, ignoring the code of conduct and inviting the wrath of the Match Referee.

"As for betting it has escalated to huge proportions with millions of dollars changing hands. No wonder the bookies pay vast amounts to the players to underperform and fix a match. This has resulted in tainted cricketers and anti-corruption squads organised by the ICC. Today cricket is loaded with money and goodies and the Indian cricketers are some of the richest sportsmen. However, since the competition is so severe, some players want to make hay while the sun shines and make money before they lose their place."

"What about established cricketers who were captains of their respective teams. Hans Cronje, Azharuddin and Salim Malik were classic examples. Raju is a poor boy totally dependent on you. You should ingrain in him not to fall to temptations such as money and other incentives that the bookies offer."

"Okay, I'll teach him all those aspects and make sure that his name doesn't get sullied but aren't we putting the cart before the horse?"

"As to getting him his rightful place in Team India you leave that to me. I'm confident of success. I've never failed in any project so far and I'm sure that I won't fail this time either."

"I admire your confidence. Attagirl, from now on he's all yours and I'm only your assistant. I give you full freedom in his training. Get results and get them fast as age is catching up with him."

Usha left having succeeded in her difficult mission. She had not thought that she would have crossed that particular hurdle so easily.

For the first few days the Colonel made Raju throw the ball at full speed, then bowl full speed with a throwing action while Usha took countless pictures. Back in the living room they analysed the bowling action and then made plans to correct the action to comply with the rules. After a strenuous work out for a month, Raju was bowling at speeds in excess of one hundred and fifty kilometres per hour. Then they concentrated on reducing the angle that the arm was bent at. They also worked on gripping the ball and turning the arm slightly to produce the swing. Lastly, she painted lines outside the off stump and at points of good length on the pitch. She promised Raju incentives if he bowled at a correct length and within the corridor of a correct line but penalties for balls pitched short or out of line. With the help of the Colonel, she placed coins at selected sweet spots on the pitch and asked Raju to bowl, ensuring the ball hit the targets so he could claim suitable rewards. This system of the carrot and stick worked beautifully. Raju bowled to claim the rewards as he could ill afford to pay the penalties.

The way Usha attended each practice and analysed the bowling action every day surprised the Colonel and his student. They found her commitment to achieve the common goal of all three, Raju's progress, to be complete. Usha with her laptop and other gadgets provided the greatest inspiration both to the Colonel and his student. Raju worked very hard and by the time the season started was bowling at speeds that he had never dreamt of and was producing a great degree of swing too. When Usha showed the replays on her laptop she shouted, "Gotcha."

To the great surprise of the Colonel, Usha declared that her product was somewhere very near to what they desired and ready for field trials. She proposed that Raju bowl at Ramu who by then had truly established his name as one of the leading batsmen of the country.

"How can we get him now?" Raju asked.

"I did my homework. He's back after an overseas tour and if I invite him I'm sure he'll oblige and provide you with a target for practice," replied the ever-confident Usha.

CROSSBAT SHOT

Most of the shots executed by batsmen are played with a straight bat as given in any cricketing manual. Such shots enable the batsman to keep the ball low or along the carpet and out of the reach of fielders positioned to take a catch. Any shot played with a cross bat is considered 'not cricket' as it looks ungainly and makes the purists wince. The batsman has little or no control over this type of shot and it may either kiss the ropes or just as likely land in the hands of the fielders.

A cross bat shot is normally played by a novice or an established batsman who wants to play for broke. However, with the advent of one-day matches of limited overs, the batsmen have started taking calculated risks and have begun improvising. Cross bat shots and reverse sweeps have fetched runs in critical situations and thus have gained popularity. The purists have stopped criticising the batsmen as long as the unorthodox shots fetch runs and win games. In a one-day match, what it comes down to today is the number of runs scored and not how they are scored. Winning has become the end and the means matters little. When the purists stopped groaning, the batsmen started using these shots even in Test matches once they were settled in and sighting the ball properly. Nothing succeeds like success and when the batsman is on a roll, he has no moral compunction not to use a cross bat shot to pile up more runs.

Ramu by now had become a permanent member of Team India and had signed a contract with the BCCI for a handsome annual salary. He had won the mental battle with his father and had started endorsing several products ranging from suiting and cosmetics to engine oils on the TV for lucrative contracts. With his newfound wealth, he broke away from his father and bought an excellent house in the upmarket area of the city where the rich and famous lived.

He also gained in popularity and had a good following of fans, who admired his square cuts and cover drives. The crowds used to go 'gaga' every time he scored a century and would give him a standing ovation. The spectators used to display placards reading 'GO RAMU GO!' Some of the young female spectators held up placards stating that they wanted to marry him and, whenever the TV cameras panned towards the audience, these beautiful girls would blow kisses to him. His fan mail, which increased enormously, often included letters from many attractive young women. Their letters, invariably, showed their physical and material assets and expressed how keen they were to marry him.

Ramu had had little or no contact with girls as he had grown up. He occasionally met Aparna and Suparna whenever they came to India but they were much older than him and treated him rather condescendingly. At times they were annoyed with him and Raju as the boys were taking away valuable time they could have spent with their father. He had had some contact with the girls at the school but before he could get to know them properly, he had got a call from the national selectors and thereafter he had had little or no time for female friends. His life was cricket and his entire focus was on cricket. Girls had no place in his scheme of things until he had cemented his place in the team. However, his body had a chemistry of its own and as he achieved success and tasted the adulation of the girls, although they took second place in his mind, he started yearning for them and even losing his concentration at times.

As part of the physical fitness programme prescribed by the team's physio, Ramu worked out regularly and this, coupled with the training given by the Colonel, had turned him into a strikingly handsome man. The vast array of clothes that he bought during his overseas tours meant he was always dressed stylishly. With his newfound wealth, looks and fame he was the guest at all the important parties held in Visakhapatnam. Every socialite who gave a social gathering included him on the guest list as he was the most eligible bachelor in the city and many girls actually swooned at the sight of him.

When he got a call from Usha, Ramu was thrilled for Usha was the prize catch in Visakhapatnam. The only daughter of an eminent lawyer, loaded with money, living in a palatial building, an MS degree and endowed with both looks and a figure that would be the envy of many girls. She was the epitome of a beautiful and desirable young woman. 'What more could a bachelor ask for?' he asked himself.

He realised that he was not from her league as he was nothing but a successful cricketer and she was, after all, a brilliant girl with all the requisites for making a lovely bride. He accepted that she was definitely from a higher social circle and he had little or no chance with her. However, he had one advantage. He was on a roll and was scoring freely. All his shots were kissing the ropes and the entire country was in awe of him. He was seeing the ball like a football. Now was the time to chance his arm and to use a cross bat shot if required.

Ramu recollected his school days and how he used to admire Usha and also ogle her. He had never had the courage to go and speak to her though. He had met her once or twice when she returned to India for a short vacation and he was at home in between tours. He had always wanted to go and say hello to her; in fact, he also wanted to tell her, 'I love you'. It is a simple sentence of three words but the most difficult to say. It requires emotional guts and mental strength to go up to a beautiful girl and say that simple sentence. It is perhaps more difficult than another simple sentence of the same length, 'I am sorry'. The latter sentence hurts the ego, but the former needs considerable fortitude. He wondered why he lacked the strength as he had faced his formidable father and had seen off the fastest bowlers from around the world and come out the winner time and time again. Why then was he scared of telling this wisp of a girl those three small words? he asked himself. He had tried to pluck up the necessary courage but always gave up at the last minute and the simple sentence had remained unspoken.

He scanned the newspapers and found some photographs that had been shown when she returned to India. The articles about her spoke of her intelligence, her excellent academic record, her wish to return to India and serve the country and of her ambition to create 'Brand India'. The papers were full of praise for her. However, what interested Ramu most were the photographs. These showed a girl with a fine figure, a sparkle in her eyes, an exquisite dress sense and, above all, a beauty that mesmerised him. Here is a girl worth dying for, he told himself.

When Usha requested that Ramu come to the Colonel's house to assist Raju he could hardly refuse even if he had wanted to. After all, the Colonel had taught him the basics and had accepted him into his team of three without reservation. Raju was his best friend and had bowled at him day in and day out as a bowling machine and provided the necessary practice required for honing his batting skills. Above all else though, his dream girl and the prize catch of Visakhapatnam herself had invited him. How could he, in heaven's name, say no to her? He readily agreed and displayed an extra enthusiasm to comply with her request by telling her, in not so many words, that he would give life or limb for her and all that was required was a call. Ramu's intentions in accepting the call to practice with Raju were mostly honourable but a trifle tinged with his desire for the lovely Usha. An occasional cross bat shot is okay, he told himself, and prayed that he would get a four or even a six and not get caught at long on. "How can I say no to you? For that matter can anyone say no to your request?" he told her.

When he reported for practice the next morning he was half an hour early as the Colonel had never tolerated tardiness and that half an hour would provide an opportunity to establish a rapport with Usha. He spruced himself up, dressed in his best with a Team India blazer and put on a front of a gentleman cricketer of fame. He also decided to impress Usha with his sincerity and commitment for the improvement of Raju and to undertake any task given to him by either the Colonel or the object of his desire.

Soon the stage was set. Ramu padded up with all his protective gear and donned his helmet; finally he took his stance in front of the stumps. He was full of curiosity, as he had heard of Usha's efforts. The Colonel stood as the umpire and Usha stood behind the net with her digital video camera as she shouted with great excitement, "Get set, go!"

When Raju delivered the shinning new ball with his new bowling action, it flew past the batsman surprising him. Ramu, by then an accomplished batsman with good scores in international matches to his credit, was completely beaten. In fact, he was beaten all ends up by both the pace and the swing. He shook his head in utter disbelief but decided to keep the shock to himself. The next ball pitched outside his off stump and again whizzed past, giving him very little time to react. He had faced many pace bowlers from different countries with hard fast pitches providing a lot of bounce and so favouring the speed merchants but never had he encountered such ferocity.

The third ball also pitched outside the off stump and Ramu could see from the movement of Raju's arm that it was swinging away from him. More by instinct and less by technique he lifted the bat up to keep it out of the way of the ball, which harmlessly swung away from him and crashed into the net. The Colonel watched the discomfort of the batsman and whispered to Raju, "Now go for the jugular!"

The next ball again pitched outside the off stump and Ramu lifted his bat up in a repeat action. This time the ball, instead of moving away, tuned inwards and crashed into the stumps sending the off stump cart wheeling.

"Hurray!" the Colonel shouted in unbridled glee.

Ramu stared at Raju and said, "Excellent! When did you learn to bowl like this?" Then the smile left his face as he continued, "But I think your bowling action seems suspect. I wonder whether you will pass the scrutiny of the umpires."

"Don't you worry about that. This whiz kid of a girl has got all that worked out," replied the Colonel.

"I can't believe it. Anyway let him continue." Ramu was definitely unsettled by the events.

The game progressed. Raju, the hopeful, bowled his heart out. Ramu, the batsman with a reputation to keep, tried to defend and if possible hit him. At the end of about six overs, the hopeful emerged the winner for the batsman could not execute any of his masterly strokes and was beaten repeatedly by the pace and swing of the ball. All four of them returned to the living room where Usha replayed the six overs and analysed the bowling action. She explained to a sceptical Ramu that Raju's new action was in conformity with the new rules of the ICC and that he should have no problems with the umpires.

She was proved wrong when Raju played the next match. The stumps went crashing repeatedly but the umpires called no balls on many occasions. The umpires held a meeting at the centre of the pitch and, after a long discussion, called Raju and his captain to declare that Raju's bowling action was suspect and he would not be allowed to bowl. The captain and Raju protested. The matter was referred to the third umpire. When all three umpires met and discussed the action, they could not decide one way or another. Finally, they decided to give the benefit of doubt to the bowler and allow Raju to continue. Bowl he did, with ferocity, and created a record by taking six wickets for a mere twenty runs. The batsmen could score only when he was tired and erred in line or length. At the end of the day, the opponents were bundled out for a paltry score of seventy-five.

Cricket is a media friendly game. Before the advent of the

TV, the cricket scribes, and there were plenty of them, wrote extensively about each match. They gave free rein to their power of expression, used flowery language, indulged in calisthenics of words and exercised their turn of phrases. Several cricket writers made their copy more interesting than the game itself. Cricket is the only game, next to chess, that had had so many books written about it. Scribes like Jack Fingeleton and, back home, writers like Prabhu, Mohan, Rajan Bala and many others wrote with a flourish that would make novelists like Salman Rushdie and Vikram Seth happy. The radio commentators were also equally up to the task. They have described the game in lucid terms and presented a vivid picture so that even the distant listeners have virtually felt like spectators watching the game from the stands. The whole media circus has the ability to make a game of cricket an event of national importance.

While some sections of the media hailed Raju as the new rising star on the cricket firmament, some called him a chucker and recommended that he be banned from bowling. Some moderate scribes recommended sending him to the MRF Pace Foundation or the Australian Academy to get his action checked. However, they all agreed that he was the fastest bowler not only in the country but also, possibly, in the world. While the controversy raged, the success of Raju in the next domestic match made headlines in the media all over the world.

The BCCI in its wisdom decided to send him to the Australian Academy. At about this time Usha wrote an article explaining the bowling action of Raju. She added photos of his bowling action, frame by frame with the software that produced angular measurements superimposed on every frame. She also compared the photos with the photos of the bowling of the world's known quickies and the extent to which the others bent their arms before the delivery of the ball. Usha proved conclusively that the bowling action of Raju was within the prescribed norms of the ICC and needed no further scrutiny. At the end of the article, she added that the author of the piece was a computer engineer from the IIT and Penn University. She also gave her e-mail address.

The article created uproar. Firstly, the last male bastion, cricket, was felled. Until then the members of the fairer sex played the game within their own group. Some ladies from West Indies and South Africa ventured as commentators. Mandira Bedi from India added glamour to the game with her designer clothes but no lady had ventured to write about cricket and the intricacies of the game with so much knowledge and authority.

Usha captured the imagination of the cricket loving youngsters of India with one article. Letters poured in from readers saying that the old scribes, who had criticised Raju's bowling action, did not know what they were talking about and the girl from the prestigious IIT could not be wrong. No chance! Absolutely, no chance of her being wrong, they all wrote in the same unmistakable words. Usha's article became the hottest news and several TV channels descended on the city asking her for interviews. She handled the situation with great aplomb and showed them all the software that she had designed.

Usha explained that it was way ahead of 'Hawkeye' in that it showed the movement of the bowler's arm in slow motion from the start of the run up until the delivery of the ball, frame by frame, whilst also showing the angle to which the arm was bent in each frame. The media loved it and showed the entire footage on TV. Usha claimed that she was ready to take on any representative from the ICC to prove that Raju's bowling action was within the new norms and that there was no need at all to send him to Australia for a check-up. She also argued that India was miles ahead in the field of software and it would be an affront to all software specialists in the country if any bowler were to be sent overseas for a check-up. She also asked the senior specialists in IT in India to check her work and point out any possible fault. She dared the cricket pundits from the other countries to prove her wrong.

Her challenge caused an almighty stir in the entire software industry from the Silicon Valley to Bangalore. Most of the experts analysed her product in depth and could not fault her. A leading exponent of cricket software from Wisden at Bangalore finally endorsed the views expressed by the girl and complimented her for working out the problem and producing something that should be accepted as standard in all the cricket playing countries and by the ICC. This confirmation removed any lingering doubts from the public or the players.

ONE DAY INTERNATIONAL

One Day International matches, the shorter version of cricket with fifty overs for each innings, were introduced to try to draw in the spectators that were failing to attend the gruelling five day Tests. Modern life has put a heavy premium on time and spending five days watching a cricket Test was often way beyond what even the ardent cricket fans could afford to give up. The shorter version was modified constantly to attract more spectators and to keep them glued to their seats. While most of the Tests, played over five days were drawn and inconclusive, the ODIs as they were called were designed to produce a result unless the heavens intervened in the form of bad weather and curtailed the play completely.

The ODIs were made TV friendly as the players wore coloured clothing to stand out in sunshine or under floodlights and played with a white ball. Several modifications, like restrictions in field placing in the first twenty overs and power play of ten overs each as decided by the team fielding, were introduced. Technology was brought in and replays were shown to settle dubious run outs, stumpings and other decisions, which the field umpires could not decide accurately without causing acrimony. Soon the third umpire formed a very important link in the game.

The results were astonishing and the stadiums overflowed for most of the matches and the TV channels paid huge amounts for the rights of live coverage. As the matches were broadcast live via satellites the action could be seen in living rooms all over the world. The interval between each over, which lasts about two minutes as the fielders change from one side to the other, provided an opportunity to air advertisements. With growing consumerism, the companies advertising their products competed for the short time and paid huge amounts for a ten second spot. Some large companies spent fortunes in sponsoring the national teams and insisted on the players wearing clothes prominently showing their company logos.

The increased revenues by way of the gate receipts, TV rights, sponsorships and personal endorsements of commercial products brought money flowing into the cricket board's coffers and to the individual players. In comparison, the players of yesteryear had been paid a pittance and only those who had formed part of the national team had earned pots of gold through various means. India, with the largest base of middle class that could afford TV, having something in the region of more than eight hundred million sets in the country, became the financial hub of cricket and its clout on the international scene rose several notches.

The process of players making more money was started by Sunil Gavaskar who is considered a living legend in India. It was furthered by Kapil Dev and finally fine-tuned by Sachin Tendulkar, who is reputed to be worth one hundred crores of rupees, a mind-boggling figure for an average Indian. He may not be in the same league as Michael Jordan, Tiger Woods and Roger Federer but he is undoubtedly the richest cricketer and richest sportsman in the subcontinent.

With the advent of the cricket *moolahs,* the game spread into every nook and corner of the country and even small children started playing the game. Taken out of colleges and schools it spread into every highway and byway, anywhere in fact where a set of stumps could be placed and then, with great fervour, boys played endlessly. If the ball broke a windowpane, the unfortunate victim rarely complained and, if they did, the parents of the young street players had no objection to paying for the damage. The shortage of playgrounds was more than made up for by the narrow lanes of the cities and towns and taught the aspiring players to defend their wicket with a vast number of close in fielders. Heroes were born in this way; Gavaskar, for example, learnt his cricket on the streets before playing for his college, university and later for his country.

The love Indians had for cricket received a great boost when Kapil Dev's team won the Cricket World Cup in 1983 against all odds by beating the all-conquering West Indies. This victory did to cricket what Dr Man Mohan Singh's economic policies did to the country's prosperity. Unfortunately, the TV was confined to only some cities and the bulk of India could not see the match. The Government introduced colour television in 1984 for the Olympics in Los Angeles so when the Benson and Hedges competition was held in Australia all the matches were televised and seen by large number of Indians. The Indian team, then under the captaincy of Gavaskar, won the tournament to prove that their success in the World Cup had not been a flash in the pan and thereafter Team India became a force to be reckoned with.

Ravi Sastry was declared Champion of the Champions and was presented with an Audi car, which was transported for free by the Shipping Corporation of India and the government waived the import duty. India had finally arrived on the cricketing map with a bang. Cricket fever swept the whole country and the following for the game has been growing in phenomenal proportions ever since.

The second of the five ODIs against the visiting Pakistani team, India's archrivals, was scheduled for Visakhapatnam. The rivalry between the two countries started when the country was divided on the basis of religion. Pakistan, a predominantly Muslim state, believed that every Pakistani soldier was more capable than three Indian soldiers. With this concept, they have waged war with India four times and come a cropper on each occasion. Smarting under these military defeats, especially the 1971 war, which resulted in the dismembering of the country and India taking ninety thousand prisoners of war, the largest figure in the annals of warfare, the Pakistanis desperately wanted to beat India on the cricket field. The matches were to be played at Sharjah, where not only were the Muslim supporters in the majority but the games were organised by Pakistan's supporters too. The overwhelming partisan nature of the crowd and the organisers was so blatant that the Indian team refused to play at this venue, ignoring even the huge financial gains to both the cricket board and the cricketers of yesteryear.

When relations between the two countries soured due to terrorism sponsored by ISI, the Pakistan Intelligence Agency, cricket matches were either abandoned or played at neutral venues such as in Canada. The Indian government, with the idea of improving relations with its neighbour, resumed the playing of cricket between the two countries.

Visakhapatnam was chosen as the venue mainly because of the new stadium that had been built according to international standards but also because of the infrastructure. The roads in the area formed part of the famous golden quadrilateral and a beautiful four-lane expressway to the stadium had been opened. Situated twenty miles from the ever-expanding city of Visakhapatnam amidst green verdant fields, the stadium looked picture-perfect. The special bahamas grass, which had been imported, provided a carpet-like outfield. The important industries, especially the Vizag Steel Plant and host of public and private sector companies, provided full support to the Visakhapatnam Cricket Association by way of funds, material and technical know-how. The ambience of the stadium then provided an ideal arena for the eagerly awaited contest.

The whole city was agog with excitement a full month before the match. The officials concerned busied themselves to ensure the stadium was fully fit in all respects. The contractors hurried to complete their jobs and put the finishing touches in place. Several hoardings of consumer products were erected alongside the road leading to the stadium and the whole city spruced itself up for the occasion. The public made a beeline for the ticket counters and it was a complete sell-out. Those that could not get tickets tried on the black market but each ticket was fetching a margin of two hundred per cent.

The hotels earmarked for accommodating the players spent a fortune on advertising their honoured selection and upgraded the furniture and fittings. Several banners welcoming the visiting Pakistani team and Team India were put up all over the city, especially along the road from the airport to the hotel and from there to the stadium. The Indian tricolour was displayed at every nook and corner of the city. The cricket lovers from all over the state of Andhra Pradesh rushed to Vizag, as it was called earlier, and filled the hotels to capacity. They wanted desperately to watch the match but, failing that, a glimpse of the fifteen-man squad of Team India would suffice.

The scribes wrote several columns describing the stadium, the pitch, the final eleven to be selected and the tactics to be employed in the match. All the scribes who had a good penmanship but little knowledge of cricket wrote lengthy columns and filled the pages of the newspapers and magazines. The TV channels called cricketers who had hung up their boots to the studio to air their views on the impending event while local companies and corporate houses paid huge amounts to display their advertisements around the boundary line. Even the rope marking the boundary was auctioned for a large amount. Meanwhile top officials scurried around and called in favours to gain free passes for the match, often using their official clout.

The police brought in extra reinforcements from all over the district and the state to control the huge crowd expected. Although the stadium had a capacity of only thirty thousand compared to one hundred thousand at Eden Gardens in Calcutta, now called Kolkata, the police expected an influx of about one hundred thousand people to catch a glimpse of the players of both teams. The entire city then was in the grip of cricket fever.

"Are you going to the match, Raju?" asked the Colonel.

"Yes, I've got special tickets as I'm part of the state team. I'm going along with the others in the team bus."

"The crowds will be unmanageable and may get rowdy if our team doesn't do well. I don't want you to come to any harm. I'd rather you come with me. I've passes for the special enclosure."

"My buddies in the team'll be disappointed!"

"Let them think what they want. I don't want to compromise your safety. You've a future ahead of you and promises to keep."

"Why are you worried about my safety? It's only a cricket match."

"I wish life was so simple in our country but if someone bungles up some aspect of the game it might stir the crowd into a fury. Sometimes with such a huge number of cricket fans, they can get boisterous when things don't go their way. Once in New Delhi the authorities issued more tickets and passes than the capacity of the stadium. People who had paid huge amounts were denied access and, naturally, they created a ruckus which was only controlled when the police opened fire. Five or six spectators holding genuine tickets lost their lives through no fault of their own. Another time at Calcutta, despite the huge capacity of the stadium, several cricket enthusiasts found themselves at the gates without tickets. They waited for an hour or so and, when they realised they couldn't gatecrash the party, they indulged in some petty arson. Of course the police took action and there were several connected deaths. Even the mounted police squads find it difficult to control the crowd."

"The spectators inside the stadium should be no trouble."

"True, but the fans always want our team to win and can't stand it when the opponents beat us. When our team wins, they celebrate with fireworks and start several fires by lighting newspapers and anything they can lay their hands on. Once in Eden Gardens our team was losing badly and the spectators couldn't stomach it. They started pelting stones, empty bottles and all sorts of stuff. The police couldn't control them and all hell let loose. The match was abandoned and awarded to the visiting team. Into the bargain some of the peaceful spectators got hurt, so you see either way there's likely to be trouble."

"Why can't the police control the crowds? I don't understand."

"In all such events the mob psychology is unpredictable. The police don't want to open fire but they are left with no other option and all too often they kill some innocent spectators while the real trouble makers get off scot-free. The police usually have to face an enquiry later but they're like men caught between two stones."

Finally, the much awaited day arrived and huge crowds thronged the airport but thankfully caused no trouble to the police. They wanted to catch a glimpse of their heroes but the players quietly and secretively got into their buses and drove to their respective hotels without risking exposure to the large number of fans.

The teams were received at the hotel in the traditional Indian way. Girls, especially selected for their beauty, welcomed them with silver plates filled with vermilion powder which they applied to the foreheads of the cricketers. They sprinkled rose water, placed garlands around their necks, presented them with bouquets of flowers and finally showered them with rose petals. The visiting team was overwhelmed on experiencing the warmth with which they were received. The top brass of the hotels then met the guests and personally escorted them to their individual rooms while the crowds outside shouted at the top of their voices wishing them good luck.

After the ceremonial reception of both captains, they held a press conference in which each captain praised the talent of the other team but predicted success for his own. They fielded questions from the press with relative ease and finally withdrew. For the next two days before the match both the teams practised on adjacent grounds to acclimatise themselves to the local conditions. When they practised in the nets, a large number of spectators turned up to watch their technique, showed their adulation and collected autographs whenever possible.

The police made elaborate arrangements to divert traffic from the main road along which these gods were expected to proceed to the stadium. This caused complete disruption to the city's traffic, which the local populace suffered willingly. The teams were whisked away well before the start of the match and taken to their respective dressing rooms that had all the amenities. The spectators began to turn up an hour in advance and found their seats. They went fully prepared taking packed lunches, water bottles and numerous snacks. Under strict police control, they filled the stadium; not a seat was left unoccupied. The enthusiasts who could not get the tickets climbed the nearby trees and perched on top of buildings to get an aerial view of the match. The organisers watched with delight as the stadium filled and with everything going so smoothly.

The ODIs are either day matches or, in venues provided with floodlights, day and night matches. This match, which was a day match, started promptly at nine. Earlier India had won the toss and elected to bat first. When the gong struck the two umpires marched to the centre and took up their positions. The fielders walked on led by their captain and finally the two opening batsmen for India, Sachin Tendulkar and Veranda Sehwag, walked to the crease fully kitted up for the purpose. As they walked they swung their bats and flexed their arms and the entire crowd stood up and wished them good luck. The cheer for Sachin reverberated not only in the stadium but also in the hills around the whole city and probably all over India.

The entire crowd prayed to their respective gods; in fact they had probably been praying since first thing in the morning for the success of their team. In addition to the crowd present in the stadium, there were the vast numbers of viewers in front of TV sets throughout India and those who could not watch the game no doubt had prayed too.

The Hindus, who form eighty-seven per cent of the population, prayed to their respective gods and goddesses for there are many in the Hindu pantheon. Muslims on the other hand believe in only one god and, no doubt, the Muslims from both countries prayed for the success of their respective teams, putting their god in a dilemma, as the Muslims in India total more than the population of Pakistan. The presence of three Muslims in the Indian team must have made His task even more difficult as Allah would have found it impossible to answer the prayers of all His devout followers; perhaps He decided to favour the teams alternately. No wonder the matches between Pakistan and India go to the wire time and time again and are decided so often on the last ball.

Seth, although not a devout Hindu, was not prone to praying for such trivial things like a cricket match.

"Are you praying for the success of Team India?" he asked Raju.

"I've never seen you praying and even the teacher in the village never prayed. So how could I pick up the habit of praying?"

Meanwhile the game started. The umpire tossed the new ball to the Pakistani captain, who in turn tossed it to his star bowler. Virendra Sehwag is a batsman with good eyesight and quick reflexes and he has excellent coordination between his various faculties. Above all, he believes that every ball bowled at him must be hit and hit hard without any thought of consequences. He started hitting every ball from the word go. In three overs, he scored twenty-four runs while Sachin his partner scored only two. Then disaster struck.

Sachin Tendulkar, revered almost like a god by all the cricket lovers of the country and number more than the population of countries like the USA and Russia, ran for a cheeky single. A direct throw by Yousuf Yohana, the only Christian in the Pakistani team, hit the stumps and the umpire referred the matter to the third umpire who, with the help of technology, replayed the scene frame by frame. He came to the conclusion that the batsman was short of the crease by more than a metre. He gave a red light, which indicated that the batsman was out. It was like dropping a bombshell. A sudden hush descended in the stadium. A similar hush must have descended on the whole country and in many parts of the world where the Indian Diaspora was watching the match.

Sachin always scored heavily whenever he played and the country always took it for granted that he would score nothing less than a half century. He, with so many records to his credit, had obliged his fans on many occasions but he was also human and fallible. He put his bat under his arm and walked back to the pavilion. The entire crowd almost wept and gave up the hope of victory. The great disappointment of the crowd could be seen clearly.

In came a new batsman, MS Dhoni. The crowd had never heard of him and did not expect much from him. They pinned all their hopes on Sehwag who obliged them by scoring at a brisk rate. Undaunted by the dismissal of Sachin, Sehwag continued in his inimitable style. He did not know that the new batsman had taken a leaf out of his book and batted in a similar manner. Dhoni matched his illustrious partner shot for shot and the scoreboard raced away much to the delight of the spectators. Every time the batsman hit the ball for a four or a six the crowd responded with a huge round of applause and soon forgot their earlier disappointment. They thought all was not lost as long as these two batsmen were at the crease. Both Sehwag and Dhoni played like batsmen possessed and hit all the bowlers all over the place. The crowd created Mexican waves, beat drums, played martial music and egged on the players to hit the Pakistani bowlers to kingdom come. When the excitement mounted, Sehwag got carried away and was out after scoring a blistering seventy-four. The scoreboard read one hundred and twenty-two for two wickets after 13.4 overs. It showed a run rate of more than eight runs an over.

Next came Ganguly, the captain, but before he could find his feet he was out. The crowd were not too concerned as the next batsman, Dravid, popularly called 'Wall', had a good reputation. He played a steady innings and gave most of the strike to Dhoni who was in a punishing mood. As he scored off almost every ball, the crowd erupted in a massive roar and applauded him in one voice. Dhoni was on a roll and his confidence grew with every ball he hit to the ropes. It was his day, he thought, and he chanced his arm even with balls of good length.

With Dravid playing steadily and Dhoni putting the bowlers to the sword, the pair took the score to two hundred and eighty-nine when Dhoni was out in the forty-second over after scoring one hundred and forty-eight in one hundred and fifty-five minutes out of one hundred and twenty-five balls, an astonishing record. That was his maiden century as he was a new member of Team India. As he walked back to the pavilion, the entire crowd gave him a standing ovation and clapped all the way until he got into the dressing room. The other batsmen came out in succession and fired rapid bursts and departed. At the end of the stipulated fifty overs, Team India had scored a commanding total of three hundred and fifty-six runs for nine wickets and had set a target of three hundred and fifty-seven for the Pakistani team.

During the lunch interval the crowd spoke of nothing but Dhoni, his gutsy batting and his ability to take the fight to the enemy camp. On that day, he became an instant celebrity and his long unkempt hair became the fashion of the day. The crowd soon learnt that he hailed from Chattisgarh, a backward state, and from a rural background. They also learnt that he had derived his strength from the two glasses of buffalo milk that he religiously drank every day. The entire nation hailed the arrival of a new star batsman on the Indian cricket firmament. His hair became a hot topic for discussion and during the Indian team's tour of Pakistan, the crowds in that country also found it very appealing. Despite being a general, the President of Pakistan, an ardent cricket fan himself, watched the game, admired Dhoni's batting and his hairstyle and advised him not to cut his long hair.

When play resumed after lunch and the Pakistani team came in to bat, they thought that they could match the Indian batsmen. They immediately suffered a great setback when Shahid Afridi, their star batsman with a reputation for lusty hitting, got out for a duck. Demoralised to a certain extent they never recovered and despite good scores from Abdul Razzaq and Yousuf Yohana they could not force the pace and lost their wickets at regular intervals. They were all out after 44.1 overs for a score of two hundred and ninety-eight runs so losing by fifty-eight runs. Dhoni was declared the Man of the Match and when he went to receive his award the entire stadium gave its approval and hailed him in one voice.

The huge crowd celebrated the victory by lighting fires, fireworks and endless drum beating. Some did the *Bhangra*, a popular Punjabi dance, and the crowd frolicked its way home singing and dancing. The celebrations lasted for a long time on the beach road but the police did not raise any objections about the din the crowd caused as they joined in. They too were happy with the outcome of the match, as the crowd could have caused them trouble if the result had gone the other way.

The print and electronic media reported the match in graphic detail. They indulged in verbal calisthenics to describe the batting of Dhoni and how a new star had filled the gap created by the early departure of the cricket icon of the country, Sachin Tendulkar.

"What did you think of the match?" the Colonel asked Raju when they returned home.

"Dhoni batted well but the Pakistan bowlers didn't bowl well. They didn't pitch the ball in the right place and provided easy pickings for the batsmen."

"It all depends on your perspective I suppose as to

whether the bowlers bowled badly or the batsmen played magnificently."

A normal fever lasts for seven days in a tropical country like India but cricket fever goes on unabated. The entire population continued to savour the delight of the match for many days afterwards. Their enthusiasm was not dampened even by the subsequent loss of the next three matches and the series to Pakistan.

CLEAN BOWLED

Every bowler dreams of getting the batsman clean bowled. When the ball beats the batsman all ends up and crashes into the stumps sending the bails soaring into the air, the bowler's soul takes flight. His self-esteem increases, his confidence snowballs, he jumps with joy and pumps the air with his hands. If it is a prized wicket, he will leap in triumph as it may prove to be the turning point of the game. When the bails are dislodged in this way the bowler need not even turn to the umpire for his decision. The batsman invariably accepts his downfall and walks off the field, as the result is irrevocably clear except when a no ball is called and cases of batsmen being declared not out because of a no ball are few and far between.

In other dismissals, by way of catches and leg before wicket, the bowler has to wait for the umpire to raise his finger and declare the batsman out. When however the woodwork is disturbed, the bells ring a peal of jubilation for the bowler and toll a death knell for the batsman. It is a signal for the defeated player to walk back to the pavilion and for the scorer to add one to the tally of wickets for the bowler. When the batsman is claimed out for any other reason he stands his ground and waits for the umpire's decision, not walking off until he sees the raised finger.

In the earlier days, when cricket was played more as a gentleman's game, the players walked without waiting for the umpire's decision whenever they realised that they were out. Such batsmen were called 'walkers' and were recognised for their honourable trait. However, with the advent of professionalism, the game became more competitive and 'walkers' have become almost extinct. The present-day players feel that the umpire has been charged with the task of deciding whether the batsman is out or not and, therefore, they hold their ground until a decision has been made. In modern cricket the third umpire, who sits in the cosy comfort of the pavilion, is asked to decide on close decisions and give his verdict electronically either on a TV screen or by showing a coloured light.

The batsman can be clean bowled by any type of ball. An in swinger, out swinger, off break, leg break, googly, armer or flipper: any can do the damage and the end result will be the same. Every batsman defends his wicket against all types of deliveries and would like to stay in the middle for as long as possible. Only the talented few play long innings however and score double and triple centuries. Sachin Tendulkar, for example, has scored a century or more thirty-five times, setting a record. Brian Lara, of the West Indies, amassed a phenomenal score of four hundred and has played other massive innings, but many others simply meet their Waterloo at some stage or another. The situation then, is akin to the lifespan of all mortals. While some play long innings and score a century or more, the majority lose their wicket when the Lord Almighty bowls one of His deadly deliveries.

The Colonel had batted fairly well in his innings until he faced a googly, which he was unable to read. He was batting on sixty-six and still seeing the ball well when he faced this particularly devious delivery in life. During one practice session, when Raju was bowling and Usha giving him directions, Seth felt a sudden pain in his chest as though a bouncer had hit him. The pain lasted only a few seconds and he ignored it completely. As a prudent man, he had always kept himself physically fit and had adhered to moderation in his smoking, drinking and eating. He took it for granted that he was playing well and would continue his innings for some years yet.

The triad of the Colonel, Raju and Usha waited for feedback from their field trials of the new product. Unfortunately for them, Team India had a break for some time and the next series was three months away. The players of Team India enjoyed their well-earned rest but the media, especially the cricket scribes, did not. They kept the pot boiling and raked up the controversy about Raju again. Their main gripe was the intrusion of a girl into their domain, which until then they had lorded over completely. They sought the opinions of the eminent cricket players of yesteryear and brought out several articles.

The foreigners also jumped into the fray. Barring a few, most of the cricketers from around the world, who had had their innings and had hung up their boots, supported Usha's theories while the present day cricket players and those waiting in the wings to join the big league welcomed her ideas. They all agreed that the game of cricket was undergoing a revolution with the new theories and techniques suggested by the girl and expressed their solidarity with her. The ICC also stepped in. It appointed a technical committee to investigate the latest ideas and technology advocated by Usha who had caused ripples across the entire cricketing world. Soon Raju the bowler was forgotten and Usha the female intruder had became the centrepiece.

Usha, being the gutsy girl she was, did not get ruffled and asked Raju to continue with his practice while she busied herself in establishing her own IT company. With the reputation that she had gained in such a short span, she encountered no problems in headhunting. Quite quickly, some well known IT specialists agreed to join her firm and lend their support to her. As the controversy continued, the BCCI arranged the Challenger's Trophy and selected the players to play for India A, B and C teams. The august body could ill afford to neglect Raju's claim to a place and included him in the India B team.

The Challenger's Trophy provided a good opportunity for all the hopefuls to exhibit their skills and for seniors, out of form, to prove themselves and regain their place. Usha decided to attend all the matches as she wanted to see for herself the product and programme she had launched and carry out any debugging if required. Thanks to the celebrity status she had gained so quickly, she was given pride of the place in the VIP enclosure, close to the dressing rooms. The sight of Usha, with her stunning smile sitting beside the Colonel, and both of them encouraging him, inspired Raju to great heights. In the first match the captain of his team tossed the new ball to him and wished him good luck.

Raju bowled his heart out with his new action and achieved spectacular results. In the second and the final matches, he finished with such a fantastic bowling analysis it left the selectors no option other than to include him in Team India. The entire country hailed the arrival of the new bowling sensation and wished him success. The only voice of dissent was from the bowler who had lost his own place in the team.

Raju thought that his life had at last taken a sudden and favourable turn and his fortunes, which were on the up, were all due to the girl of his dreams. He was very upbeat about his life until the Colonel complained of a recurring pain in his chest. This time, Seth had told him, it was unbearable as though a missile had hit him. Raju took the Colonel to the best doctors, ignoring the latter's protests and had him thoroughly examined. Seth had several scans and a complete check-up. Finally, they uttered the dreaded 'C' word. Immediately Raju had him admitted to the top hospital, then asked his sister from the village to come and look after the Colonel while he contacted Seth's daughters.

The girls, with their children in tow, arrived post-haste and their very presence made a lot of difference to the Colonel's health but eventually they took him to the Tata's Cancer hospital in Mumbai. The tests conducted by the oncologists showed that the cancer had started in his left lung and had already spread to various parts of his body. With a sombre voice, the senior specialist declared that the malignancy had reached the fifth stage, it was terminal and the Colonel had only few days to live.

The teacher and his daughter joined Seth's family to lend a helping hand. Usha left her company in the hands of one of her deputies and set up camp in Mumbai. Even Ramu felt duty-bound to join them and to provide any help he could. The Colonel, now confined to bed with life supporting medicines and appliances, looked a completely defeated man. He could not accept the idea that cancer, which he had read so much about, had finally caught him in its net. He felt like a batsman surprisingly clean bowled and looking behind to confirm that the bails were in fact dislodged. He looked around the hospital room, the IV drips and various sensors connected to his body to monitor the functioning of his heart and other organs. He felt like crying for the first time in his life.

By then, the visiting Australians had arrived in India and Raju was included in the first preliminary match scheduled a few days after their arrival. He requested the BCCI to be spared from the first two preliminary matches before the commencement of the first ODI at Mumbai. Taking into consideration the Colonel's health, the Lord High Commissioners of Cricket in India agreed readily. It suited them anyway as they wanted to use him as their surprise weapon in the first match.

One day on visiting the Colonel in hospital, Raju found his mother at Seth's bedside. She looked totally different; she was well attired and turned out like a society lady. This really surprised him and he turned to the Colonel who quickly solved the puzzle. "She's my distant cousin and played a role for me."

"What role?" Raju asked in a shocked voice.

"I requested that she play the role of your mother for some time to try and produce the results that I wanted. She kindly

285

agreed and endured quite some hardship for a period of time. You should thank her for all the trouble she took over your progress."

"You mean she's not my mother and she play-acted all this time to try and spur me on? I can't believe it! You've taken enormous trouble haven't you over the years, but I think that this lady has done much more than you in a short span of time. She managed for the first time in my life to instil a sense of pride in me. I started believing that I wasn't an orphan after all." Raju turned to the woman sitting quietly by Seth's side and said, "I can't thank you enough, Mother."

"We're all just happy that you've finally made it and are due to play your first really big match. But I'm beginning to doubt whether I'll be able to come and see the game that I've waited for all these long years," the Colonel said so sadly.

Raju was desperately upset but tried to keep Seth's spirits up. "I'm sure you will. We'll pray for you to be well enough. You've endured many things in your life and always come out a winner. I'm sure that you will conquer this problem too."

"Your maxim has always been never say die. Why do you want to change it now?" joined in Usha quietly.

Finally, the long-awaited day arrived for Raju. The Colonel desperately wanted to attend the match but the doctors ruled it out completely. After much wrangling, they did agree to arrange a TV in his room. "It's the day I've been waiting for for so many years and you'll not allow me to go the stadium! It's the most unkindest cut of all," the Colonel cried but the doctor turned a deaf ear.

The first ODI between Team India and the visiting Australians started on schedule. The whole country wanted to see Raju in action against the Aussies, known for their penchant to play fast bowling with ease. The stadium filled to the brim as usual and many disappointed fans lined up outside the turnstiles. Only Usha and his sister turned up at the stadium and took their seats in the enclosure close to the dressing rooms. The daughters and distant cousin of the

Colonel stayed in the hospital at his bedside.

India won the toss and elected to bat and consequently the Indian captain immediately wanted to relegate Raju to a 'super sub' and strengthen his batting by including an extra batsman. He was quickly talked out of it by the rest of the team. Unfortunately, the Australian quickies had a field day and played havoc with the famous Indian batting line-up. Although the conditions suited the Indian batsmen, the Australian bowlers extracted enough bounce and pace from the pitch and sent many of the Indians back into the dressing room all too quickly. Ramu fought a lone battle and with the help of the tail-enders blunted the attack to some extent. He posted a reasonable score and stood like a colossus amongst the ruins. When the stipulated fifty overs finished, India had managed to score only two hundred and twenty, which was considered a far too low a score to defend.

During the interval, Usha got a call on her mobile telephone. The Colonel had taken a turn for the worst. She ran up to the dressing room and, ignoring the protests of the security personnel, rushed in and informed Raju of the awful news. Shocked, Raju began to cry and almost broke down. His only thoughts were of leaving the game and running to the hospital; he no longer wanted to play. The coach then admonished him.

It was Usha however who said, "Have you given a thought even for a second what the Colonel would have liked under such circumstances?"

Raju suddenly realised how the Colonel had been the focus of all his attention and not playing the match. He realised it would be the greatest disservice to the outstanding man that he loved if he did not perform to his very best. It would be for his mentor that he would bowl. Raju discarded all other thoughts and decided not only to play but also to give it his very best shot.

When the match resumed, the captain tossed the new ball to the debutant Raju who measured up his bowling run and marked it. Normally Indian bowlers making a debut touch the ground reverentially and say a prayer but Raju started his career in international cricket in a different manner altogether. He turned towards the pavilion, clicked his heels and saluted smartly. He also blew a kiss. Then he bowled.

He mesmerised the Aussies with his pace and swing. He did not err in line or length and had them into all sorts of trouble. Whoever tried to chance his arm and flex his muscles came a cropper and found his stumps crashing down. India won the match mainly due to Raju's bowling. He was declared the Man of the Match for taking five wickets in his maiden appearance and the whole stadium erupted with joy when he received his award. This was in marked contrast to how Raju was feeling as he had learned from Usha that Colonel Seth had passed away shortly after the match.

Immediately after the match, Raju rushed to the hospital. On his way, he stopped at a florist and picked up three rose buds with long stems. He cut off the flowers, removed the thorns, smoothed the stems and finally shortened them so they resembled stumps. When he entered the Colonel's room and found Seth wrapped in a white sheet he bowed before him reverentially and placed the improvised stumps on Seth's chest. He then stood up and saluted the Colonel.

"I got you five wickets…and…this as a present. I know it's what you dreamed of all your life." Gently he placed his first Indian Cap on Seth's still form. "It's my bad luck you aren't here to receive it." Then he broke down sobbing but, when he finally pulled himself together, he found Usha with her arm around him reassuringly. "India won the match, I've won my place at last but the Colonel lost his battle," Raju said quietly.

"I won too," Usha added with love in her voice.

"My father lost nothing. He also won," Aparna said softly to Raju.

"We watched you on the TV," explained Suparna. "You should've seen the look on his face when you took your fifth wicket. He died a proud and happy man."

GLOSSARY OF INDIAN AND HINDI WORDS

NDA	National Defence Academy
IMA	Indian Military Academy
IAS	Indian Administrative Service
IPS	Indian Police Service
BCCI	Board of Control Cricket India
MRF	A pace academy in India run under Denis Lillie
IIT	Indian Institute of Technology

Salwar kameez	An ensemble which covers a girl from neck to toes
Dupatta	A broad strip of cloth worn round the shoulders and covering the waist worn with salwar kameez
Didi	Sister
Akka	Sister in Telugu
Sarpanch	Elected village headman
Uncle	A respectful form of address
Lakh	100,000 rupees
Crore	10 million rupees
Moolah	A Mullah, who calls the faithful to prayer

Printed in the United Kingdom
by Lightning Source UK Ltd.
125255UK00001B/14/A

9 781905 988310